Roxie Applesauce

Tonya L. Matthews

HALEYA PUBLISHING—Bowling Green, Kentucky.
Cover design by Print Media
Cover photo by Tonya L. Matthews

First Edition © 2021 Tonya L. Matthews

ISBN: 978-0-578-24369-6

Dedication

Haley Angelica
God has been with you since day one.
We love you!

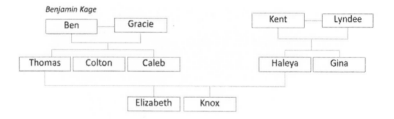

Benjamin Kage

Ben	Gracie

Thomas	Colton	Caleb

Kent	Lyndee

Haleya	Gina

Elizabeth	Knox

To the readers of Roxie Applesauce,

Someone special wrote this book for me and gave it to me. In that alone, it fulfilled its purpose. I will forever treasure this gift.

Many times in life, I've underestimated the potential of something, and this is one of those times. His plan was much bigger.

As I worked with the author, editors, and publisher as we prepared this book for print, one asked me, "Exactly who is the main character?"

I thought for a few seconds then answered, "God."

I love—with all my heart—the people in this book. I pray they will bless your life as well.

Haleya Kage

One brow lifted and his other eye squinted,
he countered,
"You sure that's what you want?"
"Yes," Haleya nodded.
The gentleman's grave demeanor fit his occupation.
He read the epitaph aloud once more
for final confirmation:

Marcella Ciscal
AKA—Roxie
Born on March 12, 1948
Died on November 25, 2010
"The best day of my life!"

Prologue

I'm ready to tell my story. It's a wonder that I'm still alive to tell it, and I'm blessed beyond words to share it like this. I know my days are few. So here it is:

My name is Marcella Ciscal, but you can call me "Roxie." Roxie Applesauce helped me escape the tough times. There were a lot of them. She provided me with happy memories. She may not have been real to the world, but she was real to me.

It's been a hard life. I know addiction and the resulting feeling of self-loathing, only to choose the lies again and again. I've sought out danger, comforted by the possibility of the worst. I've known disappointment as if the Earth's rotation stilled and the sun rose no more. But today—this day—I know a joy worthy of praise for the first time in my life. Today is the best day of my life.

You'll meet God's greatest gifts to me as you read this. I couldn't have written this alone though. Not just because my hands are crippled with age and I never graduated from high school, but because, for most of it, I wasn't there. In the end, that is a very good thing. You will agree. The fact that I'm part of it now is nothing but a pure miracle. As I speak, I look at the most beautiful one as she writes, fixing my words and making them sound pretty. Just the sight of her alone would have been all I needed to draw my last breath in peace.

Chapter 1

MARCELLA—1952—age 4

Roxie Applesauce worked her way through the crowd. She stretched to see over her mob of fans to make eye contact with her friend, Lawrence. He had the limousine door open, welcoming her as she pushed through the people calling her name, reaching to hug her, and holding small slips of paper in front of her. She smiled at each one but continued to swim against the current toward Lawrence. Her thoughts only on the triple fudge ice cream sundae they'd soon enjoy.

When the whiskey barrel came to a halt, Marcella's head spun. In the dark she wasn't sure if her damp hair and the repulsive stench were from remnants of the barrel's former life or the result of her breakfast coming up. Her cousins, laughing and yelling obscenities, kicked the barrel as it tumbled across the yard, down the bank, and rested finally near the creek. Marcella, kicking and banging, detached the top and slid out face-forward onto the muddy creek bank.

MARCELLA—1969—age 21

The room spun like an unrestrained carnival ride, yet it had been years since she'd been to a fair. Marcella closed her eyes, sinking left, then swaying right. Behind her eye sockets, colors flew by, waving as they passed. Opening her eyes, she stumbled into the living room, each step equal to the effort of wading through the ocean in a snowsuit. The TV blared, though she couldn't make out the image on its screen. A news reporter announced that a man had just walked on the moon. Marcella lifted her knees high and took big steps toward the kitchen, mimicking someone walking on the moon.

She tried to focus on the refrigerator. Its handle leapt toward her. Grabbing at the life-filled target, she sliced through nothing but air. Distracted then by her hand, she drew her arm to her face, leaning into her hand and edging her nose along her arm inch by inch toward her elbow. Entangled splashes of orange and turquoise enveloped her arm like a living tattoo. She stroked the tip of her nose against the deep shades of red sunken into her forearm. A burst of flowers tickled her nose.

Pulling away, she reached her hand out, separating her fingers. The pattern on each finger moved independently, and a brilliant pallet of hues wrapped each digit. Marcella staggered again toward the refrigerator and grabbed its handle before it could attack. Pulling out a jug of milk, unaware of its expiration date, she filled the baby's bottle. Milk spilled onto her seemingly tattooed fingers. Last time, she'd poured vegetable oil, mistaking it for apple juice, into the baby bottle. Her baby had instantly rejected it. Marcella turned to the makeshift crib and rearranged the bath towel that kept the little one warm. She patted the stained pillows used as a mattress, leaned forward, and placed the bottle where her baby slept.

MARCELLA—2010—age 62

Marcella slowly unwrapped the aluminum foil, more aware than even yesterday of the ache in her hands. Arthritis, she assumed, though she had no means to see a doctor. She leaned close to the scraps to sniff the fatty edge of prime rib, mixed in what appeared to be a concoction of mashed potatoes and something green, maybe string beans or wilted

2

lettuce. The food, raked from Lexington Steakhouse's patrons' plates, had been saved for her.

"Thank you," she muttered, nodding to the kind, young man. "For my cat," she explained as she had done each evening. After rewrapping the foil, she licked the leaking juices on her fingers. Her cat had been dead for years.

Chapter 2

FALL 2007

Benjamin Kage leaned against his truck with his keys in his hand. He'd managed to blend into the crowd so far, during the ribbon cutting ceremony. Healing from knee surgery, he limited his steps and lingered toward the back while the mayor spoke. But if he were honest, his knee was doing fine, and his distance from the podium was more about not being seen and planning a quick get-a-way.

When the mayor turned the microphone over to Ben's son, Thomas, his words were few. He introduced his wife, son and daughter, and a few key people in attendance. Ben took a tiny step to the side, so he was directly behind the person in front of him, making sure he was out of Thomas's view. Ben didn't want to be recognized. The day wasn't about him. It was about the family who'd lost their home in a tornado and those who'd come together to build it back for them.

Thomas concluded his remarks by simply mentioning that he hadn't done this alone. Though the attendees were sure to think he was referring to those who'd volunteered their time to help with the project, Ben knew what Thomas was really saying. It was the reason he'd driven from Ridgewood to Lexington for the event. Thomas had been referring to his mother, Gracie. Without her, there wouldn't be a new house or a ribbon cutting celebration. Ben had wanted to be there to feel a part of the blessing that his wife, Gracie, had initiated with a message and gift to each of her sons.

Cheers and applause soared as the mayor used oversized scissors to cut the long ribbon stretched out in front of Thomas, his family, and the new homeowners. That's when Ben's grandson Knox spotted him. Knox wove through the crowd and into his arms.

"I think you've grown!"

"I'm nine now, you know," Knox boasted and took a step back, standing tall.

"I know."

"In dog years, I'm 56. That's the right calculation because it isn't just seven years to one human year like people think. Dogs age faster in the first couple of years, then it's five years per each additional year."

"Still smarter than your grandpa, that's for sure," Ben said, looking through the crowd, glad to see Thomas occupied by the people surrounding him.

"Hey look, Pen-Pa!" Knox tugged Ben toward a nearby trickling creek.

Ben stayed in step with his grandson. His knee was doing fine, and his quick get-a-way was no longer a priority.

Knox squatted near a frog he'd spotted. "Do you like frogs?"

"Sure," Ben answered as the frog hopped onto a rock.

"I watched a video on YouTube about how to catch a frog." Knox inched closer. Within seconds, the frog dangled between Knox's fingers, croaking.

"Noisy fellow."

"He's a little nervous," Knox said placing the frog on his palm. "When I pet his back, he quiets down."

"Like a pro," Ben remarked watching the frog ease.

"You can pet it."

Ben stroked his finger on the frog's back. "When I woke up this morning, I sure didn't think I'd be petting a frog today."

"Me either!" Knox cupped the frog in his hands. "I gotta show Mom!" Knox trotted off.

Ben watched Knox work his way through the crowd. Pleased that he'd come, he turned toward his truck.

*   *   *

Thomas Kage, relieved to have the speaking portion of the ceremony behind him, knew that the lady in the trendy business suit, next to the man holding the WBKN news camera, was motioning toward him. Still, he turned to look over his shoulder hoping she pointed to someone else.

Thomas shook the mayor's hand. "Have a good Labor Day weekend," he said and stepped away. Walking toward the reporter, he waved to his wife, Haleya. She was standing talking with her parents, Kent and Lyndee. Kent held his grandson close, as he looked at the frog. Knox looked as if he were telling Kent everything he knew about frogs. Lyndee's arm rested around the waist of her granddaughter, Elizabeth. Thomas shook his head. *How did that happen so quickly?* His daughter, a freshman in high school, stood as tall as her grandmother.

"Thomas," the news reporter approached. "I'm Riley Welch." She extended her hand as her words rushed out, "You've been chosen for this week's Hometown Hero. It will air on tonight's news, and I would like a quick interview with you, please."

Thomas hadn't expected this; he needed to get back to work. The event today had been the mayor's idea. "I don't think so," Thomas said with a nervous laugh, then looked over toward his wife. Haleya gave him two thumbs up.

"I just need a few quick comments. I am familiar with the story about how you built this home for the family who lost everything in the tornado."

Thomas noticed the camera man adjusting the camera on its tripod and then he saw its red light come on.

"Is it true that you didn't know the family, but when you saw our report after the tornado, you decided to coordinate building them a new home?"

"They were staying at Lexington's Ronald McDonald House. Their daughter was sick," Thomas stammered looking away from the camera. "They'd let their home insurance lapse and needed help."

"So, you organized the subcontractors to donate their time, and you purchased the materials and managed the project?"

"It wasn't my money. I mean, it was, but—" Thomas said and leaned forward a bit toward the reporter and said in a whisper, "I really don't like doing things like this."

"What do we have?" she asked the camera man.

"We've got scans of the home—inside and outside, the mayor cutting the ribbon, and an interview with the family." He shrugged his shoulders. "Should be enough."

She turned to Thomas. "I'd like one quote. It can be short. Anything that you'd like to say. Just look at me, not the camera." She paused, waiting for him to say something.

A movement distracted Thomas. He saw something in his peripheral vision and then felt someone at his side.

"Hi, Dad," Knox said.

Thomas looked over. "Where'd you come from?" Knox had quietly edged away from his mother and grandparents and over to Thomas. He stood with his frog-friend displayed in his palm.

Knox looked up at his dad and then at the camera. "Frogs can jump 20 times their own length, and they don't drink water with their mouths. They drink by absorbing it through their skin."

"How does he do that?" Riley asked.

"What?" Thomas asked, putting his arm around Knox's shoulders with a squeeze that pulled him closer.

7

"Hold the frog? It's not jumping away," she said looking both disgusted and impressed. "I've never been able to get close to a frog. But then again, I don't know that I've ever tried."

"He likes me," Knox said, extending his palm slightly forward so she could see the frog better.

"He's cute," Riley said.

"Not all frogs are this cute. Some have big bumps and bulging eyes. Actually, I think that means they're toads, instead of frogs."

Thomas chuckled. "Yes, *he's* cute," he acknowledged.

"He's smart too," Riley observed.

"I skipped first and third grades," Knox added.

"So, he's super smart," Riley said wide-eyed.

Knox added, "Yeah, I just started the sixth grade. I'm almost 10."

Thomas nodded. "But he still can't remember to brush his teeth before he goes to bed."

"Daaadd! Don't tell her that."

"So, your frog probably wouldn't let me hold him like you are?" Riley asked.

Knox shook his head. "Nope. Are you going to be on TV, Dad?"

Thomas looked from Riley to the cameraman and back to Riley. "Well, I guess *we're* going to be on TV, actually," Thomas said and motioned toward the cameraman. "I'm ready."

"Great," Riley beamed. "Ready when you are." She smiled and mouthed, "Remember to look at me."

Thomas said to her, "Ask me that question again. Your first one about how the tornado hit, and the family lost everything."

Riley nodded and asked the question, "What inspired you to re-build this home for a family who'd lost *everything*?"

With his arm around his son, who held his frog proudly toward the rolling camera, Thomas looked at Riley and not at the camera and said, "They didn't lose *everything.*" Then Thomas nodded thanks to the cameraman. "That's it," he said as he reached out and shook Riley's hand before turning and walking in the opposite direction.

Knox, alongside him, lifted the frog closer to his dad's face. "Did you know that frogs can lift nearly twice their body weight with just their tongues?"

"No, Knox, I didn't know that." Thomas watched the frog move slightly on Knox's palm and come to rest again. "Are you sure it's not sick? Or just really scared?"

"Nope, he likes me. It's a tree frog."

"How do you know that?"

Knox pointed with his other hand toward his grandfather, Thomas's dad. "Pen-Pa told me," he said.

Ben stood beside his vehicle, keys in hand. Thomas shifted his steps toward him and said to Knox, "Hey, why don't you go show your mother the frog?"

"She's seen it," Knox said.

"Okay, show it to her again." Thomas pointed to Haleya.

She saw his glance and yelled, "Hey, Knox. Come here. Grandma Lyndee wants a hug goodbye."

Thomas called to his father, "Hey, Dad."

"Haleya called me about the ribbon cutting." Ben fidgeted with the keys he held.

"Glad you came."

"It's a nice house. Good family, too, it seems."

"You got a new truck!"

"Had to. It was gonna cost more to get the other one fixed than it was worth." Ben placed one hand on the vehicle's hood. "It's got a bunch of fancy buttons that I still don't know how to use."

"You miss your old one?"

9

Ben nodded.

"Are you headed back to Ridgewood?"

"Yep. Just wanted to see you and what you'd done," Ben said.

Thomas heard Knox running toward them. "Pen-Pa, don't leave yet. I've gotta give you a hug," Knox called with his arms wide open. Ben slid his car keys into his pocket.

"He's missed you," Thomas said to his dad as Knox reached his arms around his grandfather. Then he asked Knox, "Where's your frog?"

Knox, still in his grandfather's embrace, turned to look at Thomas. "I showed it to Elizabeth." He looked up at his grandfather with a devilish smirk. "I don't think she likes frogs."

Ben chuckled.

"Mom made me let it go." He squeezed his grandfather around the waist one more time and stepped back. "Do you have to go? You just got here."

Ben nodded and opened his truck door, causing Knox to take notice of the brand new 2007 Chevrolet Silverado.

"You got a new truck!" Knox trotted around the vehicle to take a look, then climbed in. "Okay, let's go!"

Ben looked at Thomas.

Thomas nodded. "Sure, for a quick spin. But he's skipping school right now for this. I'm sure it's of little concern to him, but we told the school he'd be back before lunch. You want to drop him off there?"

"I can do that." Ben used the roof handle to pull himself into the driver's seat. "Glad to have the knee surgery done, but this truck was built for the younger me," he grumbled. "I'm thinking about trading it in, and I've had it for less than a month." Ben shut the door and lowered his window.

"No, no—" Knox squealed, bopping the dashboard with his hand. "I love it!"

10

"Well, if Knox likes it, I might just have to keep it." Ben winked at Thomas as he started the engine and pulled away.

"Where are they going?" Haleya walked up with Elizabeth.

"For a ride."

"What about—"

"Dad's dropping him off at school."

"Okay." Haleya took Thomas's arm and began walking, Elizabeth at her side. "Was he happy with what you did with the money?" Haleya asked.

Thomas only nodded. He didn't want to talk about it.

"He's headed back to Ridgewood?" she asked.

Thomas nodded.

"Hey, Dad?" Elizabeth asked. "Can I have a phone?"

"You got a job?"

"I have good grades. I've been getting along with Knox," Elizabeth mentioned before adding, "I can help Mom more around the house."

"She's got my attention," Haleya said.

"Emma Lee's got one," Elizabeth continued.

"Who's Emma Lee?"

"Dad!" Elizabeth said. "My best friend. You see her every Sunday at church."

"Oh, the kid who sits with us?" Thomas teased. "That girl that comes to the house almost every week?"

"Dad, you're trying to change the subject. You know who Emma Lee is!"

"Yeah, she's the kid with the cell phone. Gosh, her parents must love her," Thomas teased, winking at Haleya.

"Please, Dad," Elizabeth begged.

"We'll talk about it."

Elizabeth snapped her fingers. "That's an almost yes!" She nudged her mother.

"I think so," Haleya agreed.

"Heavy on the *almost*," Thomas noted, as he turned to give Haleya a hug. "Thanks for coming."

"Wouldn't have missed it!" On tiptoes she pressed her cheek against his and held it for a few seconds. He tightened his squeeze before letting go.

Thomas turned to Elizabeth for a hug.

"Do I have to go back to school?"

"You, my daughter, have already used up your '*Dad, please!*' today." Releasing her, he added, "Have fun making those good grades."

Haleya pointed to the car. "Let's get you to school. I'm missing work."

"Yeah, but you love your work," Elizabeth said, giving her mother a look. She raised an invisible phone to her ear and grinned at her dad. "You said we'd talk about it."

"You said you'd do more chores around the house," he shot back.

"I will, I promise!" Elizabeth called as she got in and rolled down the window.

As they drove past, waving, Thomas admired their identical smiles. Haleya's had hooked him when he was in college; his beautiful daughter's smile now tugged at his heartstrings. He knew he'd be buying a phone.

Chapter 3

"Happy Labor Day!" Thomas hadn't reached the front porch of Kent and Lyndee's house before Gina swung open the door. She called out to Thomas, "I thaw you on TV, Thomath." Holding the screen door open with her foot, Gina lifted the digital camera in her hands and snapped a picture. Gina had moved in with Kent and Lyndee when she was eighteen. Now at twenty-three, she was part of the family—her Down Syndrome embraced and her joyful spirit treasured.

"They're here!" Lyndee yelled, sliding the baked beans into the oven, and dashed from the kitchen to the front door to greet Thomas, Haleya, Elizabeth, and Knox. "Happy Labor Day!" Lyndee called out and gently tugged Gina out of the way so everyone could get into the house. "Gina, I know you love your new camera, but you have all afternoon to take pictures. Give them some space."

"But Thomath is famuth!" Gina snapped another picture, just as Lyndee leaned in to give him a big hug. He wrapped his arms around her, jug of tea in one hand and bag of chips in the other.

"Famous for my ability to knock out more barbeque ribs than Kent every Labor Day," Thomas called out over Lyndee's shoulder to Kent who'd stepped into the room.

"Gina, you need a picture of this one too," Lyndee said as she released Thomas and hugged Elizabeth. "This year's 4-H Personal Narrative Winner!"

"I got it," Gina said, snapping several more pictures.

Lyndee, noticing the dish in Elizabeth's hand, cooed, "You didn't!" Lyndee pinched at the foil covering the pie and peeked inside. "That's *exactly* how an apple pie should look and smell. Kent, you gotta see what Elizabeth baked!"

"I can cook, too," Gina said to Elizabeth who worked her way past Lyndee now hugging Knox as if she hadn't seen him in months.

Haleya stood in the doorway, a grocery bag hanging at her elbow and both hands full. Dodging Knox, she fought to keep the creamed-corn casserole and the seven-layer salad upright.

The clamor and near fumbles reminded Thomas of an episode of *The Three Stooges.* He chuckled aloud, but then his smile weakened. He still missed the holidays he'd spent at home in Ridgewood with his father, mother, and two brothers. He stepped into the other room.

After four rings, Thomas heard his father's voicemail greeting. He didn't leave a message. Instead, he made another call. "Colton," he said when his brother answered.

"Hey, Big Brother!" Colton answered. "I missed the special gig celebrating what you did. I wish you'd let me know."

"No big deal," Thomas said. "How's Ridgewood these days?"

"Treasure Fest this weekend," Colton chuckled.

"So, you're saying I'm not missing anything," Thomas joked.

"Exactly."

"Do you know where Dad is? I tried to call him just now."

"Nope, haven't seen or heard from him today. Been at church getting everything back in order. Big crowd yesterday. We had to put extra chairs alongside the pews."

"My brother, the preacher," Thomas said.

"My brother, the TV personality."

14

"Far from that."

"You know they put you on the front page of the *Ridgewood Daily News*."

"No!"

"Oh, yes. Dad didn't tell you?"

"I haven't talked to him since he made his drive-by during the event."

"Says the guy who does the same when he comes to Ridgewood," Colton jested.

"I've been busy. Haven't you read the paper?" Thomas shot back.

"Good one. How's the family? Elizabeth and Knox doing good?"

"Elizabeth leaves for a Youth Group retreat next weekend. Knox surprised us with a new pet he's been keeping in his room."

"A surprise, huh?"

"His pet wasp," Thomas shared. "He's trained it with sugar to sit on his finger. Now the wasp tinkers around on his left hand the entire time he does his homework."

Colton laughed. "I love it! That reminds me of Caleb's cockatiel. He actually potty trained that thing! Remember?"

"He did. Our little brother—" In the quiet, neither said anything for the space of a long breath. "Have you heard anything?"

"No. What has it been now? Two years?"

"He's somewhere, right? Has to be," Thomas said. "I try not to think the worst."

"I don't let myself."

"It just doesn't make sense."

"Not at all," Colton agreed. "I'll text you when I hear from Dad, so you'll know he's okay."

"Thanks. When you talk to him, tell him that I said it was good to see him the other day."

15

"Will do."

Thomas dialed his Dad's number again. No answer.

*　　　*　　　*

The phone on Ben's hip buzzed. He'd put it on vibrate and didn't plan to answer any calls. He used both hands to steady himself, careful to favor his right knee as he climbed onto the boat. Though his knee was stronger after the recent replacement surgery, he knew he had no business boarding the cabin cruiser. He missed *My Gracie* though and wanted to see her. He wasn't ready to say goodbye. He grabbed the *For Sale* sign and tossed it into the water.

"Looking good!" Camille waved as she strolled past.

He'd been invited to her houseboat for her 70th birthday party. He'd declined. When she'd insisted, his upcoming surgery had worked as an excuse.

Camille, looking slender in walking shorts and a sleeveless pink polo shirt, turned nearly every old codger's head, but Ben preferred his boat.

"Glad you're home," she added.

"Home's in Ridgewood. Just here at the lake visiting *My Gracie,*" Ben called back and busied himself wiping down the captain's seat. Beside the steering wheel, he adjusted the picture of Gracie and himself posing for their 35th wedding anniversary. Later that month, the doctors had told Gracie that she had cancer. This year would have been their 40th anniversary.

He'd purchased the modest boat when she'd gone into remission and named it *My Gracie.* Together they'd eased along the Barren River Lake, Ben steering and humming along to Creedence Clearwater Revival, as Gracie sat close by, writing in a thick, spiral-bound notepad. They savored every hour, rising early from the boat's cabin, stretching in the sunshine, and star-gazing while listening to tree frogs until the evening chill drove them to their bunk.

16

When the breast cancer returned, the boat stayed docked, but Gracie continued to write. Beside Ben, in their bed at night, she'd read to him portions of her book. Ben smiled through his tears then, just as he did now, as he sat with her notepad in his hand and looked out over the water, ignoring the Labor Day celebrations.

He thought of the day he'd asked Gracie to marry him. He was 19 and had nothing; he'd wanted nothing else in the world. He glanced toward the picture of Gracie again. Now, even at 65, he wanted only her. He opened the notepad to the page where she told of their wedding day.

> There with Pastor Ted, Benjamin Kage took Gracie Howard's hand and slipped the wedding band onto her finger and, without Pastor Ted prompting him, he kissed her. Gracie stood still, hoping somehow that this moment would never end. It had been his idea to marry on top of the hill, but it was Gracie's choice that it be only the two of them.

He looked out onto the calm water again. His gaze came to rest on the lake's bank of clay, rock, and worn tree roots. The afternoon sun was low in the sky, and he listened to the birds. A mix of tweets and chirps drifted on the light breeze. He knew that when evening set in, the crickets' chatter would start. Then, at nightfall, he'd hear the familiar sound of the tree frogs singing.

*   *   *

Thomas retained his rib eater title, though he'd been kidding about out-eating Kent. Sitting on the deck, they watched Knox hunt butterflies and Elizabeth play Uno with Gina on a blanket in the backyard.

"Glad to make it to your event Friday," Kent said.

17

"It was no big deal. I would've understood if you missed it. Saving a life is a lot more important." Thomas downplayed the hype.

"Hey look!" Knox held up a butterfly in the large pickle jar with holes in its lid, compliments of Kent.

"Did you get a good one?" Kent asked. Butterflies hovered from one zinnia to another in Lyndee's flower garden.

Knox nodded. "Gina, I got this for you."

Gina squealed, "A butterf'y!" Holding the jar high, she called toward Kent, "Look! Knox got a butterf'y por me."

Kent gave her a thumbs up.

"I'm goin' name it L-i-z-z-y, after Wizabeth, 'cause we are friends!"

"Gina loves Elizabeth," Kent said to Thomas.

"Elizabeth loves Gina," Thomas responded.

"Lyndee's turning the garage into a bedroom."

"You need another bedroom?"

"Lyndee wants to start taking in teens again," Kent said.

"That's good."

"Gina hasn't had to *share* Lyndee before."

Kent's phone dinged. He pulled it from his pocket to read the text.

"You gotta go?"

"No, I'm not on call this weekend." He put the phone back into his pocket. "Back to what I was saying earlier—"

"About Lyndee and the garage?"

"Before that, about the event Friday and what you did for that family. I was proud to tell the other doctors that you're my son-in-law. And that TV interview was the best ever with Knox holding his frog." Kent chuckled. "You did a good job too."

"TV cameras make me uneasy. It reminded me of how nervous I felt when I asked *Dr. Kent Lambert* for his

18

daughter's hand in marriage," Thomas said. "I didn't think you liked me."

"Oh, I didn't." Kent casually pointed toward Gina and Elizabeth couple-dancing to the beat of Knox banging two sticks against the wrought iron table.

Thomas's gaze followed Kent's, and then he jerked it back. "What?"

"Nobody's good enough for my daughter."

"You're kidding!"

"I had a guy in mind for her though. Dr. Brummer's son, Kyle. He was older and doing well. Finished with his residency. Nice looking. Good genes."

"You gave us your blessing, though."

"You had good jeans too—just a different kind. The ones that go well with those farmer-boy boots you were wearing."

"My Red Wings?" Thomas squawked. "Haleya never liked them either." He looked down at his flip flops. "These were last year's birthday present." He wiggled his toes.

"Well, you didn't turn out too bad," Kent said. Under his breath, he added, "Though Kyle just happens to be New Hampshire's top neurosurgeon."

"Brain surgeon?"

"Your Red Wings sold me."

"How's that?"

"I knew a man wearing those boots wasn't leaving Kentucky," Kent said and pointed to Elizabeth, now helping Gina find a hiding place. "I'd have missed this," Kent said.

Knox finished counting, uncovered his eyes, and waved his hands in their direction. "Where is she?" Knox mouthed, pointing in every direction for a hint.

Kent pointed to the left, and Knox headed in that direction.

"Well, I missed dessert," Thomas said. "This flip-flop wearing guy, thanks to your daughter, is headed inside for a piece of apple pie." Pausing inside the door, he watched his wife talking with her mother.

"How's the new job's going?" Lyndee asked as she put leftovers in the fridge.

"I love it!" Haleya said, snacking on the last bite of apple pie. "Almost as much as this apple pie."

"I just can't get over you not working in the hospital anymore," Lyndee said.

"I still work for the hospital. I just provide the new technology training instead."

"No more patients. That's a big change."

"Exactly!" Haleya said. "No more rounds. No more nights and weekends!"

"What about the overnight travel?"

"A few conferences, certification requirements, trainings or whatever, no big deal." Haleya picked up a pretend phone. "Room service, please," she giggled.

"You know, I'll be glad to help with the kids," Lyndee offered.

"Thomas's got it. But, sure, if he needs it," Haleya said, scraping her spoon along the pie pan's edge. "This is so yummy! I wish you'd never taught Elizabeth how to make an apple pie." Haleya licked the spoon.

"Always glad to help." Lyndee took the spoon and put it in the dishwasher.

Haleya spotted Thomas. "Need something, handsome?"

Thomas shook his head and stepped back outside. He'd missed out on dessert, but he had everything he needed.

Chapter 4

Roxie Applesauce stepped onto the stage, carefully walking on her tiptoes so that her three-inch heels wouldn't catch on the stairs as they had once before, causing her to nearly trip in front of millions. It had been embarrassing, but her fans hadn't wavered. The anxious crowd screamed for her. "Roxie—Roxie! I love you!" Roxie bowed, appreciating their admiration. She planned to sing one of her original melodies and unveil her Spanish-inspired dance.

Roxie twirled, her dress flowing to the rhythm of the piano and the accompanying instruments spewing high notes, octaves above anything she'd ever heard before. Yet her vocals soared, and her feet followed in perfect timing. She could feel the music flowing through her and out her fingertips that circled elegantly above her head. The piano drowned out the tones of the big oversized-looking guitar between Lawrence's legs. Smiling at her, he stroked the cello, and she nodded his way, knowing that after the show, they'd go out for an ice cream soda just as they had celebrated after her last performance.

"Marcella, you better get your stinking hind-end in here right now!"

The music silenced and the crowd dispersed instantly, with no applause or adoring farewell this time.

"Marcella, right now! I'm gonna slap the—" The curse words whipped in the wind.

Marcella jumped off the hay wagon and ran for the house. Mud caked her shoes, and her heart sank. She considered pulling her shoes off and leaving them there, her young mind calculating quickly if bare feet were better than muddy shoes. But before she could decide, her grandfather was there, and as the swats came, she realized it wouldn't have mattered.

MARCELLA—1970—age 22

Marcella dug through her purse for another dollar. "Ride ag'in!" the tiny blonde called from the carousel horse. The mall was crowded, and Marcella stepped aside to let several people pass in the line as she finally pulled out another dollar bill. She gave it to the man operating the ride.

"Must be a special day," he mumbled and nodded to the two-year old on the carousel who understood that the piece of paper handed to him meant she could ride longer. She squealed, and the man seemed to get as much pleasure watching the child as the little one did in riding. As the carousel circled and Marcella came into sight, the toddler started bobbing on her horse and giggling. But Marcella knew she didn't have another dollar left and as the music slowed, she heard, "Ella g'in! Ella, g'in!"

Marcella reached for her baby, who squalled, holding the horse as if she'd melted into it. She kicked Marcella and pulled away, causing Marcella to lose grip. Her baby slid down the horse's tail and onto the wooden base of the amusement ride. The child wailed, saliva stringing from her top baby teeth to her bottom lip. Her eyelids clenched. She balled her fists as she flip-flopped like a fish pulled from water. Marcella grabbed for her, and the toddler squirmed, rolling left, then right.

Finally, Marcella reached both arms around her child and pulled her to her chest. The little one shrieked louder, and she swatted her bare leg. Placing her hand over her baby's mouth, she sprinted toward the pay phone. She had been contemplating calling the social worker all day. In fact, the trip to the mall had been part of her plan.

She'd almost changed her mind. The tiny fingers waving from the carousel were nearly more than her heart could bear. She'd forever have that image in her mind. The picture of her precious baby girl looking for the sight of her mother every time the carousel rounded the corner. The sound of her tender voice calling, "Ella!" And that sweet face lit with joy, elated beyond anything Marcella had ever known herself.

She sat her baby on the floor, hiked her purse up on her knee, and dug for change. She'd meant to save that last dollar for the phone call, but she'd instead handed it to the man for one last ride. At that point, she'd decided she couldn't do it. She couldn't walk away. But now she dumped her purse out in the middle of the mall, digging on the terrazzo floor through everything she owned for a few quarters. Seeing her baby shrieking and sprawled on the floor reminded Marcella why she'd started the day off planning to actually do it this time. She'd been thinking of it for weeks. On her hands and knees, Marcella tossed everything into her purse as quickly as she could. She didn't have a cent of change to make the call. She scooped the little girl into her arms, covered the baby's mouth, and turned running directly into an elderly lady who stood a foot shorter. The lady looked up at Marcella and the baby in her arms.

"Is this yours?" she asked so quietly that Marcella had trouble understanding her. The woman held a twenty-dollar bill. The baby was rocking and bumping her head against Marcella's shoulder, not wearing down.

"What?" Marcella asked.

"I said—" She instead stuck her hand out and waved a twenty-dollar bill in front of Marcella.

It took a second for Marcella to register that the lady was trying to give her the money. "No." Marcella motioned. "It's not mine." She pushed past the lady.

"Ma'am?" the little lady called trying to raise her voice. "I thought it maybe fell out of your purse."

She turned toward the lady as people pushed their way past, eager in their Christmas shopping. For a second she thought that maybe it had. Marcella noticed her child was the only one without a coat or stockings on her legs. The dress she'd put on her daughter was stained and its hem unraveled. But it wasn't her twenty. Someone else must have dropped it.

The baby quieted, reaching toward the lady, "Da-la."

The woman pressed her lips together in the most satisfied smile. "You are a beautiful little girl." She handed the money to the child which satisfied her, until the lady brought out a cherry sucker with a sugar-white Santa on it. The baby clapped her hands and reached for the sucker, dropping the twenty-dollar bill to the floor. Marcella and the lady both stared at it.

"It's yours," the lady insisted and nodded toward the bill, "because I want you to have it. I don't need it." As if she thought proving it to Marcella might help, she opened her purse and pulled out a stack of bills. "I really don't need it."

"You shouldn't show everyone your money," Marcella said.

"I don't," her voice shook with age when she quietly spoke, yet it held great confidence. She tucked her money away and clipped her purse closed. Her four-foot, six-inch frame stood proud as she nodded her head at Marcella and reached out to touch her sweet baby girl's hand. "See? All better now." Then she stooped, picked up the twenty-dollar bill from the floor, and tucked it in Marcella's purse, dangling open at her elbow.

"I don't need that," Marcella insisted. "I just need enough to make a call."

The lady nodded, scrabbled in her purse, pulled out a quarter, and handed it to Marcella. "Here you go," she said and walked away into the hair salon. Marcella pulled out the twenty-dollar bill, crisp and unwrinkled. She wondered what the lady would have thought had she known that Marcella would use the money to pay for a taxi to the social services office, where she'd give her baby a final goodbye kiss. Or what she'd have thought had she known that with her last twenty, Marcella had purchased drugs to support her addiction. She pulled a scribbled phone number from her purse and made the call.

When Marcella arrived, the social worker was waiting at the door as promised and took her little girl from her arms. Marcella handed over the change from the taxi, as a distraction as she left and because she didn't want to spend the lady's money on the habit that had forced her here. Walking away, she felt a sense of relief that she'd not expected, along with the fear of being alone with nothing to keep her grounded.

MARCELLA–2010–age 62

The first night she'd met Travis, he'd opened the trash bag and let her pick through it before he tossed it up and over the dumpster's edge. When Travis introduced himself as a waiter at the steakhouse across the alley from where she slept behind the dumpster, she'd told him that her name was Roxie. The next night he'd wrapped the scraps neatly in foil for her. A week later, he still did the same.

Holding the foil wrapped scraps in one hand and a trash bag in his other hand, Travis approached the dumpster, where Marcella waited. "There he is!" Travis said.

Marcella jerked her head, looking around quickly, afraid that Papa Mack or Roger had found her. She would have had a better chance to outwit or outrun Irene or Flora. She'd left her panhandling partners a week ago as they'd slept on South Broadway's sidewalk. Where she'd gotten the courage to set out on her own, she wasn't sure. She just knew that she didn't need to cuddle to stay warm. It wasn't winter yet, and Papa Mack hadn't understood. In the middle of the night, she'd fumbled through their bags and taken the little bit of cash and a few pills she'd found. She slept behind a dumpster that night—alone—and proud of herself.

"He's a good kitty," Travis said.

Marcella relaxed when she realized Travis was talking to a fluffy, gray cat.

"Here, kitty, kitty," Travis said. The cat came closer. Travis unwrapped the edge of the foil and pinched off a piece of bread. The cat came to him.

"I like cats," Marcella said.

"He's not your cat?" Travis asked.

Marcella shook her head.

"It's been a while since I've seen him around here," Travis said, leaning down to scratch its neck. He pinched another piece of bread for the cat then re-wrapped the scraps and handed them to Marcella before walking back into the restaurant. Though Travis was no longer looking, Marcella waved until he was out of sight.

Marcella pulled at the foil and pinched off a piece of the roll. "Kitty-Kitty," Marcella repeated as she fed him a bite. "Your name is Kitty-Kitty." Between bites, Kitty-Kitty rubbed up against her leg.

When his belly was full, Kitty-Kitty trotted off, stopped, and looked back at Marcella. She took a few steps toward him. He walked on, then paused again to look at her. She followed.

26

Chapter 5

"Haleya, you've got to see this," Haleya's supervisor, Janice, spoke into the phone.

"What've I got to see?" Haleya asked, relaxing on her patio with her Bible and a cup of coffee.

"I'll forward it to you," Janice said. "It's the past month's participant survey summary."

"Their thoughts on my training?"

"Yep! I knew bringing in a peer to facilitate was a smart move! The tech company presenters rated an average of 5 out of 10."

"What's my average?"

"Get this! Last week you averaged an 8½ out of 10."

"What!"

"I know! It's incredible! Listen to this. The first month, you averaged 6½. Of course, we were pleased. Then last month, your overall rating increased to 7½. Our goal was an 8, and you blew right past it!"

"Wow!" Haleya scooted to the edge of the glider.

"For me, this is an answered prayer!" Janice gushed. "Do you know how hard it's been to get the morale up? The nurses have been pushing back and literally retaining nothing. Oh—oh, and the scores from their after-training assessment," Janice's words rushing out. "Doubled!"

"Really?" Haleya covered her mouth with her hand. "You're kidding."

"You're a natural!"

"No, I'm not! I read the training manual three times. Highlighted nearly everything. Made note cards. Practiced on my kids. They could fill in for me."

Janice chuckled. "So, here's the best part. These progress reports are posted online for hospital leadership. UK's Healthcare Physicians Group asked for you to present to them. Not your training presentation but how you do what you do. They want to evaluate the possibility of developing a train-the-trainer component and expand the program."

"Janice, this is crazy." Haleya patted her heart with her hand. "The Physicians Group!"

"I know! I've never been invited to present!"

"I still get nervous presenting to the nurses. I mean, it's nervous energy. I want everything to go well, and they're stuck with me all day. I remember how it was—"

"Exactly!" Janice interrupted.

"I don't think I want to do this. I'm not sure what I'd say."

"They aren't asking you; they're *inviting* you. No one declines this."

"Dear God." Haleya's hands started shaking. "Okay, okay. When do I do this? I've got to start working on it."

"It'll be their October meeting. I just forwarded you the reviews. Read the top comments. Those are the ones that got Dr. Livingston's attention."

"Who's Dr. Livingston?"

"Haleya, you've been too busy wowing your fellow nurses. He's the group's chairman."

"Wow, okay. I'll get started on an outline," Haleya said, ending the call.

She dropped her head and laid her hands on the open Bible in her lap. "Dear God, I'm going to need you for this one." She sat quietly, and then started laughing as she thought of her conversation with Janice.

"Hey, is Elizabeth back from the youth retreat tonight or tomorrow?" Thomas stepped outside, interrupting her thoughts.

"Tomorrow evening."

"What's up with you? You okay?"

"What?" Haleya felt her smile grow. "So, Janice called. Thomas, UK's Healthcare Physicians Group wants me to present to them."

"Wait," Thomas said. "The Physicians Group?"

Haleya nodded.

"Even I know that's big! How'd that happen?" Thomas stepped toward her with his arms out.

Haleya stood. "I don't know. The nurses gave me high presentation scores. Higher than the goal." She embraced Thomas and sank against him, releasing her anxiety.

"You'll do great. I just feel sorry for Knox and Elizabeth."

Haleya leaned back and looked at him. "Why?"

"Because they're going to be sick of listening to your presentation."

"You're right. I'm gonna need to step it up. I need you in my audience."

Thomas looked at his watch and stepped back. "I've got three houses under construction. Two are my largest square-footage. I'm working on more contracts—" Thomas said, retreating.

"Okay, okay, I get it. You'd probably make me nervous anyway or make faces at me. It took tons of threats to get Knox and Elizabeth to stop giggling." She leaned over, picked up her phone, and opened her emails. "YEEE," Haleya screamed as she skimmed.

"What?"

"Read this," Haleya thrust her phone toward Thomas.

"What is it?"

"Janice sent me the nurses' comments."

"Can you summarize for me?" He looked at his watch again. "I was headed to get an iPhone for Elizabeth, and it's time to replace the house's air filters," he paused. "You're not going to let me leave until I look, are you?"

Haleya shook her head.

He took the phone and read aloud:

> *It was a great two days.*
> *Best training I've ever attended.*
> *Can I request her for future trainings?*
> *I give her a 10+.*
> *The family stories she intertwined and their association with the memorization portion really worked. I aced the assessment!*

Thomas squinted his eyes and looked at Haleya. "What family stories?"

"Good ones. Association aids memorization. Keep reading."

Thomas scrolled. "These go on forever."

"Give it to me." She snatched the phone.

Thomas snatched it back and put it in his pocket.

"Why'd you do that?" Haleya reached for it.

"Because I want you to look at me, not the phone." Thomas took her hands.

"But you've got errands to run, things to do, remember?" Haleya said playfully fighting his grasp.

"Stop for a minute." Thomas cupped her hands in his and pulled them to his chest.

Haleya quieted and looked into his eyes.

"I'm proud of you. I don't have to read strangers' comments to know you're a 10+."

Though they'd been married for almost twenty years, she blushed.

Thomas pulled the Saturday newspaper from the mailbox and noticed another newspaper beneath it. His first thought was that he had forgotten to get yesterday's paper, then he saw *Ridgewood Daily News,* Thursday, September 6th.

Colton answered on the second ring. "Thomas Kage, it has to be a record. Didn't I just talk to you Monday?"

"News travels."

"Meaning?"

"I'm reading the paper I found in my mailbox. Front page reports an anonymous donor paid for 75 Ridgewood Middle School kids' registration to attend youth camp during fall break."

"Heard that too."

"I did the calculation. That's about $50,000."

"Sounds about right," Colton said.

"I gotta give it to you. Avoid the cameras and sit back and watch. I'm a bit jealous."

"I'm not sure what you're talking about."

"You did the best, brother. No one'll suspect a preacher on his salary."

"Rumor is that Dr. Bridgeman did it. He's having fun with all the attention."

"I think you're safe."

"Still don't know what you're talking about," Colton insisted.

"Why do you think Mom did it?" Thomas asked.

"The money? I'm not sure."

"I keep the note she wrote in my wallet. I just wish I knew more."

"I asked Dad. He said there's a story behind it."

"And?" Thomas pressed.

"Oh, that's all I got," Colton chuckled.

"That man drives me crazy."

"He has too much time on his hands, and he apparently thinks he's a newspaper delivery boy."

Thomas chucked. "So, he drives nearly two hours to my house, leaves a newspaper in my mailbox, and drives home."

"That's Dad. You know, for me, whether it's what Mom intended or not, it's kept me busy thinking instead of being sad when I thought of her. For the past two years, I've been considering what I'm supposed to do with the money. Church building upgrades would have been easy and needed, but that's not what she had in mind. I prayed and waited. Now, it's like I've been skipping everywhere I go this week. I feel good."

"I get it." Thomas remembered how he'd felt when the family first saw their new home.

"Mom's gone, but somehow she figured out a way to still teach us something about life," Colton paused, "and to help us feel joy beyond the sadness."

Chapter 6

Camille whisked by Ben's boat, this time with her poodle in tow. "We are grilling out for lunch. Join us?"

"Headed out," Ben called back.

Camille slowed. "This morning? Already?" She paused and adjusted her sunglasses.

"Yep."

"I need to know something."

Ben didn't answer.

Camille took a step closer. "Was her name Gracie?"

Ben didn't answer.

Camille ran her fingers along the words *My Gracie*. "Was she someone special?"

Had she asked anything else, he could have ignored it, but that question could not go unanswered. Ben nodded.

"Special like, 'we had some good times' or special like 'the love of my life?'"

Ben smirked. She was good at this. That question couldn't go unanswered either. "The love of my life."

"Will you tell me about her?"

"I can't imagine why I would," Ben said, firm but kind.

"Was she pretty? Pretty like you could have looked at her all day. Or was she beautiful? Beautiful like you couldn't take your eyes off her."

"Both," Ben answered.

She continued to stand on the dock, her pale blue maxi skirt shifting in the morning breeze.

Camille smiled. "You're a good man, aren't you?"

Picking up his cup of apple cider, he took a couple of steps toward the edge of his boat, closer to her. "Why would that matter?"

"The only good man that I ever knew was my father," Camille said. She flicked a strand of hair from her eye.

"You aren't going to invite me on your boat, are you?"

Ben shook his head.

Camille nodded. "My husband said he loved me, but his passion was golf," she paused, "and the stock market and then—" Camille's voice trailed off. "My friends say that I divorced well." She tucked the strand of hair behind her ear.

"I guess that's a positive way to look at it."

"So, you're headed out this morning?"

Ben nodded.

"When do you think you'll be back?"

"I won't," Ben said. "Just came to say goodbye."

"You're going to sell it?" She pointed to where the *For Sale* sign had been.

"I should."

"I know Kim and Frank, several boats up," she said. "They say that they know you."

Ben nodded.

"And *your* Gracie. They said that she lost her arm in a fire and that you have three sons."

"Well, that's about all there is to know."

"They said that you grew up in an orphanage."

"Well then, I guess they know everything."

"They told me you're a good guy, but I'd already figured that out."

Ben took a long sip of his apple cider.

"Well," Camille said, pausing for a deep breath. "You know, before I was just being friendly—a little flirtatious." She grinned, looked away for a second, and then back to Ben. "But now. Hearing you talk about her—"

Ben interrupted, "I just answered your questions."

Camille wrapped the end of the dog's leash around her wrist. "Your eyes say it all." She bit the edge of her lip. "But now, something tells me it's going to be hard for me to get you off my mind." She gave the leash a tug and waved bye.

Ben picked up the *For Sale* sign he'd fished out of the water last weekend and placed it on the cabin cruiser's front window.

*   *   *

Thomas started the DVD player as Haleya slid under a cozy blanket. Elizabeth was out of town at the youth retreat, and Knox was staying overnight with a friend. Haleya lifted the corner of the blanket for Thomas to scoot in next to her as her phone rang. She didn't recognize the number.

"Mom."

"Lizzy, are you okay?"

"Yes, I'm going to get baptized!" Elizabeth said with a squeal.

"Oh, my! That's great! I'll call the preacher and next Sunday—" Haleya scooted toward the edge of the couch. She turned to Thomas and said, "Lizzy's ready to get baptized."

"Mom, I'm getting baptized tonight. Right now!"

"But you're at camp?"

"I know!"

"It's eight hours away." She put the phone on speaker. "Thomas, Lizzy wants to be baptized at camp."

Thomas shrugged, wide-eyed. "Lizzy, you sure?"

"Yeah, there's nine of us. Emma Lee got baptized last year. I gotta go." Elizabeth hung up.

"Lizzy, wait!"

Elizabeth was gone.

"Thomas! She's getting baptized!"

"I heard her."

"Tonight!"

35

"Yes."

"But we're not there!"

"I know. We're home. She's there," Thomas said kindly.

"But we haven't even been talking about it!"

"Maybe we should've been." Thomas's phone rang. "This'll be quick. It's Colton."

Haleya went to her bedroom, pacing while she dialed her mother. "Mom, Lizzy's getting baptized. Tonight! At camp. In Gatlinburg, Tennessee."

"That's a good thing, right?"

"But Mom, I'm not there. She's all by herself!"

"Emma Lee's there, right?"

"Yes. In fact, she said that nine kids are getting baptized. It's like she's jumping on the bandwagon."

Lyndee was quiet.

"Mom! Are you there?"

"I was just thinking."

"Thinking what?"

"Jumping on the bandwagon for Jesus might be a good thing."

"I just thought we'd all be together. I didn't picture it this way." Haleya sat on her bed, cross-legged. "I wanted to be with her."

"I know, but this might not be about you," Lyndee offered sweetly. "Here, talk to your Dad."

Haleya whimpered, "Dad, Lizzy's at camp, and she's getting baptized tonight."

"Praise God!" Kent said.

"Yeah, but I'm not with her."

"She's a young lady. She's going to be making a lot of grownup decisions, often without consulting her parents. Next thing you know, she'll be bringing some strange boy home from college and telling you that he's the one."

Haleya looked up. Thomas stood at the bedroom doorway with the popcorn bowl. "He's not so strange."

"He's lucky," Kent said.

"Lucky to have me?"

"Lucky that your Mom calmed me down before he asked me about marrying my only daughter," he confessed. "And that, too."

"I think I need some popcorn. Thanks, Dad." She pointed to Thomas, still standing in the doorway and motioned 'come here.'

He stepped toward her.

"Not you. Just the popcorn," she teased.

He drew a circle around his face and the bowl. "We're a package deal."

"Good." She patted the spot on the bed next to her.

Chapter 7

MARCELLA—1954—age 6

Roxie Applesauce accepted the call even though she knew it would be impossible to incorporate their request into her schedule. "Yes, I'd love to perform with Cinderella. Yes, I do realize what an honor that is." Roxie had to rest—doctor's orders. She'd nearly collapsed on her tour. Traveling had never been a challenge until they had booked a last-minute show in Italy directly after her recitals in France.

Marcella's tiny wrists burned as she tried to free herself from the twine knotted to the chair spokes. She hardly had the weight to rattle the heavy chair, yet she tugged and twisted. She stopped crying when there was no avoiding the taste of snot pooled on her upper lip.

She had just wanted to rub the cat. She couldn't resist the urge even though she knew the ramifications. Last time when she'd caused Whiskers to growl, she'd been literally kicked out of the room, her body rolling like Whiskers' catnip toy out the back door.

MARCELLA—1970—age 22

Marcella hadn't touched a needle or swallowed a pill after she'd found out about the baby. She was clean when her baby was born. She didn't know why it was different now that her baby wasn't bulging at her waist but was instead in her arms. Had she cared less about her child when she could touch her soft skin and feel her warm breath? With her baby against her chest, she had raised the needle, examined its tip, and sunk it into her arm. That was the day she had chosen a meaningless existence over her baby.

She could blame Rich, who was long gone, for offering it to her. She could blame the father she never met, the stepfather she wished she'd never met, her mother for abandoning her, or her grandparents for unending torture. Or she could, with just a small prick of a needle, forget about them all. Marcella rested her eyes as the bright lights danced like melting crayons. She pulled her pink polka-dot cat close and tucked him under her chin. He purred. Marcella didn't know the cat or recognize the walls surrounding her. She had knocked on the door and the strangers had welcomed her, just as she'd been told they would. She knew the price when she'd entered the doors, but she'd already lost her baby. Nothing else mattered.

MARCELLA—2010—age 62

Marcella followed Kitty-Kitty to the street corner. He ran to the back steps of a house with boarded windows. Prodding her to follow, he'd dart back to her and rub circles around her leg. She stooped to rub him, and he curled into her fingers. She set down her bag and tucked herself next to a bush. When she fell asleep, Kitty-Kitty was resting on the backdoor step. When she woke up, he was nestled against her. "You can cuddle with me," she said as he purred. The next morning, he jumped onto a side porch tucked against a wall of shrubs, then through a shattered bay window with the board torn from it.

It took all Marcella's strength to pull herself onto the edge of the cracked, concrete porch. To stand, she tugged on the porch post, and then crawled through the window. Though in bad need of repair, it was the perfect home for a stray cat— and maybe for Marcella.

Chapter 8

"4-H Personal Narrative Winner—Freshman Elizabeth Kage," the emcee at Lexington High's year-end award ceremony announced. Thomas thought, *"Only for another week."* In August, she'd be a sophomore and Knox would start seventh grade.

"Gorgeous Gina," at the podium, Elizabeth began to read.

Gina sat in the front row of the auditorium between Lyndee and Kent with Haleya, Thomas, and Knox. Elizabeth continued:

When I was 8, my grandmother decided to open her house to troubled teens. What sounded great to everyone else didn't strike me the same. The spare room at her house that was mine, now occupied a tall girl with pink hair and multiple piercings. She rarely ate anything but potato chips, which I thought was kind of cool. When I stayed over for the weekends, now sleeping on the pullout couch, she ignored me for the most part. She'd tell me and my grandmother wild stories about crazy things she'd done. When I asked a question, she'd say, "You're so stupid." I was smart enough to know that what she was telling couldn't be true. I asked my grandmother why she listened to all the lies. Grandma Lyndee said, "She wants to talk about her life; she's just not there yet." My heart didn't break when Snooty Savannah left.

Then when I was 9, my grandmother moved in another 18-year-old. She asked if she could paint the bedroom

40

black. Black wasn't just her favorite color—it was her only color. When I asked Grandma why the girl wore so much black, my grandmother politely said, "Black is slimming and quite stylish." Dark Dawn stayed for a year, then moved on.

When I was 10, my grandmother told me that the new girl moving in was named Gina. I didn't waste any time. I googled, "Negative words that begin with G." At least I'd be prepared this time when I met the new 18-year-old who'd occupy my room at Grandma Lyndee's house.

The day that Gina arrived, I was at my grandmother's. I'd already written down some possibilities: Gaudy Gina, Ghetto Gina, and Gloomy Gina.

But as prepared as I was, I soon learned I wasn't prepared at all. At 10 years old, my best friend became an 18-year-old named Gina. She loved to talk to me. She wore bright colors, even if they didn't match. She and I shared the bedroom when I came over for the weekends.

I'd never really known someone with Down Syndrome before. At first, I didn't know what was okay to say to her, and sometimes I couldn't understand what she said. But that didn't last long. Today Gina is 23. She still lives with my grandparents, and she's still one of my best friends.

It took me a while to figure out a good name for Gina. There were so many positive G names that fit. Gina was giving. When someone gave her a stick of gum, she saved the other half for me. Gina was always grateful. For Easter Sunday, I made us both headbands with purple and pink flowers. Gina wore hers every time I visited that summer. She was gentle and genuine, too. Then one day, Gina and I were playing with Grandma Lyndee's Kentucky Derby hats. We walked downstairs, using both of our hands to hold our big, fancy hats on our heads. Gina asked Grandma Lyndee if she was pretty. Grandma said,

'Gorgeous, Gina. Gorgeous.' That was it. She was and still is Gorgeous Gina."

The crowd applauded. Gina, waving both hands, stood from her seat, and the audience began standing too.

As Thomas lifted his hands, applauding, he felt his phone buzz. Colton had called three times. He stepped into the hallway. "Hey, brother."

"Are you where you can talk?"

"Yeah, Dad okay?"

"I just got off the phone with him. The Pulaski County police are looking for Caleb."

"Oooo," Thomas let out a breath and felt his chest sink. "What for?"

"Embezzlement charges," Colton said. "He failed to appear in court."

"And that means, what? That we still have no idea where he is," Thomas groaned rubbing his forehead.

"That means he's alive."

"I should feel relieved, but I just feel sick."

"Me, too."

"Someone knew where he was at some point for there to be a court date, right?" Thomas asked.

"You'd think."

"But no one notified us! Caleb didn't reach out to us either!"

"Exactly!"

"How's Dad?" Thomas asked.

"He said to me, 'Thanks for calling. Don't take this wrong, but leave me alone for a bit.'"

"I get that." Thomas understood, his mind reeling.

"I've been trying to work out the timeline. The last time we saw Caleb was—"

"Thanksgiving 2005."

"Right. Mom was sick again, and he headed back to Somerset saying that he'd be back when he could get away from work. He doesn't return any calls. No visit. Then Christmas was the turning point."

"We knew something was wrong," Thomas said.

"We learned he hadn't shown up for work for several weeks, and his landlord said his apartment was empty."

"We filed the missing person's report which went nowhere," Thomas ranted.

"So, why didn't someone contact us when he resurfaced? Why didn't he contact us?"

"We need the missing pieces." Thomas paced. "When did they find and arrest him? What did he embezzle and who from?"

"You mean, just how much trouble is he in?"

"How much trouble makes jumping bail a good option?" Thomas said between clinched teeth.

"How much trouble makes you miss your own mother's funeral!"

"None of this has ever made sense, and now—" Thomas didn't finish his sentence.

"Now we know he's in trouble and not dead."

"No. Now we know he's in trouble and yet again have no idea where he is or if he's okay."

Chapter 9

When Ben met Gracie, times were simpler. Franklin's Grocery carried one brand of apple cider, and a double-scoop ice cream cone at Swirly's cost way less than a dollar. Ben wasn't even 'Ben' back then. He was *Kage*. Today, Franklin's Grocery was no more. Kroger, three times its size, had replaced it. Lots had changed, but not his love for Gracie.

Ben stood in the grocery aisle trying to not think about Caleb. As the police walked toward his front door, it had been evident by their expression that they didn't bring good news. All Ben knew was that he didn't have answers.

Now at the grocery, he pondered apple cider options and thought of Gracie. He wanted to go back to when Gracie made homemade apple cider—her grandmother's recipe— when she believed a warm cup of apple cider fixed everything. He'd since adapted to the jugs Kroger sold, and now discovered it even came in a box: individual packs of dry powder, seven brands, various flavors from cinnamon to spiced, and an organic option.

"Good Morning!" Aaron called from behind the service desk. "Didn't see you come in." Manager of the Kroger store, he was as hometown friendly as Ridgewood got. "I think the weather is finally letting up. Enough rain to float the Ark."

Ben nodded.

"How's the family? Elizabeth's how old now?" Aaron asked.

Ben began unloading his cart. "Turns fifteen this month."

"And that little one, the boy?

"Knox's ten."

"I ain't seen Thomas around here in a while."

Ben pulled his debit card from his wallet and handed it to the grocery clerk.

Aaron, bagging the groceries, jabbered, "I remember when Thomas was little. Gracie, even with only one hand, made being a mother look easy."

"She did better than I did with both hands."

"And that Thomas, he was full of energy."

"And still stubborn," Ben mumbled.

"Actually, I think Gracie's funeral was the last time I saw Thomas."

"Probably so." Ben took his grocery bags, leaving Aaron with a farewell nod.

At home, Ben thumbed through the yellowed pages of the spiral-bound notepad. He needed to be reminded of good memories. She'd captured their story. He loved seeing her name. Sometimes he'd skim the pages, touching her name. He'd slow down for his favorite parts. Especially this one.

Gracie's left index finger rested between Ben's teeth and his quirky, yet charming, grin. As she tugged her finger free from her husband's playful grip, his arms tightened around her beneath the sheets. A tear spilled from her thick lashes. She wiped the tear with her hand—her only hand. Though her right arm lay by her side, forever etched with scars, she had never felt more beautiful and complete in her life. Nestling close, Ben's body enfolded hers under the sheets, his chest against hers. She remembered how she had felt the first time he had held her in his arms, and especially she remembered the encompassing peace that had lingered.

He knew that peace too. He needed that peace. He'd held her the first time and a thousand times, until the last. He sat still feeling at ease, almost empty of everything. The anger had no place any longer, and the anxiety had turned to a calm loneliness. Resting his finger on her name each time he saw it, his eyes fell on the word Stargazers. Flowers. Gracie had written about the flowers her grandmother had planted in the window boxes and flower beds outside of the ice cream shop, and then about how they'd gone empty after her grandmother passed. Flowers. She'd loved flowers. Gracie planted flowers every spring: around the mailbox, down the length of the sidewalk, along the front porch, in flowerpots on the front porch, on the back patio, and around the trees in the backyard.

He'd seen flowers for sale outside Kroger. He fumbled for his wallet and picked up his keys. Aaron, as always, greeted him with a hello.

"I need some flowers."

"Well, we've got flowers. Do you have a particular type in mind?"

"Those outside."

"We got petunias, geraniums, begonias, snapdragons, and marigolds. We also got the kind that come back every year. We got day lilies, black-eyed Susans, Russian sage—"

Ben cut him off, "I'll take 'em."

"Which ones?"

"I'll take 'em all." Ben walked outside.

Aaron followed. "All of which one?"

Ben pointed to the two tables of flowers and put down his truck's tailgate.

"That's a lot of flowers."

"I think we can fit them all in here."

"Uhh-mm," Aaron stammered. "What are you going to do with so many flowers?"

"Buy them, Aaron," Ben repeated, taking two containers and sliding them into his truck bed.

"Those are shrubs," Aaron pointed out.

"Even better." Ben picked up two more.

Once home, Ben called Thomas. "Son, got a favor to ask."

"Are you okay, Dad?"

"Better than fine. I've got a project that needs four hands and a set of knees better than mine. When school gets out, can Knox come for a week?"

"Sure, Dad, but Knox doesn't have much muscle power. You need my help?"

"Nope. He'll do fine."

That night when he slid into bed, he read:

As Gracie walked next to Kage and listened to him, she watched him closely. She didn't remember his face from the grocery the other day, but she had noticed that his arms looked strong. As dusk set in, the thought crossed her mind once more, and this time she wondered what it would be like to be held in those arms.

In the escaping twilight, she concluded that he was handsome. It wasn't just one thing. It was the slight dimple that flared, even when his lips were closed. It was the tranquil sound in his voice, mixed with the way his eyes shifted when he spoke. Thanks to a full moon, she could see his lashes when he blinked and the slightest shadow of a scar above one eyebrow.

As Kage awkwardly moving his hands from the pockets of his jeans to his jacket pockets and back again, Gracie felt her countenance transform. She pursed her lips, to conceal the smile on her face.

He remembered that night. The first night that he'd walked her home from the ice cream shop. Ben turned off the lamp. To himself he said, "She said I was handsome."

Chapter 10

"Roxanne Applesauce?"

"Yes."

"A gift for you, ma'am. Could you sign here?"

She pulled a feather pen from the pocket of her silk robe.

"I can't believe I'm actually meeting Roxie Applesauce! Wow!" He backed away not taking his eyes off her.

Blushing slightly, Roxie waved and closed the door, curious as to what could be in the package. She pulled the ribbon gently and the bow loosened. Lifting the lid, she couldn't believe what was inside—a white kitten, soft and cuddly.

The tag read, "For Girl." Marcella wasn't sure why she was one of only two kids in class who received a present from a stranger for Christmas, but she imagined it had something to do with Santa Claus skipping her house. She was supposed to wait until Christmas to open the gift, but then again, when was Christmas?

Marcella ran though her front door. "It's for me! It's for me!" The big bow looked like a gift itself. She carefully untangled the ribbon and tucked it into her pants pocket. As she tore the Christmas wrap, Marcella couldn't hold back her squeal, "She's beautiful." Opening the box, the baby slid out, right into her arms.

"Give me that!" Her grandmother took the baby. "Who gone and bought you that?"

Marcella shrugged.

"We ain't no charity. Get it, Buster!" Her grandmother threw the doll toward the dog like a fresh bone. Buster bit its neck, gnawing on it like an old shoe. Marcella reached for her doll. Buster growled, shook his head viciously, and scurried out the back door. Marcella never saw her doll again.

Buster had done the same to her baby doll, Roxie, that her mother had given her before she left. He'd trotted off with Roxie between his teeth. He'd returned but without Roxie. It was Marcella's birthday when Roxie came back to her. Each year Roxie grew bigger like Marcella. No one knew Roxie was there. It worked better that way.

MARCELLA—1967—age 19

When the guy she'd met had told her that his name was Rich, she heard Boaz. When she was 15, she'd heard the Bible story. She dreamed of a man who'd take care of her. The clothes Rich bought her looked just like the ones in magazines. She wanted to show her grandmother—yet she never wanted to see that woman again. His apartment had three locks. He said she'd be safe. She didn't know where he went during the day, but he was there at night.

MARCELLA—2010—age 62

When the lady from the mission who visited the libraries and parks showed Marcella the pale pink dress, she touched its soft fabric. Taking it, Marcella headed for the restroom. Peeling off her clothes, she pulled the dress over her head. She pressed her palms against her waist—a perfect fit. She stuffed her hands in its pockets, wiggling her fingers. Her dress had pockets! Retying her thin scarf around her soiled, unkempt hair, her new look was complete.

Tucking her dirty clothes under her arm, she cautiously exited the restroom. She peeked out and then around the corner. She launched straight for the door. She didn't want to run into Irene, Flora, or Roger, whom she'd stolen the money and pills from, or Papa Mack who insisted on cuddling.

Tonight, Marcella, sitting on the abandon house's dusty floor with her sleeping blanket spread out, careful not to get her dress dirty, unwrapped the foil to see what Travis had saved for her. Inside there was a second ball of foil. She opened it to find a fish stick for Kitty-Kitty. For her, there was the juicy fat from a ribeye, bread rolls, and the skin of a baked potato. She celebrated. She had a place to sleep, food to eat, a new dress, and a kitty cat.

Chapter 11

FALL 2008

The first time Haleya presented to UK's Healthcare Physicians, Janice had been pleased. The second time, exactly one year later, it went even better. She received praise for her training scores and her contribution to getting the train-the-trainer concept off the ground.

This week she'd attended a software tech conference in New York. Though Thomas had done well with the kids, the house needed her attention. Haleya pulled Knox's sheets off his bed as her phone rang.

"How was your flight?" Janice asked.

"Good. Glad to be home."

"I have news. It's bittersweet. The hospital created a new position and offered it to me."

"That's good, right?" Haleya sat on the bed's edge. She hadn't expected this. "What kind of new position?"

"They're expanding the development programing. I'll oversee implementation of the new concept. It's training for administrative personnel and upper management. When it's established, I want you to work with me. Without a doubt, your strong numbers and our progress influenced their decision. I'm so appreciative!"

"We won't be working together anymore?" Haleya's heart sank.

"You'll meet your new supervisor next week. She's a new hire, and I've heard great things. I'll keep in touch. Promise. I gotta go."

Haleya's phone slid from her hand onto the rug. That's when she saw the paper wadded up near the foot of the bed. She picked it up to toss in the trash but got curious and uncrumpled it. "Hey, Bug Boy" it said in graffiti-style letters.

*   *   *

The newspaper reporter who'd written Kent's soon-to-retire article called him "accomplished." The list was long: education, research, lecture series, volunteerism, and more. But with so much "accomplished," he'd told Lyndee that something was missing. He didn't know exactly what it was, but he'd soon have time to find out. Travel was on his mind, but not to any particular place. More volunteer work was a definite, but he hadn't decided what or where. On January 1, 2009, he'd be retired Dr. Kent Lambert, age 68, husband to Lyndee, father to Haleya and Gina, grandfather to Elizabeth and Knox, and surgeon to thousands over his past 40 years— and then what? He didn't feel old; he felt unfinished.

He sat with the week's newspapers, trying to catch up. A glance at the first article made him thankful. Earlier this year when he'd mentioned the possibility of retiring, his financial advisor suggested he sell his high-risk stocks and invest in stable ones. The newspaper he held dated, Wednesday, October 15, 2008 read:

Recession-talk scared Wall Street, sending the Dow Jones industrial average to its second biggest one-day point loss ever.

He shuffled through the newspapers on the table. The week's theme was evident:

Another blow to housebuilders as property sales hit a 30-year low; prices keep falling.

Days after the White House's $700 billion rescue plan was approved, it looks like a pebble tossed into a churning sea.

Kent stacked the papers.

"Done reading?" Lyndee asked.

"You've seen one, you've seen them all."

"I just got off the phone with Haleya. A group of boys are making fun of Knox at school."

"I wasn't a fan of him skipping grades. He can do the schoolwork, but kids are ruthless—especially older kids."

Lyndee nodded. "Janice, her supervisor was promoted."

Kent picked up the coffee pot and added a splash to his cup. "She's been fortunate to get to work for Janice."

"She meets her new supervisor next week."

"Whoever it is will like her. She's come a long way—"

Lyndee finished his sentence, "since she struggled in school."

"I remember you working with her. I knew when there was a test the next day. I had to play hopscotch around the index cards you'd made scattered on the living room floor."

"Flash cards and association strategies," Lyndee said. "She got really good at it. She worked as hard for a C as most kids did for an A. In high school, it wasn't me showering the floor with index cards. She did it herself. In nursing school, she made those grades."

"You're someone special to do what you've done." Kent sipped his coffee and pointed at the framed photos of the two teens who'd stayed with them and then at the photos of Gina taped to the refrigerator.

"I'm not sure why we renovated the garage. I expected a placement by now."

"Until then, you'll just keep sponsoring hungry kids from across the sea for, what is it? Only 52 cents a day?"

"More like a dollar a day, but they're precious." Lyndee reached for three photo cards in a basket on the table. "See, Largo is learning about Jesus." She sat next to Kent and shuffled to another card. "Raeti is growing fast because she gets healthy meals now." She pushed the third card in front

54

of Kent. "And KeYan, he skipped a grade in school; he's been working so hard."

Kent looked at KeYan's picture. Then he put out his hand and wiggled his finger for Lyndee to hand him the other two cards. He lifted the picture of Raeti's close to his face.

She leaned toward Kent and pointed to the smile on Raeti's face.

Kent looked at his wife. "I love you."

*   *   *

Ben, pulling into the church's parking lot, saw Colton, cap on backwards and paint brush in his hand. Several youth group kids, on fall break, were around the grounds helping.

"Forgot you had this going on today," Ben said as he stepped out of his truck.

"Did you come to visit your flowers? A few are still blooming," Colton teased from his perch where he was painting the hand railing.

"Good thing the church accepts donations." Ben returned the good-natured humor.

"The burning bush was appropriate." Colton pointed toward its fall red foliage.

"Good one."

Ben had called Colton to pick up the remaining flowers and shrubs to spruce up the church grounds. He'd finally admitted his eyes were bigger than his green thumb. When Knox had visited to help, he'd talked more than helped. After a week with Knox, Ben knew more about a 10-year-old's thoughts than ever before. When he was 10, at the orphanage, no one listened, and his mind wasn't free like Knox's. And now he realized that when his boys were that age, he'd focused more on the wood mill than them. He regretted that.

Ben sat on the step next to Colton. "I still can't believe he never contacted us. Turned himself in, but didn't contact us. Then ran off again." He shook his head.

Caleb had told the police he'd contacted his family.

Ben continued, "What are they doing to find him?"

"Whatever they can. Dad, if he contacts us, you know we've got to let them know."

Ben snorted, "Like he's going to contact us?" Ben stood. "I'm having a hard time with it today." He walked over to the burning bush, cut a couple of twigs with his pocketknife, and raised them in a wave to Colton.

Chapter 12

"Emma Lee, wait up," Elizabeth yelled as she got off the bus. "Why weren't you at school yesterday? Were you sick?" Emma Lee turned, and Elizabeth noticed her swollen eyes. "What's wrong?" Elizabeth pulled her aside. "Tell me!"

"My dad took a job at Murray State. He showed me around yesterday."

"Your parents are splitting up?"

Emma Lee shook her head.

"Then why did he take a job in Murray? You're not moving?"

Emma Lee nodded.

Elizabeth's heart sank. "No!"

"Yes." Emma Lee wiped a tear.

Elizabeth dropped her book bag and covered her face. "Emma Lee," she said through her fingers. "You're my best friend. You can't leave me."

Emma Lee pulled her sleeve over her hand, wiped her tears, and then ran her arm under her nose. "I knew Dad was looking for a new job, but he never mentioned moving."

"He's made the decision and that's that?"

"They cut his position. He doesn't have a choice."

"Then get another job here!" A blur of students passed as the bell rang.

"He tried."

Elizabeth tossed her bookbag over her shoulder and wrapped her arm around Emma Lee. Leaning into each another, they walked to class. She'd known Emma Lee for as long as she could remember. They'd done everything together. She couldn't imagine life without her.

*   *   *

"Whatcha doing?" Thomas asked. Haleya sat with her back against the headboard and a thick binder on her knees.

Haleya pointed to the binder from her new boss, Candice, and continued reading. Candice, displeased with the train-the-trainer concept, put Haleya's teammate, Erica, on a 30-60-90-day improvement plan and had Haleya take progress tracking responsibilities during her co-worker Leslie's maternity leave.

"Are you going to be doing that for a while?" Thomas asked.

Her highlighter between her teeth and both hands flipping pages, she nodded.

Thomas winked at her, pulled out his phone, and left the room.

*   *   *

Ben was used to short conversations with Thomas. They'd developed a comfortable routine, "Hello, how are you? No time to talk." Tonight though, Thomas hadn't rushed off. He shared how Haleya's new boss was changing up everything, and she was working a lot. Elizabeth's best friend was moving. Guys at school were making fun of Knox, and he'd signed him up for the swim team. Thomas downplayed concerns about the economy. This year he'd done well, though not as well as the year before. He had no worries with two houses under construction and three contracts signed for the New Year.

Ben had seen the news reports specific to homebuilders that said gross revenue was down 60 percent from the prior year with a continued drop anticipated, as much as an additional 60 percent over the next two years. The report

58

ended stating that industry sources expect only half the home building companies will remain once the market bottoms.

With Thomas on his mind and Caleb weighing on his heart, he knew just what page of Gracie's notepad to turn to:

"I wish I could make it all perfect for you. I wish I could fix it." He kissed her neck, and Gracie welcomed the tingling sensation.

"It doesn't matter that you can't fix it," Gracie spoke to the distance. "You can't. It can't be fixed." Then she looked directly at Kage. "But you do make it better. You have already made it so much better." Gracie shut her eyes and once more breathed in the cool night air. "As hard as I tried to go on and to escape it, nothing's really changed. I'm still, and always will be, the little girl who ran from that house the night of the fire, that was ... is me." Gracie said the words, though difficult, for the first time aloud.

Wrapping her arms around him, she added, "No matter how many brothers and sisters you hunt up and find, you're still going to be the little boy who grew up in an orphanage, but that's okay." Gracie hoped he understood. Before she had a chance to say another word, Kage's lips pressed against hers, and she knew he did.

Ben placed the notepad in the bedside drawer, on top of Gracie's journal to Caleb. Ben was to give Caleb the journal—if he ever saw him again.

Chapter 13

MARCELLA—1956—age 8

Roxie's private jet floated through the clouds. She'd performed for the President of the United States. It wasn't her first performance for the First Family but her most memorable. She even had her own room at the White House. She didn't want to leave, but she would be back. They'd invited her for Easter.

Marcella, tucked behind a tree, counted nine bonnets.

A lady, peeking beneath her lace bonnet, smiled. "You like my Easter bonnet?" she asked. "I always look forward to Easter. Did you know Jesus rose today?"

Marcella shook her head and bit her tongue.

"You ever been to church?" she asked.

Marcella hugged the tree tighter and shook her head.

The lady's daughter wasn't smiling. The ruffled bonnet with its big bow beneath her chin didn't distract Marcella from the girl's wide-eyed stare as if she were deformed or worse—poor.

"Scat! Scat now! Get out'a here!" Marcella's grandmother stumbled from the porch and ran them off as if they were stray dogs.

MARCELLA—1967—age 19

"Hey," Marcella welcomed Rich home. She leaned forward in the recliner for a kiss. It didn't matter that no one had looked for her when she'd left home at 18. Rich had his own place, and he wanted her.

"Uhh, we got company. There's someone here for you to meet."

"Okay," Marcella stood up, brushing cat hair from her pants.

Rich backed out the door and in came a large man. "Ugly" was the first word that came to mind—his head, shaved and tattooed, and his face acne covered. Frightened by his gaze, she backed against the wall. Rich shut the door, and Marcella was alone with Ugly. Though she'd been betrayed many times, she'd never felt it more so than when she learned Rich had left her with this man to settle a debt.

After he left, Marcella dug in the dresser drawer and found the plastic bag of pills. She swallowed one, waited, and then swallowed two more. On the bed, she rocked, feeling like vomiting but holding back the urge. She scraped her fingernails down her face and scratched her tender forearms.

As the drugs took effect, her body collapsed on the bed, and she was thankful to be numb again. Marcella no longer needed Roxie—she'd found something better.

MARCELLA—2010—age 62

Marcella's pale pink dress made it worth waking up. She felt fancy and dressed for a day out. Marcella waited for the pedestrian signal to indicate she could safely cross. She used to ignore crosswalks. When she was younger and could dodge traffic, she didn't follow rules. Abiding by the law let others control her. Hate had pumped through her veins; anger had become her identity, and she'd held as tightly to it as the drugs. Though she'd never been hit crossing the road, she'd felt life had side-swiped and hit her head-on.

But now she obeyed traffic signals. She hoped doing right would make up for all her wrongs. Though the signal said walk, she looked left and then right. She stepped slowly onto the street and in front of the vehicles. She held her palm

61

forward as if they needed to be reminded not to move. Once she stepped onto the curb, she turned and waved.

It occurred to her that she'd missed out on so much in life, even something as simple as waving. Angry people don't wave. She decided 'Hi' was her new high, and there was no harm in overdosing. She waved through three lights.

Sitting on a park bench, she fumbled in her pocket and felt the three remaining pills. Once, there was a time she would have started the day with all four. They'd been easy to access as long as she'd associated with the right people.

She pulled Dr. Seuss's Green Eggs and Ham from her handbag. Unwanted most anywhere, Marcella had spent most of her days dragging her belongings with her. She felt inconspicuous behind the book—invisible to gawkers.

Today, feeling pretty, she felt gutsier than usual. She peeked around her book. Making eye contact with a mother and son picnicking on a blanket, the mother smiled at her. Marcella sat a bit taller as she flipped a page.

Glancing over the top of her book, Marcella surveyed her surroundings: a couple strolled, relaxed in their chat; two teens sat, heads together, peering at a digital device; and a sharply dressed man, pacing with a furrowed brow, held his phone to his ear. To her left, a boy sat beneath a beech tree. Knees pulled to his chest, back against the tree, he tucked his head. His fingers were woven through tousled hair laying uneven in chopped strands.

"Mama, my faborite book!"

The book, instead of hiding her, had drawn the attention of the boy in light blue striped overalls on the blanket. "My faborite book, Gween Eggs 'n Ham."

She smiled and curled her fingers into a wave.

"Mine!" he stood, dropped his sandwich, and waddled toward Marcella. In one step, his mother had him. She stepped closer.

Marcella glanced at the book, then to the sleeve of her pink dress, and then to the sky. She wasn't hallucinating. The pill she'd taken at best eased her joint pain. Most parents sneered at her and her homeless companions. She hadn't expected kindness.

"She likes that book, too. She has one just like yours."

The mother sat next to Marcella, close enough for him to stretch and touch the book. "You know the story. Tell her the story. 'I am Sam—'"

"Gween Eggs 'n Ham, I AM!" he said and clapped.

Marcella turned the book toward him, as if he were reading it, and flipped the page.

He said, "Sam I Am. Eat eggs 'n ham!"

Marcella flipped to the first page and began reading, "I am Sam. Sam I am—" When she got to the last page, she closed the book.

"I think that made his day." She stood. "My name is Ashley. This is Mason."

"My name is Marcella, but you can call me Roxie."

"Roxie. That's a fun name." She glanced toward the beech tree. "Do you think she's alright?"

Marcella looked toward the tree where the boy sat. "Who?"

"That girl," Ashley tilted her head toward the tree. "She was here yesterday, too."

Marcella glanced at the mud-stained tennis shoes that peeked beneath raveled jeans and the skinned elbow looking for any indication to why the lady thought it was a girl. From her purse, she pulled a small pack of Nab crackers, handed them to Ashley, and pointed toward the tree.

Ashley walked toward the tree. "You've got a sandwich," she told Mason when he grabbed the crackers. "Food," Ashley offered.

The girl lifted her head—striking cheek bones, weak eyes, and a bruise that connected them.

Ashley knelt and placed the crackers on the ground.

The girl looked at them, looked at Ashley, grabbed the crackers, and darted away.

Ashley glanced at Marcella and shrugged. Before leaving the park, Ashley and Mason waved goodbye. Marcella waved until she couldn't see them anymore.

Chapter 14

SPRING 2009

"Can you get that?" Haleya called to Thomas to grab her phone.

"Why does your boss call at bedtime?" Thomas handed it to her. "Doesn't she know you have an early flight?"

"So, quick update," Candice got straight to the point. "Things didn't work out with Erica. Friday was her last day."

"Wow. She'd made it through the probationary period."

"Shouldn't have been a surprise to her. I've got to call Leslie. Her workload just increased. What's your take on Leslie?"

"Leslie's efficient. She follows up and contacts me when she has questions. She's very competent."

"Good. Contact me if you need me." Candice hung up.

"Mom—"

Haleya heard Elizabeth come into the bedroom. "What's wrong?"

"I don't feel good," Elizabeth said.

"Come here," Thomas motioned. He felt her forehead. "No fever."

Elizabeth dropped her head. "Can I stay home tomorrow?"

"School's no fun without Emma Lee," Haleya said to Thomas.

Elizabeth sat on the bed beside her dad and leaned her forehead against his shoulder. "I hate it—"

"So, these bees are for my school project," Knox, entering the room, interrupted.

65

Elizabeth squealed. Thankfully, the bees were in a plastic container.

"What school project?" Thomas asked.

"Science fair," Haleya explained.

"My presentation's tomorrow. If I place, I go to regionals." Knox tried to scoot his hind-end between Elizabeth and his mother who'd sat beside her.

"Get away!" Elizabeth squirmed.

Knox started to take the top off the container.

"Dad!" Elizabeth screamed.

"Knox," Thomas said sternly.

"Wait. If I get stung by bumble bees, do I have to go to school tomorrow?"

In unison, Thomas and Haleya said, "Yes."

*   *   *

"Hey, Bug Boy!"

Knox kept walking toward the bus. When he saw his dad parked along the curb, he remembered swim practice.

"Good job, Knox," another boy mimicked their teacher. "Congratulations on being selected for the science fair."

"Wait! Wait!" one boy said, causing the boys and even Knox to stop. "Bug ... Bee ... Boy!" he said. "His new name is Bugbee Boy!"

Knox jogged toward his dad's truck.

"How was your day?" Thomas asked.

Knox shrugged.

"Did your presentation go well?"

Knox nodded.

"Remember what we talked about?"

Knox looked at his dad.

"The swim strokes. You've got to have your head in the right place. Otherwise, you create resistance, and it slows you down. For the breaststroke, you've got to—"

Knox wasn't listening. Chants of "Bugbee Boy" were in his head.

*   *   *

Since retiring, Kent spent time with Lyndee and Gina, volunteered at the Salvation Army, and occasionally missed his patients. He'd been praying for how God could use him.

"How about Haiti?" Kent asked on the way home from church.

A Northwest Haiti Orphanage Mission group had visited their church. The kids sang and thanked the church for its support. Volunteers who'd been there reunited with orphans they'd gotten to know.

"I'd like to do that. Go there," Kent said to Lyndee.

"I want to go," Gina said. She began to read the promotional pamphlet. "Childr'n born in Haiti with sebere dis'bilitieeth and 'pecial neeths are of'en outcasth at an eawy age. Dozenth have pound hope—" She tapped Lyndee's shoulder with the pamphlet.

Lyndee took it. The Medical Ministry was outlined on the inside panel. "Treating the sick was a cornerstone of the ministry of Jesus Christ, and it's a cornerstone of Northwest Haiti Christian Mission. This amazing ministry can be viewed changing lives regularly in our surgery wing, eye clinic, and general clinics." Lyndee looked at Kent.

"That would be pretty incredible," Kent said.

"No doubt, but you'd be so far away."

"How far?" Gina asked.

"A whole different country," Lyndee answered.

"I just wish you could be satisfied with what you're doing here—what you could do here."

Kent nodded, letting her know that he heard.

Chapter 15

"Dad, please!" Most kids begged for the beach, but Elizabeth wanted to go to Murray for spring break.

Thomas got to thinking. He could drop Elizabeth off at Emma Lee's, then take Haleya and Knox to Land Between the Lakes.

"How about we go somewhere for spring break?" he asked Haleya.

"There's no way!" Haleya pointed to the binders on the counter. "Candice has me covering for Leslie two days a week so she can be with her baby. Essentially, she's handed me what Erica did. It's a load on top of my trainings."

"You need a break." Thomas stepped closer to pull her into his arms. "Elizabeth wants to stay with Emma Lee that week, and we can get a cabin—"

"Thomas!" Haleya busied herself warming up supper. "Money is tight. Your contracts are falling through."

"Just that one. I'll sign on two more to replace it."

"Look at my schedule," she pushed the printout toward him. "Take Lizzy. Take Knox. I can't go!"

"When did your job become more important than your family?" He raised his voice.

Haleya slammed the cabinet door shut. "I can't believe *you* just said that!" She stormed from the room.

*   *   *

"Benjamin Kage?"

"Yes, it's Ben," he answered his phone.

"This is the Palaski County Police Office. Caleb Kage is in our custody."

Ben didn't respond.

"My name is Blake Sanders. I'm the person your sons originally filed the missing person's report with."

"Yes," Ben managed to say.

"I apologize for not contacting you or your sons to properly close out that missing person's report when he resurfaced in 2008. He'd told us he'd contacted his family."

"I understand."

"I'm learning in this job not to trust so easily."

"Trusting isn't the worst mistake."

"He knows that I'm contacting you. He's refused his phone privileges, sir."

"Thank you," Ben said, his voice catching. He cleared his throat. "How does he look?" Ben asked.

"Healthy," Officer Sanders said.

"Dad!" Colton bolted through the door without knocking.

Ben shook the phone, indicating he was talking.

"They've arrested him on illegal gambling charges now," Colton said.

"Officer, I appreciate the call." Ben hung up.

"What'd they tell you?"

"He said Caleb looked good—healthy." Ben started cleaning the kitchen, wiping the counter as if trying to remove stains. He pictured Caleb—a baby bouncing on his knee, a boy on Christmas morning opening presents, and a man hugging his mama for what turned out to be the last time.

When Colton left, Ben flipped to where Gracie had written about his years in the orphanage. Tonight, he didn't feel like Ben. He felt like Kage. He felt raw, bruised, and beaten.

The cruel caregiver's tone rang in Kage's ears as intensely as the rain now beating against his face. He shook his head, willing the memories to be forever

69

buried. The only hint that she was a woman was her uniform's white, knee-length skirt. Her voice echoed deep and coarse, harsh like a man's, and her words were profane and indecent.

Again, Kage shook his head, unconscious of its motion—his mind unrelenting. Maureen's hands were large, much larger than his even now. She hit him across the face with the back of her hand when he didn't speak up. He received the same reward when he did talk, and when he didn't eat quickly enough, and again when he ate too quickly.

Because of Maureen, he even hated the sound of his own name. It was the way she said it—Kaaaedge. She would hold out the "a" as long as she could in one breath, setting the "K" apart from the rest of his name. She would grit her teeth together, moving only her lips. "Kaaedge, sit down." "Kaaedge, get up." "Kaaedge, your heart's too tender, boy!" His name was printed on the inside tag of his shirts, pants, and even his stained underwear. K A G E, stamped on his waistband, served as yet another reminder of his prison.

Ben looked around the home he'd shared with Gracie and his boys. He felt the walls closing in, as they had at the orphanage.

*　　　*　　　*

"Whatcha doing?" Thomas asked.

Haleya turned, a hanger in each hand. "Trying to decide what to wear to Knox's science fair presentation tomorrow."

"They found Caleb."

"What? Really! Where?"

"Jail."

Haleya dropped the clothes and stepped to him. He let her pull him into her arms, his head resting on her shoulder.

70

Thomas mumbled, "I can take Elizabeth to Murray on the first Saturday of spring break and pick her up the following Saturday."

"Okay." Haleya put her hand on Thomas's head.

He felt her fingers in his hair. "I'm sorry," he mumbled. "For what I said."

Haleya nodded. "I'm sorry, too. I wish we could do it."

Thomas liked it when Haleya ran her fingers through his hair. His mama used to do the same.

Chapter 16

Lawrence collected the roses tossed on the stage while she accepted the boxes of chocolate she'd soon be sampling. Minty, nutty, and cream filled—she couldn't decide which was her favorite.

Marcella knocked on the door and turned to look at her cousins in the truck. One yelled, "Go!" She knocked on the door again.

"Hi, you sweet thing. Are you a monster?"

"A ghost." Marcella muttered, although the sheet over her head was yellowed with stains.

"Well, that deserves some candy." The lady dropped a piece of taffy and a pack of Juicy Fruit into Marcella's bag.

"Look!" She showed the taffy and gum to her cousins.

"Good job, little monster!" Taffy Teeth muttered.

"Yeah," said Juicy Fruit.

That night Marcella lay in bed wondering what kids with full bags of candy did. She imagined sorting the candy first by its type: taffy in one pile, suckers in another, and a big pile of gum in every flavor. Then she'd divide it by her favorites, then by color. She reached under her mattress and pulled out a butterscotch. As quietly as a plastic wrapper could be undone, she opened it.

When Mrs. Swander had dropped three pieces of candy in her brown paper bag, Marcella's eyes nearly popped out of the circles cut in the sheet. She knew if anything, they'd flip a coin for the extra piece. So when Mrs. Swander reached out to hug her, Marcella's arms and bag went around Mrs.

Swander's waist. Marcella reached in, grabbed the butterscotch, and slipped the piece of candy into her underwear.

MARCELLA—1967—age 19

Marcella pulled the shard of glass from her eyebrow. She'd waited to tell Rich, not because she'd been scared, but because she didn't want him high when she let him know he was going to be a daddy. She wiped the tears on her cheeks along with the blood trail from her upper eyelid. Once her hands stopped shaking, she steadied her fingers and dialed the only person she could think of.

"Grandma?"

The conversation was short. "Don't you bring no baby around here." The dial tone met her ear with an ache deeper than the beer bottle flung against her face.

MARCELLA—2010—age 62

Marcella had one pack of Nabs left. She had saved them for the girl in the park. She'd been behind her book for an hour—no Ashley, no Mason, and no girl that she'd thought was a boy. It was Papa Mack and Irene that she saw when she peeked around her book. Papa Mack circled from one side, while Irene circled the other. Marcella stuffed the book in her bag and darted to the beech tree. She crunched down covering her face with her hands and started counting. She was at 92 when she felt a tap on her shoulder.

"Hey, that's my spot."

"Oh, it's you!"

"You don't know me. That's my safe spot. Give it back."

Marcella looked for Irene and Papa Mac. They were gone. She stood awkwardly and picked up her bag. "I brought these crackers for you."

The girl stepped back. "No!"

"But you're hungry."

"They sent you. I know they did!" she stepped backwards again, ready to run.

"Who?"

"You know who!" she shouted, turning in a full circle. "Where are they?"

"Is Papa Mack looking for you too?"

"Who's Papa Mack?"

"He was here with Irene."

"I don't know any Irene." The girl dropped to her knees and crawled under the tree.

"Then who are you running from?"

The girl didn't answer.

"But you're hungry?"

"It's a trap. Yesterday I got away. I wasn't going to come back." She leaned forward readying to sprint.

"But this is your safe place," Marcella said and cautiously sat. "My name is Marcella. I want to help."

"I don't trust you. You're lying!"

"I know you're hungry. I'm just gonna sit here. Run if you get scared. I'd never catch you." Marcella opened her bag and let the girl glance in. "See, nothing in there that could hurt you."

After a long glare, the girl settled against the tree, hiding her face.

"Where are you sleeping?" Marcella asked.

The girl didn't lift her head from her knees but shook it.

"Right, you think I'll tell them. I ran away when I was 15. Best thing I ever did. It was really good, and then it got bad. I left home again when I was 18 and never went back. That was good, then really bad. Did you run away?"

She shook her head without looking up.

"Do you know there's a shelter where you can stay? You can sleep there, and they'll feed you."

74

She fiercely shook her head. Not the kind of 'no' that says, 'I didn't know,' but the kind of 'no' that says, 'no way—not safe.'

"There are places that keep women who are in danger—secret places."

The girl looked up, peeking out above her knees like a turtle from its shell.

"I can take you there," Marcella offered.

She shook her head again but kept her eyes on Marcella.

"It's just a tad ..." Marcella started to say, "cooler today."

The girl whipped up on her feet, her arms swinging.

"What?" Marcella shuffled to stand.

"Tad! You said Tad! Where are they?"

"They?"

"They find me! They always do!"

"Are they going to hurt you?" Marcella asked.

She looked toward Marcella with cold, empty eyes.

"They've already hurt you," Marcella said under her breath. "You're safe, I think." She unclasped her handbag and pulled out the Nabs. "If I hand you these, you're going to run."

The girl looked at Marcella and then the Nabs, and with her back against the tree, she slid into her safe position.

Marcella opened the Nabs and pulled one out. "Your name?" Marcella asked. "Doesn't even have to be your real name. Just any name." Marcella shook the Nab in her hand to show that she'd give it to her if she answered.

"Raquel. It's Raquel." Raquel grabbed the Nab and stuffed it in her mouth.

"You can call me, Roxie."

"You're not going to hurt me?"

Marcella shook her head and pulled another Nab from the plastic wrapper. "You don't have to tell me your exact age. I just had rather know than guess."

75

The girl said nothing.

"Older than 16 or younger than 16, how about that?" Marcella asked.

Raquel nodded.

"You have to answer." Marcella pinched off a corner of the cracker and tossed it toward a bird.

"I'm 17. Seventeen!" She took the Nab.

Marcella pulled out the third Nab and held it. "Just anything you want to tell me. Don't care if it's your favorite color or favorite animal."

Raquel was quiet and then she said, "I used to be pretty."

Marcella smiled, encouraging her to say more.

Raquel rested her cheek on her knees and Marcella could see the side of her face. "I had long hair, not this chopped up mess. It smelled clean too. I wore make up, but not too much. I had cute clothes and modeled in middle school. Nothing big, just mall fashion shows and one pageant. I didn't win."

Marcella nodded, listening.

"Dad got in trouble. He was gone for a long time. He owed lots of people money."

She handed the Nab to Raquel.

Raquel pushed it into her mouth. "Mom quit caring. She quit caring about everything–even herself. She left me with my Dad," Raquel said and then was quiet. She breathed deeply as if her soul cried.

Marcella watched with a sense that she knew how the girl felt, even while wishing that she didn't.

Without prompting, Raquel continued, "I was with my Dad when they took me." She looked past Marcella when she talked. "He let them take me."

"Social services?" Marcella asked.

"No. Tad and–" her voice broke off.

76

Marcella thought about ditching the last Nab and digging in her bag for her last two pain pills. "Tell me that your dad came looking for you," Marcella said handing the last Nab to Raquel.

She shook her head. "Can I ask you a question?"

Marcella nodded.

"When did you decide that it was worth living?" Raquel sat up straight. "Sometimes I'd rather be dead."

Marcella gulped. She felt like she was looking into her own eyes. She took the hem of her dress and blotted her face. "I just never died," Marcella said. "It could have happened. It should have happened. I wanted it to happen. It just never did."

"I'm so scared," Raquel blurted out, her tears letting loose.

When Marcella reached for Raquel and pulled her into her arms, Raquel didn't pull away. Marcella realized it wasn't only waving that she'd done too little of in life. As they sat under the beech tree, Raquel's tears turned dry and became the kind that well-up from the soul when the wet ones were used up. Marcella rocked Raquel in her arms, both faces hidden in the other's shoulder where no one could recognize them. Find them. Take them. Or hurt them.

Marcella stood slowly. "I know where there's food—real, restaurant food. I know a place to sleep that has a roof and walls. It's just me and my cat."

Even in the fading sunset, Marcella saw in Raquel's eyes something she hadn't seen in her own for years, until recently. Hope.

Chapter 17

"Have you heard from Emma Lee lately?" Haleya asked, sitting next to Elizabeth as she practiced driving.

"Nope." Elizabeth braked at the stop sign.

"You had a good time when you visited her."

"Spring break was awesome. She has new friends now."

"You should invite her to stay with us fall break."

"She'd just talk about her new friends the whole time. She hasn't even responded to my last text."

"Turn left when we get to the end of this road."

Elizabeth nodded.

"Well, starting in December, you won't have to ride the bus any longer. That should make you happy."

"Which way?" Elizabeth asked.

"Left," Haleya repeated. Elizabeth didn't use her turn signal. "You—"

"I know. No turn signal."

"I know it's not for several months, but you have prom to look forward to."

"Not excited."

"Why? It'll be fun."

"Probably not. Mom, which way?" Elizabeth asked as she slowed.

Haleya pointed right, and Elizabeth clicked on her turn-signal. "So, do you talk with Sophia at school?" Sophia was the neighbor's daughter.

"She's no fun."

"Who do you talk to?" Haleya pointed to the speed limit sign.

Elizabeth slowed down, a little.

"Kara," Elizabeth answered.

"You should invite her over."

"Kara isn't the 'chill at the parents' house' type."

"What kind of type is she?"

"Super cool. No lace or ruffles."

"A tomboy?"

"Not really. She jokes around a lot, but you wouldn't think her jokes were funny."

"Why not?"

"She cusses."

"Do you like dirty jokes?"

"Mom, I didn't say they were dirty. I said they were funny."

"You just drove straight through that stop sign!"

"Oh." Elizabeth glanced back.

"Use your mirrors!" *So much for having a pleasant afternoon together.* Haleya thoughts were interrupted by Candice calling. "Pull over up here. I have to take this call."

"Whatcha need?" Candice asked.

"Did you listen to the message I left?"

"No, it was too long."

"Okay, well. I told you that I did the best I could, explaining everything to the consultant." Leslie had turned in her notice the week before.

"I showed you the restructure outline—"

"It's been challenging to work Erica's groups into my schedule. I really don't see how I can do my job and cover Leslie's too. I need some help."

"They can provide that, if needed."

"Can the contract with them be written for extended personnel support?"

"I make those decisions," Candice said.

Haleya swallowed before she continued, "So in today's meeting, I shared my upcoming month's schedule with them."

"Yeah, I heard that on your message."

"But you said you didn't listen to the message."

"Not all of it."

Haleya breathed deeply and sat back. "We can talk later if you're busy."

"No, now's good."

"Okay," Haleya said exasperated that this was typical of their conversations. "It's just that you told me there was no need to prep for the meeting with the consultant because you had it handled. Then when we got into the meeting, you took a call and motioned for me to cover the meeting. I'm sure the call was important, but I didn't have the answers they wanted."

"It's your job always to be prepared. You know your stuff. You know the responsibilities."

"I know, but I don't think we accomplished much. They'd already read everything we'd sent about the responsibilities and expectations. They sounded like this may not be a fit for them."

"How's that? This is exactly the kind of thing they do."

Haleya knew what the consultant would do. He'd assess the overall situation. Justify that it could be accomplished through one position. Help outline the implementation timeline, goals, objectives, and required resources. He'd create the operation manual and reporting processes, stick around for a few months assessing the situation, and sign off on it. Somehow Haleya was to do the jobs of Leslie and Erica in addition to her own, at a level to meet Candice's satisfaction.

"They had lots of questions," Haleya continued.

"Is it that you don't think that they're qualified?"

"Not that. They just needed answers."

"You couldn't answer them?"

"Not all of them."

"Which ones?"

"They said that they could negotiate the rate."

"Good."

"They wanted to discuss that in the meeting, so they had an idea of how to prioritize our request."

"Our request should be top priority. We give them lots of business."

"But they are booked this month and only have a few dates available," Haleya explained.

"Okay, which ones?"

"The ones they can work in their schedule didn't work with mine. I'd have to reschedule several things."

"What would you have to reschedule?"

"My certification. I'll be in Alexandria at the end of this month."

"Alexandria?"

"Virginia," Haleya said.

"Can't you do it on another date?"

Rescheduling would delay her pay increase. "Yes."

"What about your trainings? Which can be rescheduled?"

"The nurses' trainings or the training I have in New York?"

"I was referring to the nurses' trainings. What training do you have in New York?"

"You have access to my schedule, you know."

"Cancel New York."

"That'll effect the following month's progress."

"That reminds me, I'm going to send you an email about your presentation length. I've marked through some of the sections and activities to cut your training time."

"You'd said that you might make some suggestions once you sat in on the presentation. Some of those activities may be more valuable than you realize—"

Candice cut her off. "So, what dates this month are you meeting with the consultant?"

"We didn't figure that out yet."

"Do I just need to tell them which dates they're taking?"

"They have other contracts and limited availability. They told me which dates they could make work," Haleya explained.

"You didn't just tell them what dates you need?" Candice asked.

Haleya shook her phone and gritted her teeth. *Was Candice even listening?*

"What are the other questions?" Candice asked.

Haleya sputtered, "none." She wanted off the call.

"Okay, work with Tina to schedule a time for us to meet about this."

"Yes," Haleya said trying to manage the quiver in her voice.

Haleya pointed toward the road for Elizabeth to pull out. "Head home."

"Which way?" Elizabeth asked pointing in both directions.

Haleya dropped her head and growled, "You head left to go home."

* * *

Thomas rushed to trade the truck, loaded with porta potties, for his vehicle. With only two houses under construction, he'd offered to help their neighbor, Carson Wyatt. Carson owned a porta potty company with his brother who was recovering from surgery.

Thomas didn't want to provide any ammunition for the boys making fun of Knox when he picked up Knox for swim practice.

"Hey, Dad. Can I have ten bucks for the book fair?"

"Whatcha got your eye on?"

"Ten Creepy Insects that Make Great Pets," Knox said wiggling his fingers.

"What are the other guys reading?" Thomas hoped Knox would take interest in other things.

"Guys my age or guys in the eighth grade?" Knox asked.

"You know what I'm asking."

"They don't read. That's why they sell candy."

"So I should just be thrilled you're not buying ten-dollars of candy."

"Exactly."

"No problem. Remind me tonight. You ready for swim?"

Knox shrugged.

"What are you supposed to think about when you do the breast stroke?"

"Uh, face down—" Knox couldn't remember.

"It amazes me that you can remember dozens of weird facts about spiders, but you can't remember what I told you."

Knox looked out the window.

"Knox!"

"Freestyle, look straight—" Knox tried again.

"Just forget it."

Chapter 18

The Senior Level Executive Coach position Janice asked Haleya to consider provided training to upper-level management and physicians.

The synopsis read:

> Over the past 15-20 years, the awareness of the importance of health care leadership and the value of formal training for such positions have increased dramatically. Historically, advancement to leadership positions in medicine was based on candidates' academic and clinical accomplishments, with no expectation of knowledge of the so-called differentiating competencies, such as team building, communication skills and emotional intelligence.

Candice came to mind. Haleya called her father.

"That's not an easy group to train. We focus on what we do well."

"Honestly, I think it would be intimidating."

"What makes it appealing?"

"Working with Janice. I see why they picked her for this program."

"How's the new boss?"

"Different."

"What's her name again?

"Candice. She's combined two positions with mine."

"What happen to the others?"

"They let Erica go, and then Leslie resigned because the workload was too much with a new baby. They hired Candice to increase efficiency and decrease costs. I think it was her plan all along for one person to do everything."

"What's the time commitment of this *newly created* position?"

"I need to ask. I know it comes with a pay increase. I have lunch with Janice to learn more about it. I'd love to work with her again."

"It's a great opportunity to work with upper administration and obtain the training certifications," Kent encouraged.

"It's a lot to think about." Haleya had ditched her scrubs for business casual when she became a trainer. She pictured herself in a business suit working the room.

*   *   *

Ben had declined all Thanksgiving invitations and ate leftover meatloaf. The quiet house got to him though. With no one to stop him, he did what he'd talked himself out of a hundred times. He typed in his son's name on the public records website. Just a few clicks, there was Caleb's picture. He skimmed offenses one through three. Bail denied—flight risk.

He called the Pulaski County Regional Detention Center, but Caleb didn't accept his call. He reached into the bedside drawer and pulled out the journal Gracie had written to Caleb. He had left her thoughts private. He didn't know what he was to gain by reading them. Maybe he just didn't want them to go unread. He began reading: Caleb's first birthday, the day he was baptized, when he'd learned to ride his bike, a day when he'd helped her plant flowers, funny things he'd said as a boy, and a Mother's Day when he'd given her a 'Treasure Fest' rock. She'd dated each page. Ben flipped to her last entry. She said goodbye. It was an emotional overload to read her words.

Haleya opened the front door for Kent and Lyndee.

"This is Whitney," Lyndee introduced the teen staying with them.

"What up?" Whitney greeted her.

Elizabeth, slouching on the couch, pointed to Whitney's tattoo. "I like it."

A snake wearing a crown wound her arm. "I'm getting more."

"My friend Kara would love that!"

"I'm going to get a tattoo too," Gina said.

"She wants the kind that doesn't hurt," Lyndee winked.

"I can do that." Elizabeth jumped up, dug through the drawer, and pulled out a black Sharpie. "What do you want Gina? A rose or a heart?"

"A heart, a rose, and one like Whitney's."

"Sweet tattoos, please," Lyndee said as the girls shuffled out of the room.

"S'il vous plait," Knox said repeating "please" in French.

"Knox is learning French this year," Haleya explained. "I have to google what he says half the time."

The girls returned, found several colored Sharpies, and headed out of the room.

Lyndee laughed at them. "I've been so nervous about Kent leaving for Haiti in January that it feels good to laugh."

"I'll be fine," Kent said.

"When will you be back from Haiti?" Thomas asked.

"April," Lyndee answered.

Kent clarified, "April is when the others are returning, but I can adjust my return date at any time."

"Four months and they call it a *short-term* mission trip," Lyndee scoffed.

"Life of the retired doctor," Thomas said. "He can't let go."

"Pen-pa, if you're bored, you can help dad haul poop. La merde."

Though everyone chuckled Haleya noticed Thomas didn't particularly like Knox's comment.

Kent put his arm around Haleya. "I ran into Janice. She said the two of you had a good lunch. Sounds like she really wants you in that Senior Executive Coaching position."

Haleya started sharing its pros and cons.

"What position?" Thomas asked.

"Janice wants me to work with her. I'm not really sure about it."

"A new job? Doing what?" Thomas stuffed his hands in his pockets. "I guess you'll tell me about it later." Thomas walked outside mumbling, "When I'm done hauling poop."

"Look at my tattoos," Gina came into the room. A smiling snake wearing a princess crown circled her arm.

"Oh, those are nice," Lyndee said.

On her shoulder was a large heart with *Lizzy & Gina BFFs* written inside.

"What does BFF mean?" Lyndee asked.

"Bwest Prenths Foreber," Gina gleamed. Then Gina lifted her shirt to show everyone "Whitney Waz Here" and the rose around her belly button.

"Okay." Haleya clasped her hands at her chest. "Let's have Thanksgiving dinner."

*   *   *

Thomas wasn't interested in talking though Haleya had tried to explain.

"Janice wants me to work for her. Candice has me covering three positions. I've actually thought about asking for my nurse's job back—"

"But what? It pays less and we need the money or your daddy might be disappointed?"

Thomas saw the color leave Haleya's face. When she was mad, her face turned red. He'd hurt her feelings, but he didn't care. "Maybe if the new job pays well, I can just haul poop for a living."

"No, stop—" Haleya said, waving her hands.

"Not a single contract for next year. Not even a good lead." Thomas hit the kitchen counter with his fist. "Haleya! Do you get it? It's almost December. I don't have a *single* home to build! If I don't have any homes to build, then I don't have a business!"

Thomas grabbed a beer and headed into the garage. The beer went down easy. He rummaged around and found four darts. He took a dart, aimed and threw it—bullseye. When he'd started his own business in February 2007, he had building opportunities lined up. Out of the gate, he'd turned away smaller jobs because he could get bigger ones—more profitable ones.

He threw the second dart. It was off from center. In 2008, he'd made less, but it was respectable.

He threw a third dart. It hung loosely, farther off center. This year had hurt—2009 was a tough year.

He threw the last dart. It bounced off the board—*2010, nothing.*

Chapter 19

MARCELLA—1958—age 10

When Roxie opened the velvet box from Lawrence, she couldn't believe it was a diamond bracelet. She spent her birthday turning circles watching her bracelet sparkle and humming "Somewhere Over the Rainbow."

Marcella snapped buckets full of green beans all day by herself for a week. Her webbed fingers ached. When her grandfather brought sugar snap peas, she felt rejuvenated. As she hulled and watched the bowl in her lap fill, every so often she popped a pea in her month. She discovered the smaller the pea the sweeter. All went well until Grandpa caught her sucking on a pea.

"Meercellee's eatin' the peas." Everyone for a half mile heard. "Maybe she wants some green beans too." Grandma pulled Marcella's head back by her hair and stuffed a handful of unsnapped beans in her mouth. Their sharp pointed ends poked her cheeks. She couldn't chew or swallow. Unable to eat the beans, too scared to spit them out, she cried.

MARCELLA—1971—age 23

The rhythm of the rocker recliner halted mid-motion when Marcella heard the knock. Marcella's back stiffened, and she held her cat tight. Another knock came, hard and mean. They wanted Randall. Though the cat in her arms was quiet, she hushed it. "Shhh. Shhh. They want to take you. If we're quiet, they'll go away." She pretended it was her baby.

When she'd met Randall, she was 21 and still had her baby girl. She wasn't concerned if it would last but just that he

89

was there. She soon learned he had no interest in the toddler that came along with the marriage papers she'd eagerly signed.

Randall never held her baby or played with her—he simply ignored her. Marcella could accept that, as the little she remembered of her stepfather, he hadn't been so kind. Her mother even once told her while she cuddled Marcella that she hated him too. Yet 'Mom' had chosen him over her. She remembered the day they dropped her off at her grandmother's house with a few clothes and her rag doll Roxie. She was four—old enough to know what goodbye meant.

When she saw the dark spots on her little girl's leg, at first, she'd thought it was dirt. Then she wondered if her mind was playing tricks when the smudges wouldn't wash away. She slowly placed her finger tips, one by one, across her baby's thigh and wrapped her thumb around the back of her tender leg. Her finger tips and thumb matched each dark area.

When she'd accused Randall, his angry words haunted her. "What makes you think you didn't do it?" The sting of the back of his hand that burned her cheek and busted her lip paled compared to the realization that he could have been right. Marcella made sure there was no chance she could hurt her baby again.

The front door of the apartment rattled on its henges. "Last chance! You'll regret this!" Randall wasn't there.

Marcella heard a car door shut and the engine turn. Slowly the recliner inched back to its easy rhythm, though Marcella's heart beat didn't.

MARCELLA—2010—age 62

Raquel licked her fingers. "Thank you."

"Thank Travis," Marcella said. For the past couple of days Travis had wrapped food for two.

"I'm so glad I'm not outside in the rain."

"We can thank Kitty-Kitty for that."

"I feel safer with you," Raquel said.

"What are you going to do now?"

"Whatever you do."

Chapter 20

JANUARY 2010

"What up, Whitney!" Elizabeth had stopped by to introduce her friend Kara. "This is Kara."

Lyndee reached to hug Kara, but she shied away.

"Nice to meet you," Kara stretched the gum she chewed and twirled it around her finger.

"You're gonna like 'What up, Whitney.' She's cool," Elizabeth said to Kara.

"Well, here's Gorgeous Gina," Lyndee interjected as Gina bopped down the stairs.

"Wizzy!" Gina ran into her arms. "My tattoos are gone." Gina held out her arm. "I wike your jeans."

Elizabeth turned showing off the ripped jeans. "They're Kara's."

"You girls don't go cutting up Gina's jeans," Lyndee said.

"We won't." Elizabeth shot a sneaky look Whitney's way. "We're headed to watch football practice. Kara's got it bad for Joey the quarterback. She's staying overnight at my house."

"On a school night?"

"Grandma, I'm almost 17, and Dad said it's fine. Mom's not home tonight."

"That's right. She is out of town with her boss."

"I don't mind that she's working all the time. It's like she has homework, and I don't."

"No homework?"

"Not much. How's Grandpa?"

"He called from the airport."

92

"He's bringing me a necklace from Haaities," Gina said.

"A necklace from Hades—like Hell?" Kara asked.

Whitney snorted laughing. "That's good! You're funny!"

"Haiti," Lyndee said. "He's volunteering in Haiti."

"I want something too," Elizabeth said.

"Yeah," Kara said. "I want something cool from Hell."

"Actually, it would be hot, not cool," Elizabeth said and pulled her car keys from her pocket.

Whitney cracked up. "I gotta hang with you two."

"Come with us," Elizabeth invited Whitney.

"You won't find me at a high school anything."

"Who says we're actually going to football practice," Kara winked.

Elizabeth gave Kara a push.

"You girls aren't up to something, are you?" Lyndee asked.

"She's kidding. She wishes we had something better to do."

Lyndee pulled a twenty from her purse. "Get something good to eat. You both could stand to gain a few pounds."

Elizabeth took the money and hugged her grandmother.

*   *   *

With no houses contracted and nothing in the pipeline, Thomas signed on with a temp agency.

"Dad, what does the company you're working for make?" Knox asked.

"Paper towels and paper plates, things like that. When you're at the store and you see Dixie, Brawny, or Quilted Northern, that's what we make."

"Quilted Northern, the toilet paper?"

"Don't you have homework or a wasp that's lonely?"

Taking two steps at a time, Knox's shoulders jerked in laughter. He turned. "Can I call Pen-pa?"

Thomas handed his phone to Knox and pointed to his room.

Thomas took two Advil. The constant dull pressure had started after Thanksgiving. He hadn't apologized for the hurtful things he'd said to Haleya. Days passed with few words. Then life pushed them into their regular routine. Their conversations centering around Elizabeth's attitude and questioning their decision to accelerate Knox in school.

He used to see the little girl in Elizabeth's eyes, but not anymore. No longer content at home, she always wanted to be with Kara. Emma Lee had spent time at their house, where Kara rarely came over. Haleya had compared them as wildflowers—Emma Lee a bellflower and Kara a thistle. Thomas had asked what flower Elizabeth was. Haleya had answered, "Whichever flower her friend wants her to be."

"Pen-Pa says, 'Hi.'" Knox whisked by on the phone.

Thomas stepped around the corner and listened. Knox told his grandfather that the Hercules beetle is considered the world's weirdest insect, recited French words he'd learned, and shared his plans to try out for the school musical.

Thomas stepped around the corner and motioned that he wanted to talk before they hung up.

"Hey, Dad wants to talk to you." Knox headed upstairs.

"Anything wrong with that picture, Dad?" Thomas asked when Knox was out of earshot. "French, school musical, bugs as his best friend."

"I heard a happy kid."

"I'm not sure how to parent the kid," Thomas said. "I feel like I should be teaching him how to be a man. Like you did, making us work at the wood mill."

"You hated the wood mill."

"I just didn't want to do it forever or live in Ridgewood forever."

"Truth be told, I didn't plan to stay in Ridgewood either."

"I know you wanted me to take over the business. Then Colton never took interest, but who can argue with God's call, right?"

"Who was I foolin'? Wood mills are nearly a thing of the past. Others have done well, though. One in Louisville, another in Lawrenceburg, others in Morehead and Tompkinsville, several in Elkton—"

"Dad, I get it."

"I wanted to pass it on."

"You passed on something as important. I've done well because of the start I had. With Knox, I just feel something's missing. We don't do boy things. I don't want Knox to grow up a—"

"Sissy," Ben finished the sentence.

"He needs some toughening up."

"Not necessarily. Don't take the sweet outta that boy. That's what makes him special."

"He's not going to always be a boy."

"Don't take the sweet outta him," Ben repeated. "How's business?"

Thomas made up an excuse to end the call.

*　　　*　　　*

With Knox on his mind, Ben read what Gracie had written about him as a boy capturing it even though she hadn't been there.

Kage couldn't remember her face or her name, but he could remember feeling his arms wrapped around her tiny frame. She was the orphanage lady who read Bible stories to him—not Maureen, the mean one with the big hands, but the one who was full of hugs. She was the one who taught him right from wrong as she rocked him, whispering in his ear that he was a good boy until he could no longer hold his eyes open. Then her name came to him—Lady. Kage realized now that it was probably spelled Lattie, but as a boy she'd been his "Lady." She made rounds each night and said prayers with the children.

He remembered asking Lady, "What does it mean to have a tender heart? Is that a disease?"

She responded, "Oh, a tender heart means you'll be a great daddy someday and a good husband when you grow up. God loves tender hearts."

Ben's love for Knox was something he'd never imagined. He wished he could keep the ills of the world far away. He'd do anything for that boy and his *tender heart.*

*　　*　　*

"I'm leaving the hotel, headed for the airport." Not sure what to expect, Haleya had hesitated to call home.

"Kara came home with Elizabeth last night. It sounded like they stayed up all night, but they made it to school."

"How's Knox?"

"Woke up speaking French, but I only know French toast."

Haleya laughed along with Thomas. It felt good and eased the tension. "At least Knox is talking to us. Elizabeth doesn't unless it's about what she wants to do and the money she needs to do it."

"I'm not sure about her friend Kara. I hid my wallet," Thomas said. "Learn anything helpful from your job shadowing adventure?"

Haleya appreciated Thomas's playful tone. "The concept is good. It's a smaller hospital, and that's why it works so well. Candice told me she'd share her assistant Tina with me," Haleya laughed. "I'd enjoy working with all the nurses on their continued progress. But—" Haleya paused.

"But what?"

"But Candice doesn't understand. We're nothing alike. She's not married, doesn't have kids, or extra-curricular activities, not even church. Honestly, I'm not sure that she could do what she's asking of me, but it's obvious she *thinks* it can be done."

"I know the kids are a handful alone, and then there's me."

She could see his dimple flare though she wasn't with him. "Thank you for saying that." With his words, she felt a wall crumble. "It's been hard."

"I know," Thomas said. "I've just got to get things worked out on my end. I've got to accept that—"

"We don't have to talk about it right now. I'm ready to be home."

When Haleya's flight landed in Lexington, she said goodbye to Candice.

Candice, though, suggested they grab a bite. "Let's debrief."

"I, I—" Haleya stuttered.

"After we grab our luggage first, of course."

Haleya didn't know if she had it in her for another conversation on "hospital alignment" *per Candice.* She felt like she'd been running on "fake" all afternoon. She needed to recharge. "I need to get home."

"We'll make it quick," Candice insisted.

After an hour with Candice, Haleya got in her car to head home. She closed her tired eyes before starting the engine. January 12! She'd accomplished few of her regular duties, having instead focused on making the new structure work. The consultant had indeed found time to start the effort just as Candice had said he would, though he hadn't followed-through on his promises. Of course Candice didn't care. She was getting her way.

Pulling out of the parking garage, she tried to focus on driving, but as she merged onto the interstate, her thoughts returned to work. Haleya had passed on the Senior Executive Coaching position. If it had felt right, then she would have pursued it. Several things Janice had said when they'd met for lunch stuck in her mind.

Haleya was on her second glass of water when Janice arrived. She sank into the bench cushion across from Haleya. "Sorry to be late. Oh, it feels good to sit down." She rolled her neck. "Getting this project off the ground has been like an unrestrained roller coaster ride."

"I didn't know what you wanted to drink. I just got us waters," Haleya said.

Janice held up her finger for Haleya to wait as she downed it. "I needed that." She waved to a server passing and pointed to her empty glass. Finally focusing on Haleya, she leaned forward, arms crossed on the table. "How *are* you? The kids good?"

"Where to start," Haleya laughed. "Lizzy's a handful. She's rarely happy. If she is, it's like she's on cloud nine and then hates the world an hour later."

"Still beautiful though?"

"Gets prettier every day."

"And Knox?"

"He's going through a tough time at school. Some of his classmates make fun of him. It's tough. Thomas signed him up for the swim team—"

"Good," Janice interrupted.

"Not so good. Knox likes to swim but would rather glide with turtles than compete with sailfish."

"Sailfish?" Janice asked and lifted her glass for the server.

"The fastest fish in the ocean. They swim 68 miles per hour. Knowledge, thanks to being Knox's mom."

Janice laughed as her phone buzzed. "So glad you called. Listen, I'm at lunch, but I know we've got to go over the numbers. I don't think we've accounted for everything."

Haleya circled her finger around the top of her water glass. Janice was so upbeat. On top of it all. So together, unlike Haleya felt.

Janice pulled a paper from her purse, read through some information, and laughed out loud. "You've got it. You're the best," she said before hanging up. "You know when you get to the top on the roller coaster and it takes off downhill and then swings you in every direction?"

Haleya nodded.

"And you don't know whether to scream or laugh, so you just do both."

"Yes," Haleya understood.

"That's my life."

"You look like you love it."

The server walked up to take their order, but Janice sent him away. She scanned the menu and continued talking. "I *do* love it, and you will too." She winked and started into the job details. Just listening, Haleya felt like she'd jumped from the tilt-a-whirl ride she was on every day with Candice to Janice's roller coaster ride. After her last real roller coaster ride, Haleya had a throbbing headache, bruises, and nausea.

Their lunch discussion nearly gave her motion sickness. Though the position sounded thrilling, in part because of Janice's enthusiasm, Haleya could read between the lines. More travel, so much to learn—quickly, and the expectation that she'd bring the same "wow" factor in this new position as she *had* the pervious one when she'd worked for Janice.

Then, Janice mentioned that her divorce was nearly final.

Haleya gasped. "Janice!" She leaned forward. "You didn't tell me."

Janice waved it off. "It was a long time coming. You know all the counseling we've been through."

"But you were better. You were happy—"

Janice cut her off, "Well, that was then, and this is now. You win some. You lose some." Janice motioned for the server to take their orders.

Haleya wasn't hungry anymore. Janice was still the passionate person who'd inspired her to be more than she thought she could be. She'd always wanted to be like Janice in so many ways, and yet now, she didn't.

The national news on the radio broke into Haleya thoughts as she drove. She nearly ran off the road.

> Haiti today at 4:53 p.m. was struck by a devastating 7.3 magnitude earthquake, about 16 miles west of the capital, Port-Au-Prince. Dozens of aftershocks are expected that could scale up to 4.5 magnitude or greater. Communication channels are broken. Thousands of deaths are predicted, with an estimated 1.5 million people being displaced.

*　　*　　*

Lyndee's calls weren't going through to Kent or any number associated with the mission. It was killing Lyndee to lay awake in bed not knowing. *Where was he? Was he okay?* Even though she knew that the Northwest Haiti mission was 140 miles from the epicenter of the earthquake, not hearing his voice was torture.

At 5 a.m. Lyndee's phone rang. She answered it, not sure if she'd been asleep, but fully awake now. "Kent! Kent!" Lyndee cried into the phone.

"We're okay."

Throughout the night she'd cried out to God to hear his voice again. He was alive; he was okay.

Chapter 21

"Pen-Pa, you've got to see what's on TV!" Knox was spending spring break with Ben. "Last month, this oil rig in Florida called Deepwater Horizon exploded, killing 11 people, igniting a fireball visible 40 miles high. It's the largest oil spill ever in America!"

"That's a really bad deal."

"Somebody's daddy probably got killed. That's sad."

"You're lucky to have a dad. I didn't grow up with a dad or a mom."

"They've been fighting a lot."

"What about?"

"Everything," Knox went on about the oil spill. "And then, there's the fish, Pen-Pa. The ocean is their world. It's going to kill thousands of sea turtles, fish, dolphins, and whales!"

"You've got a good heart," Ben said. He thought tender but didn't say it.

"The heart beats 4,800 times per hour. That means a person's heart beats over 100,000 times each day."

Fascinated by what fascinated Knox, Ben listened as he hopped from subject to subject.

*   *   *

"Then Mom, Candice calls me like it's no big deal and says 'I need to talk to you about your presentation scores,'" Haleya ranted while helping her mother clean windows. "She then said my overall score fell to a six and reminded me the goal is eight. Then she says, 'you know the tech company provides trainers at a very affordable rate. I know prior management wasn't pleased with their mediocre ratings, but that's still an option.'"

"Why would your score drop?"

"At Candice's *suggestion*, I cut out the activities to shorten the training. Now, though, it's as if Candice has forgotten that I mentioned the importance of the activities. Suddenly, it's the presentation scores that matter most." Haleya's towel flew from her fingers as she tossed her hands up.

Lyndee handed the towel back and taped a picture of her newly sponsored child to the wall.

"Mom! Are you listening?"

"Yes." Lyndee sat and turned a chair toward Haleya. "I keep thinking about your dad."

"You talked to Dad?" Haleya realized she'd been acting like Elizabeth: me, me, me. "Sorry, Mom. I don't talk to Thomas anymore about this kind of thing."

Lyndee put her hand on Haleya's as she sat. "I see the changes in your family. I miss Thomas's ease, your cheer, Elizabeth without the bad language, and Knox sharing silly facts instead of asking tough questions."

"What bad language and tough questions?"

"I didn't mean to tell on them, but I know that it's different than when they were younger."

"Mom, tell me," Haleya persisted.

"Well, when Elizabeth talks to Whitney, she says things she didn't used to say. Their conversations are PG-13."

Haleya covered her face. "I've never heard Lizzy cuss."

"I did interrupt and told them those words are not okay in my home."

"What are Knox's tough questions?"

"He's just trying to figure out why people say one thing and do another. Teachers at school, so-called friends—"

"Parents," Haleya interrupted. "He's smart. We haven't been consistent lately. When Thomas is angry, he's mean.

He and Knox aren't a lot alike, and Thomas gets frustrated. I–"

"Don't."

"But I don't always get it right either," Haleya confessed.

"Every time I put the toilet paper on its holder 'wrong' Whitney lets me know. Forget that she didn't even have toilet paper before she came to live here and that it's my house, I'm supposed to know how to put the toilet paper on 'right.'"

Haleya dropped her head and snickered. "It's like you've done this before."

"You aren't going to be perfect, and you aren't going to win with a teenager when you debate at their level."

Haleya leaned toward her mother. "Do you have room for two more kids?"

"I have my hands full with a husband who's decided, instead of coming home this month, that he's going to stay in Haiti."

"What? He's not coming home?"

Lyndee shook her head. "He's staying."

"Has everyone lost their minds?"

*   *   *

"Lizzy not home?" Lyndee and Gina had dropped by to give Elizabeth her birthday presents.

"Not yet," Haleya said.

"Where's Knox?" Gina asked.

"In his room. Since school let out, he's spent most of his time on his computer."

"I want to thee his awardz," Gina said. Knox had racked up at the 8th grade graduation.

"Go ahead."

"Knox," Gina started up the stairs. "I'm coming to thee you."

"Doesn't feel like a birthday," Lyndee observed.

"We asked her when *she'd* have time for her 17th birthday." Haleya pulled out an envelope with Elizabeth's name on it. "She only wanted money."

"Well, that's easy."

"Not a lot of fun to shop for, but easy."

"Is Thomas here?" Lyndee asked.

"No, unfortunately, the attorney ran late." Haleya said. "Shutting down Kage Construction."

"Ohhh."

"He'd set May as the decision month. If there was no business, then he'd move forward."

"What's he going to do now?"

"Maybe construction management again."

"Heeeyyyy!" Elizabeth shot through the front door with Kara and a guy Haleya hadn't met. Elizabeth called over her shoulder, "Oh, this is Sam." They darted past and up the stairs.

"Lizzy, birthday presents down here!" She called to them. No answer.

"It would be rude to cut the cake without her, right?"

Lyndee nodded.

"How's Dad?" Kent had joined a traveling surgical team in Leogane, the earthquake's epicenter.

"He's good. At least he was the last time we talked. Cell service is less reliable where he is now."

"But he's safe?"

"He's in the middle of the madness now. I can't listen to the news—so many people, so many problems, so many needs."

"Are you okay, Mom?"

"I hate this. It's selfish, but I need him too. Some days I'm proud of him. Some days I'm angry that he's not here. I miss him. I miss us."

Haleya could hear herself in her mother's words. She and Thomas were under the same roof but some days she felt as distant. "How long's he going to do this for?"

"He doesn't know."

Haleya grabbed the towel. "From my experience, cleaning a window helps. The harder you scrub, the better you feel."

*   *   *

Haleya's phone conversation with Candice started off well. "Your May presentation scores were strong," she shared. Candice had watched the scores daily. Haleya knew because she'd forwarded Haleya participant comments she thought could *help* Haleya improve.

"Great," Haleya said. "I added back in some of the exercises for information retention. I'm not getting home for dinner with my family though," Haleya admitted.

"The nurses during the roundtable assessment were full of praise."

An almost-compliment, Haleya thought. "That's great to hear. I love it when nurses email me after a training, and Janice would always forward me their positive comments."

"I get those. Most are good."

Did she need to point out that, on occasion, she received less-favorable ones or was she saying some of the positive comments weren't good enough to meet her standard?

Candice continued, "If you don't see me tomorrow, then I got tied up in a meeting."

"See you where? I have training all day."

"I know. I have a packed day too," Candice said and followed with a quick bye.

Haleya felt deflated as she did after most of their conversations. Any encouragement seemed overridden by vague insinuations that she was somehow lacking.

The next day, in the midst of her training, the doors opened and Janice pushed in a cart with a triple-layered cake. Janice and her entourage cheered, "Haleya! Haleya!"

What was happening? It wasn't her birthday or any sort of anniversary. Haleya recognized the hospital's CEO. He reached out for her lapel mic.

"Every year, three Super-Star team members are chosen from hundreds of nominations. The award is presented to honor a person whose attitude and dedication exemplifies what our hospital is all about. This year's first Super-Star award goes to Haleya Kage." Janice started jumping. The trainees stood clapping. The CEO unveiled an acrylic statue, and Janice snapped pictures.

The CEO continued, "Award criteria: consistently goes above and beyond; is known for respect, compassion, dignity, and dedication; values teamwork and collaboration; and has a history of implementing innovative ideas benefiting the organization."

Haleya wiped a tear. She thought of her mother who'd patiently helped her through school and her father who'd taught her to stand on her head. She thought of Thomas and how he'd come to her rescue when she was overwhelmed in college and insecure beginning her career.

That afternoon, Haleya forwarded a picture to Lyndee and got a response right away. "So proud of you!" She sent it to Kent, but it bounced back. She sent it to Thomas. No answer.

When she got home at nine o'clock that night, Elizabeth and Knox were goofing off. She got them to bed with a few threats and then a bribe that worked. Thomas was asleep already. When she crawled in bed with him, he smelled like liquor and cigarettes.

Chapter 22

MARCELLA—1958—age 10 ½

Roxie's fingernails were perfectly sculptured with the brightest red polish applied. The salon that catered only to the elite had named the polish for her—Roxie Rose Red. Through the front window, she saw Lawrence pull up in the limousine. Escorting her to the car, Lawrence steered away the gathering crowd. She blew kisses from her Roxie Rose Red fingertips.

When she showed her grandmother her sore foot, she'd done nothing. Marcella walked on her tiptoe for a week. When a classmate said that she smelled rotten potatoes, the teacher sent Marcella to the nurse. The nurse warned her that draining the puss from the large boil would hurt. Marcella gritted her teeth, her jaws clenched.

The school nurse said, "Wearing socks will keep this from happening again."

Marcella nodded, but without hope. She didn't have any socks.

MARCELLA—1971—age 23

Randell packed his cooler as Marcella got in the truck holding her cat. She could see the ground through the rusted-out floorboard as they drove down a dirt path and to the creek's edge. Randall took care of business first. The man they met placed a bag in the cooler, and Randell handed him an envelope.

Mittens rested in the sun next to Marcella. She didn't hear Randall approach.

"I'm tired of you bringing that stinkin' cat everywhere we go!" He grabbed Mittens and threw him in the water. The creek was up, and its current strong. "You dumb—" he cursed and laughed at Marcella calling frantically for her cat.

Marcella rushed to the water's edge and slipped on the bank, falling onto her hands and knees. Scrambling to stand, she ran along the creek. Mittens bobbed up and down. Reaching for him, she tumbled into the water and managed to grab hold of a fallen tree.

"That cat can swim better than you. I hope it drowns! You don't need no cat. You got me."

It was Mother's Day. Marcella had no reason to celebrate it. She never had. She just wanted her cat back.

MARCELLA—2010—age 62

"What?" Marcella sat up in the dark. She'd heard something. "Kitty-Kitty," she called out. *Had he knocked something over?*

Flashes of light blinded her, moving across the room and to Raquel. In seconds, they had her.

"Get out!" Marcella screamed at the men. There were three of them. The flashlight beam shined directly into her eyes. "Tad! Let her go!" She suspected it was Tad's boot that kicked her directly in the face. She felt it with horror, but then the kicks to her ribs came one after another. She only remembered the first two.

Chapter 23

OCTOBER 2010

"The software conversion has been moved up," Candice shared. "This way we get in on the front end, but we've got to move fast."

"What was wrong with the January kick-off schedule?"

"Being one of the first has advantages."

"And disadvantages," Haleya pointed out. "A later date would allow the kinks to be worked out for a smoother conversion."

"I was able to get you into their training starting Wednesday. It lasts until mid-morning on Friday."

"This is Monday. That means I have to fly out tomorrow evening? I'd have to reschedule this week's trainings."

"Tina's booked your flight and is rescheduling those."

"But we're also behind on several of the two-day trainings, and I have the quarterly progress reports completed for us to review. We need that to happen so the nurses get feedback to improve. We don't even have the official responsibility handbook for my position that you requested from the consultant. It's way past due—"

"I'll see that the consultant gets that to us," Candice interrupted. "We were talking about the software conversion. We're negotiating final costs with them for the upgrades, so it's important that you 1) notify us of any concerns as you train with them and 2) cooperate and build relationships. We are a large account for them. They are looking to determine which accounts will be low or high maintenance. We want to prove ourselves as a knowledgeable, skilled team. Call me after you get the email with the details if you have questions."

"I have questions," Haleya said. "Do we still need to do the trainings we are behind on if so much is changing with the conversion?"

"We'll know that answer soon."

"Conversions can be complicated."

"They don't have to be," Candice responded. "Once you're familiar with the new software, we'll get all the nurses and staff up to speed. That will take—"

"Wait!" Haleya said. "Staff?"

"This software also accommodates the administrative staff's needs. Everyone will need to come onboard with the new programing as soon as possible."

"Wow! That's going to be—" Haleya started as a zillion thoughts came to mind. "Security levels at log-in will be crucial."

"It may take multiple visits to New York before you feel confident with all the software's components. There's an orientation online you can start—"

"Multiple trips? You know it's difficult to stay on top of the progress assessments when I travel." The last time she'd been out of town, Thomas had started his company's shut down. Knox got a stomach bug, and Elizabeth came home twice past curfew thinking Thomas would be asleep—he wasn't.

"That reminds me, there's an online assessment you'll have to pass before you can begin to train the staff."

"This is a lot."

"You've got me and Tina," Candice said. Tina had already shared with Haleya that Candice was super-high maintenance and that she felt maxed out.

"And that's going to help me how?"

"Tina will keep your schedule, and I'll keep things moving."

Haleya burned inside. She had always been able to keep herself scheduled and keep things moving when there was a manageable workload. Haleya could predict the new norm. Tina would constantly be adjusting from the over-ambitious schedule to what was reality, taking up additional time and inconveniencing everyone involved. There weren't enough days in a week to train, travel, learn the new software, gauge nurses' progress, produce the progress reports to review—which Candice had rescheduled twice now—and then follow-up with the nurses so the initiative had any value. Candice would call out what was critically off schedule and push it forward. She'd look like the problem solver, when in reality, she was just performing sporadic, emergency surgeries to keep the monster she'd created alive.

"Did we lose connection?" Candice asked.

"No, I'm here."

"Okay, I'm having Tina send you everything you need to know in an email."

"Another question—" Haleya asked, but Candice was gone. Haleya pushed her phone away to distance herself from it and that conversation. Elizabeth shot through the front door. "How's my senior?"

"Awesome!" Elizabeth headed upstairs.

"Your day, Knox?"

"*Not* awesome! I hate 9th grade!" He headed upstairs.

Following them in, Thomas heard the exchange. "I'll check on him."

Less than a minute later, Elizabeth came downstairs holding her keys.

"Where are you headed?"

"Kara's."

"It's a school night."

"I know."

"Be home by nine," Haleya called out the door.

Knox trotted down the stairs, shoulders slumped. Thomas followed a step behind.

"Do you have homework?" Haleya asked.

Knox shook his head and opened the refrigerator.

"Who's your favorite teacher?" Haleya asked.

Knox shrugged, pulled out a whip cream can, leaned his head back, and filled his mouth.

Quietly, Thomas said, "The school kids told his science teacher that he prefers the nickname Bugbee Boy."

"Oh, no! He didn't call him that?"

"No, but it embarrassed him. I told him it sounded better than Butterfly Boy," Thomas pulled out a beer from the fridge.

"Dad!" Knox heard. Taking the whip cream can, he stomped up the stairs.

Haleya glared disapproving at Thomas. Maybe it was their lack of communication for the past six months that had built up inside her. Maybe it was seeing Knox deeply hurt and Thomas's callous response—almost as if he sided with the cruel boys. Before she thought, she spouted, "What if someone said you were an out of work lamebrain!"

The words just came out. Her point was meant to help him better understood Knox's feelings not to intentionally insult him. After his last placement ended, the temp agency hadn't called with another. Her words, a punch to his gut, wouldn't soon be forgotten.

*   *   *

Thomas shook his wrist loose and then massaged it. He'd let his anger get the best of him. He glared at the busted sheetrock. *What had he expected?* Haleya had, in fact, been screaming at him when they first met. He looked down at his lace-up Red Wing boots that she'd bought for his birthday.

112

He regretted tossing out his favorite pair of pull-on Red Wing boots like the ones he'd had in college.

He peered at the dart board hanging on the garage wall. Thomas squinted to perfect his aim, locking on his target. He mumbled, "I should have kept walking right past her in my Red Wing boots." Pulling back for the release, he stepped into a lunge and exhaled with the roar of a grizzly. The dart hurled. He'd had the choice to leave "Miss Prissy Pants" to fend for herself against the world—or planet Earth to be precise. The force of his throw—roughly the same he used on the garage wall—caused the dart to bounce off the corkboard. It hit the concrete floor, breaking its delicate tip. Its demise brought Thomas bent satisfaction.

But Thomas hadn't kept walking and let her fend for herself. He knew that even if she hadn't called out to him, seeing her struggle, he would have stopped. It was second nature for him, not because his mother taught him always to offer a helping hand, but because she had needed it. It had only taken one time, at five years old, for Thomas to see his mother on her knees, frustrated and in tears, as she gathered shattered pieces of her Fine China from the floor, to know she needed help. On campus that day, the frustration on Haleya's face had reminded him of his mother's when he'd helped her sweep up the shards of glass.

Broken against the concrete floor, the dart rested. Next to the garage door, the ragged edges of the hole in the sheetrock, where he'd tried to release his frustration, mocked him. *Would his mother be proud? Proud of his selfish choices, quick temper, idle hands.* He thought about how with one hand, his mother managed her grandfather's ice cream shop and then three rambunctious boys. With his two hands, he managed to mess up everything. Thomas's glare followed another fierce throw that brought a second dart to its demise—yet this time he felt nothing but regret.

Chapter 24

At work, Haleya functioned on autopilot. "The most advanced point-of-care systems include a digital tablet, an embedded wireless radio with an internal antenna, and a barcode reader—"

"Can you repeat that?"

Haleya didn't remember a word she'd said.

"And I didn't understand what you were saying earlier about troubleshooting," another nurse asked.

"Okay, we'll review." Haleya flipped back a few slides. She dug inside for the passion she'd once had. The thrill of demonstrating the conveniences and time-saving measures no longer brought satisfaction—not when things weren't right at home. Her mind instead was on Thomas and getting to the airport. Haleya, packed for the week, had left home that morning without a word to Thomas.

She yearned for the life she'd once had. She missed Knox's younger years and his thousand-and-one questions when he thought she had all the answers. *How is plastic made? Who discovered shrimp?* Now he went straight to his room after school, got on his computer, and found his answers on the internet. She missed Elizabeth's interest in hair bows, now replaced by an obsession with mascara and eye liner. Mostly she missed Thomas's arms encircling her as if she couldn't break free—as if he'd never let her.

"The locking docking station allows you to mount to the computer in hallways or patient rooms for easy access." Haleya continued, though her thoughts returned to a time before point-of-care technology existed, when she'd first been introduced to a simple, old fashioned hammer. She thought of the day she'd met Thomas and remembered how he'd come to her rescue.

Using her body's weight, Haleya stood, alone, on a farm wagon with her hip pressed against a bulky piece of plywood to keep it standing. Planet Earth wasn't going to be created in six days—well, its paper mâché replica. Her sorority sisters, responsible for the Earth Day float, were no shows, and she'd written off their partners, the agriculture fraternity, on the first day when the only two who showed up had other things on their minds.

She pulled a screw from her pocket and held it along the edge of the plywood board that swayed and hovered awkwardly as she tried to steady it. Like the headboard of a bed, the plywood needed to be attached with tools—that she only knew from Home Depot commercials—to the frame erected on the wagon. The electric screwdriver only had one burst of power and buzzed to a halt. "I can't believe this!"

When she thought it couldn't get worse, the first raindrop fell. "UGGH," Haleya screamed. She feared tears weren't far behind. Adjusting her hold, the board fell forward knocking her to her knees. She beat her fist against the wagon's plank floor and then pushed her back against the board trying to stand. "Hey! Hey, you! Get up here and hold this! Where is everybody?" Haleya yelled from under the board when she spotted a guy nearing.

"Okay. Like this?" He jumped up on the wagon and held the board with one hand.

"Yeah, like that," Haleya huffed.

"Now what?"

"I don't know!" Haleya turned in a circle, her hand against her forehead. She wasn't sure if her headache had started before the board attacked. "These screws are supposed to go there. See how that would hold this thing in place. But—" She picked up the electric screwdriver and allowed its pitiful moan to make her point.

"Hold this."

Haleya used both hands and her chest to keep the board upright.

"This is all we need." He found a hammer and nails. Placing the nails between his lips like four dangling cigarettes, he shifted so his shoulder held the board while he hammered in the first nail. By the third nail, the board was standing on its own.

Not letting Ag Boy get away, she fed him more nails and then a 2 x 4. "This needs nailed there. Then we have three more to put together like this, so it makes a box. It's a base to hold that in place." Haleya pointed to a large, hand painted globe that once on the wagon would tower over her five-foot four frame. "Then I need you to take that and—"

"My name is Thomas," he interrupted.

"Okay. I was thinking we use that board and prop it on the edge of the wagon to roll Earth up—"

"Nice to meet you, uhh?"

"Haleya. I'm Haleya. Do you think that'll work?"

"How do you spell it?" Thomas asked as he tugged to make sure the 2 x 4 was fastened tight.

"What?"

"Your name." Thomas looked up at her, again four nails extruded from his lips.

"You want to know the spelling of my name?"

"Yeah." His lips less skewed with each nail removed. "H-A-L—?"

"H-A-L-E-Y-A, okay?"

"Okay." Thomas completed the last nail and kicked the boxed 2 x 4s at the center of the wagon with the tip of his steel-toed boot. "Yep, that should hold your big ball."

"Earth."

"Whatever you say."

"For the Earth Day Parade. Don't you celebrate it?"

"Nope. Who did all the painting?" Thomas asked balancing the man-size paper-mâché ball with both hands as he rolled it up the makeshift ramp.

"My sorority sisters. Now you see how much they could care about the Earth. They'd let it get soaked in the rain." Haleya flung her hands above her head as if the steady sprinkles were instead a torrential downpour.

"Usually the Earth appreciates a bit of rain," Thomas ribbed.

Haleya glared at him and pointed. "It needs to go right here."

"How are you going to get it to rotate?"

"You and your brothers must think you're funny, don't you? I'll tell you what. I'm unimpressed." Haleya touched Africa making sure that the sprinkles hadn't harmed it.

"What?"

"Lazy, irresponsible—"

"Colton and Caleb?"

"I don't know their names! If you hadn't come along, I—"

"I guess it would have been the end of the world?"

Haleya tightened her lips. As much as she fought it, she laughed. "I really hate Greek Week. I hate this silly Earth Day Parade. I love my sorority sisters, but they are almost as irresponsible as your brothers."

"Why do you keep dragging my brothers into this?"

"Because it's supposed to be your project too!" Haleya pointed to the Greek letters on the board they'd erected.

Thomas scratched his brow. "You think I'm a part of the agriculture fraternity?"

"Yeah." She pointed to his dusty Red Wings, as if his boots were more telling than the crest the guys wore on their shirts.

"I'm not an AGR."

"What?"

"I was just walking past, cutting through here to get to my apartment before the rain came." Thomas looked up. "Looks like it passed."

Haleya wasn't listening, instead she looked at the work he'd done. "So, you were just walking by when I screamed at you?"

"Yeah, pretty much."

"And you got up here, grabbed a hammer and nails, and started helping?"

"U-huh."

"And you never wondered why?"

"My mom is a sweet woman, but one thing my brothers and I learned early was that when a woman starts pointing and screaming, just do what she says, no questions asked."

"Your brothers—Caleb and Colton?"

"Yeah, my lazy, irresponsible brothers. So, you think these Red Wing boots are cramping my style?"

If planet Earth had a door, she would have crawled inside and never come out.

Chapter 25

Thomas slid the menthol Marlboros from his coat pocket and tapped the package on the heel of his hand in a rhythm as natural as if he'd never quit. Peeling away the cellophane wrap, he leaned into the cigarette pack and breathed in its minty-tobacco scent until his toes felt cool and relaxed. The Thirsty Thursday drink specials had drawn a crowd. He found a seat at the bar.

"Drink?" the bartender asked as she placed a napkin in front of him.

"Maker's and Coke." It wasn't the greasy hamburgers that drew him through the doors of McCubbins. Elizabeth and Knox were with Gina celebrating her birthday, and he'd been home with only his reproving thoughts. He needed loud music to drown them out and a drink.

The oak bar welcomed graffiti. Apparently, "Brandon loved Jill" once but not anymore, since her name was scratched out.

"Here you go, hero."

Thomas, more interested in the smell of scented tobacco and everybody else's business carved into the bar, looked up at the young waitress. She didn't look old enough to bartend. Her waist was slightly bigger than the size of his arm when he flexed his muscle, and she wore little make-up. Her features were pleasant, easy. The thick orange rubber band holding her hair back was her only adornment.

"You are the guy, right? The guy who built that house for the family who lost it in the fire a year or so ago?"

"Tornado," Thomas corrected. He took a final puff and put out his cigarette.

"That was so cool—what you did. You know who I thought of? Ty Pennington. Really, it was like our town had its own *Extreme Home Makeover* show. You kind of look like him now that I see you up close."

Thomas's dimple flared, as he tried to hold back the smirk. Just what he needed to top off his day, being compared to a man who regularly cries on TV and probably doesn't know how to drive a straight nail if his life depended on it. "Not quite, but thanks for the compliment. I think—"

"No, really, I'm serious. What's it like being famous?" she lightheartedly teased, not deterred by Thomas's aloofness.

"Obama has yet to invite me to the White House, if that's what you're thinking." Thomas quipped, tossing some nuts in his mouth.

"But George W called you, right? I know. That was front-page news."

Thomas downplayed it. "Just a couple of reporters and a television camera on a slow news week."

"Oh, come on." She saddled up on a stool behind the bar and yelled to the other bartender, "I'm on break."

The bartender, looking like it might be his first night behind the bar, nodded as he juggled three drinks.

"How do you get away with that?" Thomas asked looking around at the crowd.

"Well, let's see. Two reasons. One, he's my little brother. And two, he totally stood me up last night and left me working alone."

"Younger brother? How old are you?"

"Twenty-six. Our parents own this joint. They travel to other countries now, drinking stuff we don't stock and eating fancy-named raw fish that costs more than anything on our menu, while we toss everything in a pan of grease and call it good. Speaking of grease, how about a burger?"

"Nope, I've given up solid foods," Thomas quipped, pointing to his empty glass.

"So, what are you doing now? Haven't seen much of you in the news these days."

Thomas's phone rang. He pointed to his empty glass again and put his phone to his ear.

"Hey," Haleya said.

"Hey," Thomas said.

An awkward silence followed.

"So, this is how it's going to be?" Thomas asked, kicking the toe of his boot against the base of the bar.

"No, it doesn't have to be."

Her voice felt to him as distant as the miles between them. "Having fun in New York?"

"Not exactly. After tomorrow morning's session wrap-up, I catch the next flight home."

"Good."

"Where are you? I can barely hear you."

"McCubbins," he muttered, preparing for the speech to follow.

"You got Knox and Elizabeth there with you? You aren't introducing them to the bar scene yet, I hope?"

"Knox offered to buy a few rounds, and Lizzy's dancing on the tables."

Haleya laughed.

Silence followed.

"I still like your laugh," Thomas warmed. It could have been the drink he'd downed. He wanted more than hearing her laugh. He wanted her home. "Be safe and get home to me."

"You be safe! I'm the one locked in my room while you paint the town. You know you could order in. They deliver."

"Yeah, but then you'd be having all the fun."

"I've been working."

He knew she hadn't meant to hurt him. The temp job he'd shown up for had fallen through.

"Sorry. Hey, I'll be the girl at the airport who looks like she really misses her husband."

"Then I'll be there. I'm getting a call coming through." Thomas glanced at the number. "It's Dad."

"Talk to him."

Thomas had avoided his calls. He hadn't told him there was no more Kage Construction.

"Okay. See you tomorrow," Thomas said bye. Instead of answering the call, he turned off his phone.

*   *   *

Haleya massaged her neck. Though the hotel bed was comfortable, she missed her bed, its three down pillows, and her morning stretch to hit the snooze button. She remembered the first year she married. Thomas bought, second-hand, a double bed that barely fit in their apartment bedroom. When they moved and bought a king-size bed, they wasted most of its 108 inches. She'd married a cuddler. She'd never fit in with co-workers complaining about their husbands. Thomas put away her shoes more often than she did his. He'd say she was beautiful when she was sweaty and filthy from gardening or with morning hair and pillow creases lining her cheek. She would search his face for sincerity, only to be reassured by his fascination with the moles on her chest. She had somehow snagged the man who never once left the toilet seat up and always remembered her birthday.

She hated the fighting, especially the ugly words that were new to their marriage. She hated feeling trapped—not trapped in the marriage, but caught between how wonderful she knew it could be and what it had become. The word "divorce" was unsaid but implied when Thomas woke in the middle of the

122

night the day that she'd received her award. Still affected by the liquor, he had had nothing good to say about her award or their marriage. His hurtful words lingered in her mind.

Haleya searched, trying to figure out where it had all gone wrong. When she'd accepted the technology training position, she'd wanted away from her hectic routine. In the new position, she'd felt accomplished. That same month, the Lexington Chamber of Commerce had cut the ribbon for Thomas Kage Construction. Her husband had started his own company, a life-long dream. But tonight, four years later, she lay alone miles away and Thomas sat in a bar, unemployed. *Where had their road of dreams taken them?*

Chapter 26

MARCELLA—1959—age 11

Roxie Applesauce patted her tears with a lace handkerchief. It wasn't like her to be so emotional, but the Actress of the Year honor had caught her off guard. "I would like to thank my mother for always being there for me, my father for his support from the very beginning, my brothers for always treating me special, and my grandparents for buying me everything I ever wanted." The crowd laughed. Roxie smiled at her family. They were beautiful people. Her mother adorned by the finest dress, and her father sat distinguished with his arm cradling her shoulders. Her grandfather reached for her grandmother's hand, and a tear trickled from her grandmother's sparkling eyes. Roxie held the crystal statue close to her chest. Her beaded gown glimmered in the stage lighting. Her brothers stood and the thousands followed—the roar so loud she couldn't continue her speech. She lifted the award once more and bowed.

Marcella held up the shampoo bottle and squeezed it, puffing out its pink soapy-smelling scent and posing in front of the bathroom mirror. She'd taken the shampoo from her grandmother's room where she'd seen it when she was hiding under the bed. She'd done well to steer clear of her grandfather until the dust bunnies worked up a sneeze and her cousins tattled on her quicker than the spit from her sneeze settled.

After helping her grandfather cut the heads off the chickens, she'd snuck back into the bedroom and tucked the shampoo bottle under her shirt. Marcella called out as she headed to the bathroom, "Going to take my bath, and you didn't have to tell me." Marcella darted past her grandfather watching Gunsmoke and sipping whisky from the bottle. She usually would have paused to admire Miss Kitty, but the TV was only a blur as she dashed to the bathroom and locked the door. She sniffed the shampoo, held the bottle out in front of her, and twirled. She'd watched shampoo commercials hoping if Santa ever came that he'd leave her the shampoo that made hair flow like silk. She mouthed, "Thank you," to the mirror just as the banging on the door shook it on its hinges. Marcella, knowing that the door being broke down would ultimately be her fault, hid the shampoo behind the toilet and opened the door.

"What are you doin' in here? You've had time to take three baths, girl!" Her grandmother ripped the shower curtain back and turned on the water, which hiccupped and sputtered before it came on full force. "I'd expect an 11-year-old to know how to take a bath, no wonder your head stinks like—" She pushed Marcella's head under the water, but she fought back, splashing water outside the tub, on the walls, and in her grandmother's face. Grandma cursed, reached to get a washcloth, and spotted the shampoo bottle. Marcella wasn't sure what the shampoo felt like on her hair, but she knew how it tasted.

MARCELLA—1971—age 23

Marcella used her hairbrush to brush Mittens. Randall had threatened for what he said was the last time to introduce her cat to Jesus if it kept shedding hair. He was making fun of her. She'd learned about Jesus when she was younger from a lady named Mrs. Milam and wondered if it was true that Jesus loved everybody—even her. When Randall had said that she was worthless, and nobody would love her, she'd answered, "But Jesus does." She didn't know if she believed it, but Mrs. Milam had said so.

"Jesus?" Randall had repeated.

Marcella nodded.

"Ain't no Jesus," he'd said.

MARCELLA–2010–age 62

Marcella often felt safer in an abandoned home than she had her own, but today that changed.

"Help–" but no one answered. Marcella's left eye blinked and stuck–her lashes clung like a fly caught in a sticky trap. Marcella, lying sprawled against the cracked linoleum floor, felt blood seep over her eye and into the corner of her lip. The blood trailed her chin and neck as it pooled giving new color to the dirt-ridden floor beneath her. Above her, tiny angels fluttered like sweat bees visiting her and then flying off, only to return. She'd seen the angels before when she was a little girl. Still years later, the angels glowed the same.

Roxie Applesauce swiped the delicate strand of hair from her eye. Her thick mascara tangling her lashes. She pressed two fingers to her lips, kissed them, and extended her hand to the crowd. Cheers erupted. Her chiffon dress turned from its soft pastel to a deep scarlet red.

"Help," fainter this time. Marcella tried to move her arm, her fingers, her foot, and finally her toes. Nothing.

She feared the cruel men would return, yet she feared no one would find her.

Chapter 27

Elizabeth shoved her book into her backpack as the bell rang, signaling the beginning of the weekend. "Hey, Sam," Elizabeth answered her iPhone.

Elizabeth's teacher stopped her as she passed his desk.

"Hold on," she said to Sam.

"Your paper?" Mr. Bratcher asked.

"What paper?"

"The assignment due today. I didn't get one from you."

"I turned it in." Elizabeth shook the iPhone slightly to let him know she was talking to someone.

"It's not here." He pointed to the stack of papers on his desk.

"I turned it in early. Remember?"

"No, only three students went for the early extra credit."

"Well, then you lost it," Elizabeth suggested.

"I typically don't lose papers."

"But you could have misplaced it, right?"

"There's a small chance, but I don't believe that's the case. I was looking forward to reading yours. You're a talented writer."

"I turned it in. Let me know if you don't find it." Elizabeth put her iPhone back to her ear, turned her back to her teacher, and walked out of the room. "Sam, are you there? I have to pick up Knox at swim." Elizabeth tossed her backpack strap over her shoulder.

"No," Elizabeth cracked when Sam asked about her conversation with her teacher. "I haven't even started it. I hate that class. Hey, I see you." Elizabeth waved.

"Sam, wait up!" Kara caught up with them.

"I got 'em." Elizabeth discreetly pulled the pack of cigarettes from her pocket.

"Oh, yeah!" Sam snatched them. "Nice!"

"My dad won't miss them."

Kara reached into Sam's pocket. "Give me one!"

"No!" Sam shielded his pocket. "Not now."

Kara linked her arm in Sam's. "There'd better be some left, you jerk."

*   *   *

Haleya dropped her purse in the seat next to her at the airport and called her mother. "Me not happy," she pouted.

"I haven't heard that in years."

"They delayed my flight." Haleya kicked her carry-on.

"Are you safe there?"

"Yes, Mom," Haleya said. Hearing her teen-like tone, she thought of Elizabeth. "I'm ready to be home. How's Dad?"

"We've talked a few times. I am hoping we can Skype. I want to see him."

"Me too."

"I've got someone for you to meet."

"Seriously, Mom? A stray dog? A single mother who needs a home?"

"Neither, but I bet you can guess if you keep trying."

"Another Childcare Worldwide kid you've sponsored?"

"Yep, her name is Sikia. She has brown hair and brown eyes. She loves to dance and sing. She's just starting school and likes to read."

"Mom, what are you going to tell Dad when he gets back? How many sponsored kids does that make now?

"Oh, that doesn't matter."

"I guess there are worse addictions."

"I'm ready for an overnight visit from Knox and Lizzy. I miss them."

"Knox could use a little grandma spoiling. He says he's not being picked on—"

"By the older boys?"

"Mom, all the boys are older."

"He'll be 13 soon," Lyndee encouraged.

"And all the boys will still be older. I don't even know where he got all his smarts. Not from me!"

"God," Lyndee answered. "What's his favorite donut?"

"Whatever flavor he's eating."

"Just like his mama."

"Stop. You're making me laugh, and I don't want to laugh. I'm mad, remember? I'm stuck at the airport. Thomas and I've been fighting. I don't even feel like I know my kids anymore." She paused seeing the flight schedule monitor update. "No!" The screen now flashed *Flight Delayed,* again.

* * *

When Elizabeth arrived at the country club to pick up Knox, she knew where she'd find him—far left swim lane with the kindergarteners as she called the middle-schoolers.

"Knox, let's go!" Elizabeth called, not so much for Knox to stop swimming but for his coach to look her way. She strutted over to the bench, pleased that the coach's eyes followed her. She lifted her iPhone to her ear as if it had rung, not returning his gaze but every bit aware of it. *Mission accomplished,* she thought. *I knew he liked me.*

"It'll be a minute!" Knox stood at the pool's edge drying off.

Elizabeth called back, "I'm not waiting forever!" She dialed.

Thomas answered on the first ring, "Hey, baby girl."

"Not a baby anymore, Thomas," Elizabeth smarted back.

"Still your dad, Lizzy. Please remember to get Knox."

"Oh, I'm here, and they're holding him over along with three others. So, I'm waiting."

129

"Why are you waiting?"

"You mean I can leave?"

"No, I mean why are they holding him over?"

"No idea. Hey, Dad, can I go over Kara's after I drop Knox off at home? We need to study."

"Study what?"

"I have a big paper I'm supposed to write, and there's lots of research. We save time by doing it together."

"Really? Between painting your nails and listening to the radio?"

"We listen to iTunes, not the radio."

"Okay, go. You do remember your mom comes home tonight. Well, she would have already been here, but her flight was delayed twice. I gave up waiting at the airport."

* * *

Lyndee's hands shook as she logged on her computer. She felt like a schoolgirl waiting for a call from her beau. Skype was supposed to work this time.

No picture, and her heart sank. She looked at the clock on the computer. It was only one minute passed. The screen became skewed, and, after a few bursts of light, she saw him. Kent waved. She saw his lips moving but heard nothing. "Kent, can you hear me?" She leaned closer as if that could help. "Kent?" Nothing.

She saw him work with his computer, toss up his hands, and mouth, "No sound."

She blew him a kiss.

He waved bye, and she knew he was going to shut down his computer. That was all—less than a minute. The screen went dark, but Lyndee felt lighter. The sporadic phone calls kept her going. Seeing him only for the few seconds made her feel like dancing.

* * *

Haleya, still at the airport, called her prior boss, not Janice but her nursing supervisor. The conversation went as she'd expected. She'd be welcomed back, but she wasn't sure that's what she wanted.

"Look, it's Santa!" A little girl ran to the man who looked like Santa Claus, though he wore a flannel shirt and overalls. Haleya watched the sweet interaction as the man played along. The little girl looked as if she'd been crying. Haleya had thought about crying too. It'd been a long day at the airport no matter a person's age.

Haleya moved her purse when she saw Santa looking for a seat. "You brightened her day."

"Brightened my day! You think that I like spending all day here?"

"So why do you do it? The Santa thing?"

"What are you talking about?"

"The long white beard and hair. Don't make me feel silly for asking. I know the Santa secret, and you could fool me."

"Oh, this?" He stroked his beard.

"Yeah, that. Are you one of those trendy 21st-century mall Santas?"

"Nope."

"It's good money."

"Money's not what makes me happy."

"You sound like my dad."

"I bet I'd like him."

"Everybody does. He's nearly 70, but thinks he's 25. He's been in Haiti since January."

"Haiti?"

"Yeah, he's a retired doctor. He plans to be home by Christmas." She chuckled. "If you needed to know that, Santa."

"Sounds like a man who deserves a visit from Santa."

"He likes a few sips of Gentleman Jack. He'll be ready for one when he gets home."

"Ahh, finally a sign that he's not a saint."

"My mother has her addictions, too. She has what my dad calls the 'save every sick dog on the side of the road' syndrome. Dad finally told her no more animals. So when I moved out, she started helping troubled teens."

"You must've not been enough trouble for them to get parenting teens out of their system. Mine took their toll on ole Saint Nick; that's why I have all this white hair." He laughed, and his belly bounced.

"Santa's a comedian too. That was good! I think I'm getting more gray hairs by the day."

"You have kids?"

"Two. My boy is almost 13. My daughter is 17. They're good kids."

"I'll add them to my list."

"Another good one," Haleya laughed.

"Why teens?" Santa asked.

"They don't stay small and cute forever."

"No, why does your mother take in teens?"

"It started with a mentor program at church, but as typical for my parents, they took it to an extreme. They have a 19-year-old named Whitney living with them now, well, with Mom since Dad's in Haiti. She's been a tough one."

"What's her story?"

"Whitney aged out of foster care at 18 and didn't do well on her own."

"Most don't."

"After a second run in with the law, her case worker connected her with our church. Then my mom met her and, of course, brought her home. Then there's Gina. Gina came to stay with my mom when she was 18. She's in her mid-twenties now. She has the heart of a child," she paused.

132

"Down Syndrome, and nothing but a pure delight. Then there are the Childcare Worldwide kids, you know, sponsoring children in another country."

"Your parents make Santa Claus look like a lazy guy who works only one day a year."

"Tell me about Mrs. Claus." Haleya pointed to his wedding band.

"She writes children's books." He pulled two small books from his bag. "I give them to kids who think I'm Santa." He handed a set of the books to Haleya. She read the titles, "A Girl's Christmas Gone Perfectly Wrong" and "Boys Need Santa Claus Because—"

The overhead speakers announced the boarding of their flight.

"Keep the books," Santa offered as they scurried to board like two kids dashing from their rooms on Christmas morning.

*　　*　　*

Another rejection letter, another wasted day. Instead of simply wadding the paper into a ball and tossing it in the trash, Thomas pulled out a cigarette, lit it, and held its red tip to its bottom corner. Once, he had his own business and the heart to donate time and money to a family who'd lost their home. Last night, he'd heard a stranger mutter for help from an abandoned house, yet he walked past without concern.

He placed his hand over his heart to check if it was still beating, almost sure it had turned hard. Once he had been good at everything—good at making people laugh, good at making money, and good at loving his wife.

On that thought, *she* entered his mind. Not his wife, but the girl from McCubbins—Lorie. He'd recognized the invitation, however subtle. The way she'd allowed her hand to casually linger on his as she reacted to his stories. The way she was undeterred when he mentioned Haleya. He especially picked up on her regret when he'd finished his drink and announced that was it for the night.

"You can't go. Happy hour ends at eleven."

"It ends at nine," Thomas corrected.

Lorie leaned back on the stool and with her fingers erased the "9" from the chalk board and wrote "11." Cheers erupted.

"I can't."

"Will I see you again sometime?"

"Maybe on TV."

Sitting alone in his living room, Thomas reached for his phone and dialed.

Chapter 28

MARCELLA—1960—age 12

Roxie, floating on the clear blue water, flipped and dove to the bottom of the resort pool. Coasting under the water, she felt free.

"Lick it up!" Marcella's grandmother demanded.

Marcella reached for a dish towel.

"I said lick it up!"

Marcella had spilled her glass of chocolate milk. She looked at her grandfather. "Ain't no wasting chocolate milk in this house. Do what she says."

Marcella stuck out her tongue and began licking. In the glass it hadn't looked like as much. When she finished, her grandfather pointed to chocolate milk puddled on the floor. Marcella got on her knees.

MARCELLA—1971—age 23

Marcella scratched her head, her fingers caught in her knotted hair. They'd broken the door down this time. She didn't have what they wanted. Randall wasn't there, and he'd left no money. They knocked over the card table, broke the back from the recliner, and cut the mattress on the floor. That was all the furniture in the apartment. She reached for her cat and crawled to the corner of the room.

MARCELLA—2010—age 62

"Help me," Marcella croaked. She heard people laughing, stumbling, and cursing as they passed the abandon house walking from the nearby bar.

Roxie Applesauce swung from the trapeze with such grace, as if she'd been born to be the main attraction of the three-ring circus. Hanging upside down, she flew from one trapeze swing to another. The crowd applauded as she twirled and daringly flipped high above the ground. The sunshine on her purple body suit gleamed as she flew through the air in the giant tent.

Marcella's cries now only a whisper, "Help."

Chapter 29

Haleya's eyes shot open when the taxi driver spoke. "What?" She'd been out cold.

"This your address?"

At the sight of her front door, she wasn't concerned about his perception of the snoring middle-aged woman he'd dropped off at two in the morning. Before falling asleep, she'd listened to a voicemail from Candice. Her friend, a doctor at the University of Maryland Medical Center, had a speaker fall through for his seminar series. He'd asked Candice to help with a last-minute replacement. "Tina's working to rearrange your schedule. I'm forwarding you Dr. Fogler's number so you can contact him."

She added the event to her calendar, but her stomach knotted as she wondered when and how she'd break the news to Thomas that she'd be gone again—a favor for Candice's friend. She just wanted to crawl into her bed, shut her eyes, and feel Thomas's breath on her hair.

Stumbling onto the sidewalk, she did well to balance her luggage. As she reached for her house key, her purse tangled with the cosmetic bag landing against the concrete and knocking the keys from her hand. Tripping over her luggage, she ended up eye to eye with her keys in the moonlight. Opening the door, she kicked her luggage inside. Greeted by the smell of roses, she deflated at the sight of her pillow and a blanket on the couch. She knew he'd been frustrated by the wait at the airport.

So tired that she felt nauseous, she breathed deeply. The floral fragrance grew stronger, and she realized it was Paul

Smith Rose. The perfume had broken in her cosmetic bag. Pulling the neck of her shirt over her nose, she dropped onto the couch. Just feet from her bed—and Thomas—she felt further from him than ever.

*   *   *

When Thomas called the cops to check out the house on the corner of Harpe Street, they told him it was nothing unusual, probably just a homeless bum. They'd check it out. After another Maker's and Coke, Thomas had crawled into bed. Images of his week ran through his mind; he felt like a failure on all fronts. He'd been impatient with Knox when he'd gotten home from the airport. That's why his son had avoided him the rest of the evening ...

"Hold this." Thomas had handed a hammer to Knox. Thomas had always wanted to build a shed in the backyard. Now he had the time to do it. "How was your week?" he'd asked Knox.

"I got a 99 on my science test."

"Awesome!" Thomas fiddled around in his pocket for several nails and took a sip of beer. He took the hammer back and asked, "Swim going well?"

Knox shrugged.

"What does that mean?"

"I'm not one of their favorites."

"Why's that?" Thomas climbed the ladder and started hammering.

"I'm not as good."

"Try harder. I told you what to do."

"I know." Knox traced a circle in the dirt with the tip of his shoe.

Thomas explained how his strokes could be better and his start faster and then asked for Knox's help. "Get that box of nails. Feed me one when I need it." Thomas wiggled his fingers for Knox to give him a nail. Thomas continued talking about the breaststroke. "Understand?"

"Yeah."

"Well, then just do that—like we've talked about, and you'll be swimming with the winners."

Knox fidgeted with a couple of the nails in his hand.

"Nail!" Thomas, snapping his fingers, reached toward Knox. "Wait," Thomas said stepping off the ladder. "This is a good time for you to practice driving a nail."

"What?"

"I was building dog houses and selling them at your age." Thomas pointed for Knox to climb the ladder.

Knox held both sides and stepped up slowly.

"I've got a hold of it. Climb on up," Thomas encouraged.

"Which step?" Knox asked, hesitating before going up to the next one.

"One more." Thomas handed him the hammer. "Take this, and here's a nail."

Knox awkwardly tried to hold the hammer with one hand and the nail with the other. He almost dropped the hammer but instead dropped the nail.

Thomas shook his head, picked up the nail, and handed it to Knox. "Hold it about an inch above the last nail and hammer it."

Knox positioned the nail and looked down at his dad. Thomas nodded. When he went to strike it, the nail slid between his fingers and landed on the ground.

"Not like that." Thomas picked up the nail and handed it to him again. Knox held the ladder with one hand, careful to balance himself and reached for the nail. "Hold it tighter, and give it a couple solid knocks on its head. Once it's in a little, you can focus on hammering it instead of holding it."

Knox tried again. The nail went in slightly.

"Okay, give it another solid tap."

Knox hit his thumb. "Ouch!" The nail toppled to the ground. He put his thumb between his lips.

"I don't have the patience for this," Thomas blurted. "Get down. Go inside; read your science or something."

Thomas tried to get Knox's discouraged look out of his mind. Thomas thought he'd heard Haleya when she'd gotten home. He debated on whether to get up, but too tired and admittedly too stubborn, he'd placed a pillow over his head instead and tossed and turned until he fell asleep.

The next morning when he unlocked the bedroom door, he covered his nose. *What was that smell?* Starting the coffee pot, he looked toward his wife curled up on the couch in her favorite mohair blanket. He felt a twinge of guilt—a sense of regret. Thomas watched, hoping not to disturb her yet wishing she'd wake up so he could carry her to their bedroom. She rested so innocent, sweet, and beautiful, reminding him of the morning he'd awakened next to her when they'd first married. He'd wanted nothing else in the world but her.

When Thomas got back from his morning jog, Knox was waiting, ready for his swim meet.

"Hey, Dad," Knox trotted down the stairs.

Thomas put his finger to his lips and pointed to Haleya sleeping.

He held up his swim cap and goggles. Thomas gave him a thumbs up, and they headed out.

*   *   *

Haleya twisted, tangled in the blanket. A cup of coffee sat on the coffee table with a note. She reached for the note but pushed the coffee away. After more than a dozen cups yesterday while trying to stay awake at the airport, coffee was only a miserable reminder of how she'd spent the last 22 hours before getting to sleep on her couch.

The gesture was nice though. Written on the napkin were the letters "T R U C E." She glanced at the bedroom door, wide open now, inviting. She wrapped the blanket around her and tiptoed into the bedroom. As she'd expected might be the case, he was gone—the bed neatly made. Again, she felt the same disappointing twinge as the night before. But truce was good; TRUCE was a place to start.

More than sleeping though, she wanted to see Knox's face and hear about his week. She'd even take an eye roll from Elizabeth at this point. And she wanted Thomas close again. With that thought, she remembered the semester they'd met.

"Kage! What are you doing?" The ROTC instructor made himself heard.

Haleya looked up as the student repelling from the parking structure flew down its concrete façade, wide-open, foregoing all safety measures for an amateur repeller. When the student got to his feet and removed his helmet, Haleya recognized him. A couple of guys who'd gone before him slapped him on the back in admiration.

Sergeant Bronson, wasting no time, was up in Thomas's face.

Haleya, providing first aid for minor injuries to the college ROTC repelling class, so far hadn't been needed. Picking up her bookbag, she watched who she hoped was the final student as he squeamishly hurdled the concrete ledge.

"I need this looked at. It needs bandaged up."

"I don't see anything." Haleya looked at Thomas's arm.

He pulled up his sleeve and pointed. "This here."

"That tiny scrape?"

"Tiny? I'm in pain."

"Let me see if I have a Snoopy Band-Aid for you. Oh yeah, lucky you. Last one." She dabbed an alcohol-soaked cotton ball on the spot he pointed to that at best was maybe an old rope burn. "Better?"

"Maybe, but I might need it checked tomorrow. These types of injuries can fool a person."

"I think you should be more worried about Sergeant Bronson than the freckle that's healing under that Band-Aid."

"I'm his favorite."

"I don't think so. He still looks mad."

"Nah, he likes me. So, if I have any problems with this, who do I need to see?"

"You need to go to a doctor outside of my field of study. Maybe someone in the psychology department."

"Good one. Especially coming from a girl who verbally abuses innocent strangers as they walk by *and* insults their family members as well."

"Touché."

"Hey, Thomas!" one of the ROTC student yelled as they gathered around Sergeant Bronson.

He stepped away in a backward trot. "Thanks! It feels better already."

*   *   *

What's been your greatest accomplishment?"

Thomas shifted in his seat. He clasped and then unclasped his hands. "Biggest accomplishment?"

"Yeah." The lady across from him tapped her pencil on her desk. Thomas knew Haleya would have gotten a big kick out of this picture. Of course, he'd assumed T & T Construction's owner was a man.

Starting a business only to fail in its first three years, after having been accustomed to six figures previously, wasn't something to brag about. Neither was his marriage since the kindest word said to his wife recently was "T R U C E" written on a napkin.

"Next question," Thomas responded. He wondered if they awarded extra credit points if he mentioned he could flawlessly patch sheet rock.

"Okay, we'll move on. Tell me about your biggest mistake."

"What?"

"You know, biggest 'oops, shouldn't have done that' thing. Professional is fine, doesn't have to be personal."

The questions caught him off guard. What guy, or for that matter anyone, wants to talk about his biggest mistake? But he'd been thinking about it for months now, and he actually felt liberated saying it. "Gave away $50,000 left to me from my mother."

The lady paused with her pencil suspended. He figured she was debating whether he looked more like the casino or the racetrack type.

When he didn't elaborate, she looked back to his resume. "I see you were most recently self-employed."

"Yes, a casualty of the economy."

"I see you opened Kage Construction in 2007."

"Unfortunately, just before you couldn't turn on the television without the news reporting multiple bank failures. Yep."

"Yes, tough time in the housing market."

"Commercial construction seems strong," Thomas said looking around the plush office, nothing like any construction offices he'd visited recently.

"Can't say we haven't felt it too, but we're holding on." She circled his name and phone number on the application, but then marked an X in the top corner.

"Is that it?" Thomas asked seeing her notation. He scooted his chair back and leaned forward. *Another morning wasted.*

"Yes."

"So, I shouldn't expect you to call about the project manager position?" Thomas asked with a sarcastic snort.

"No."

No word of farewell, Thomas headed for the door.

"But I'd like you to interview with my husband who is looking to hire for another position that you're better qualified for."

"Ma'am, with all due respect, I'm qualified for this position. I'm not interested in working for your company."

"Would you be available Monday?"

"What?"

"Around 2 p.m.?"

"Did you hear me?"

"Yes."

"I'm not interested." Thomas's phone rang. He saw his father's number flashing, flipped the ringer to silent, and stuffed it back in his pocket.

"Here. It's my husband's card." She extended the business card to him.

Chapter 30

MARCELLA–1961–age 13

Roxie Applesauce waved at the thousands gathered for the parade. Dressed in her tulle gown with a pink diamond crown resting on her curls, she extended her arm and waved like a princess. The children standing nearby grabbed their mothers' hands as they pointed, "There she is!" As Roxie passed each eager face, she leaned forward, blowing kisses.

Marcella watched as the boy rode by a second time. She pulled the laundry from the clothesline, balling it up in her arms. A couple of loose towels dragged the ground as she ran to the house and dropped them on the floor. Outside again, she took her time unclasping each clothes pen. On his third pass, he stopped and yelled, "What's your name?"

"Marcella," she yelled back.

"We moved in up the road," he said, pointing.

"I'm 13," Marcella said.

"I'm 14."

"What's your name?"

"Dennis."

"Like Dennis the Menace?"

He nodded.

Marcella walked toward him. "I like your bike."

"It's new."

Marcella didn't remember what they talked about after that, but she did remember how her grandfather stormed out the front door and told the boy that she had a disease that he wouldn't want and shooed him away.

MARCELLA—1972—age 24

"They aren't mine," Marcella said as she pulled the bags from her pocket and placed them on the hood of the truck.

"Who's the guy who ran off?" The lady cop lifted the flashlight so it beamed directly in Marcella's eyes.

"Randall Manning," Marcella answered, covering her face.

"And your name," she demanded. "Uncover your face, please."

"Marcella Manning," Marcella said, squinting.

"Driver's license?" The officer asked.

"Never learned how to drive."

"Identification of any kind?" The officer asked.

"Not with me."

"What's in the bags?" The guy cop asked.

"Prescription pills, I think?"

"Prescriptions written to you?" He asked.

Marcella heard the officer but didn't answer. The acid she'd taken earlier kicked in.

MARCELLA—2010—age 62

"What do we have?" the emergency room doctor asked as he made his way over to the patient unloaded from the ambulance.

"Elderly woman, beaten. Labored breathing. Barely conscious. Facial injuries. Suspected broken ribs and abdominal injury. No identification. Found alone in an abandoned building."

Chapter 31

"How did the interview go?" Haleya asked, wishing she could take the words back when she saw the look on Thomas's face. "Not good, huh?" She stepped forward to embrace him but stopped when he slammed the door with the heel of his boot.

"Where's Knox?" Thomas glared. "You didn't get him?"

"No, where was I supposed to get him from?"

"The swim meet today."

"I thought you were staying to watch."

"I had an interview," Thomas ground the words between his teeth. "I told you I would drop him off if you could pick him up. You even said that worked great because you wanted to see him swim since you've missed the last three."

"Oh, no! I forgot. It was such a long day yesterday."

"It's been a long *year* with you!"

"What happened while you were gone?" Haleya picked up the napkin where he'd written truce.

"I came to my senses. I've gotten used to hanging out by myself. Maybe I like it that way."

"If this is how it's going to be when I come home, maybe it's just better that I don't."

"That's an option!"

"This isn't workin—" Haleya's voice trailed off.

"Then leave!" Thomas spun her around and pushed her toward the door.

She tripped over her feet, landing on her knees. She no longer fought back the tears. "I'm done!" she screamed. "Done with everything!" Haleya beat her fist against the floor.

"I'm tired of this. I'm just so tired." She curled into a ball, the cool hardwood floor against her damp cheek.

"Go find you a rich doctor then!" Thomas walked past her and was gone.

"I quit," Haleya whispered in broken breaths though no one was there to hear her. "I told them that I couldn't do it anymore. No more traveling. Thomas, I quit," she said to an empty room.

*　　　*　　　*

"I thought Mom was picking me up. Why are you here, Liz?"

"My name's not Liz or Elizabeth or Lizzy. It's El," Elizabeth scolded her brother though she'd never announced this piece of information before.

"Who is El?" Knox pulled his swim bag over his shoulder.

"Me. If you call me Lizzy ever again, I'm telling Dad how much you hate swim. Got it? Now, what did your coach say about me?"

"Nothing."

"I saw him pull you aside at the end of your last race, and he kept looking over at me while he talked to you."

"He told me that I did better today."

"And that he wants to know my name?"

Knox's head fell. "And that I still need to do better if I'm going to compete."

"Oh, Dad's gonna love that when I tell him."

"Don't."

"Oh, I'm gonna tell him—well, unless you do my research paper for me."

"I'm not going to write your paper for you!"

"Come on. Google a bunch of words, read it, highlight the important stuff. You're a nerd anyway. Wait, writing a paper on how technology has changed the world, oh, that's not boring to you. That kind of thing you and your nerd friends do for a good time."

"I'm telling."

"Oh, 'I'm telling!' You sound like a five-year-old. Well, I guess that makes sense. You swim like one. It's your choice."

"What choice?"

"You know what a bad mood Dad's been in lately. When he hears that you didn't advance with the other kids, this is going to be fun to watch."

"Okay, okay. When do you need it?"

"Yesterday."

"You are the devil, you know."

"You're the one who's gonna get hell."

*   *   *

"Hey, what's up?" Lorie wiped her hands on a rag. Tucking a strand of hair behind her ear, she tilted forward, her palms on the bar in front of Thomas. "Your usual?"

"Nah, I'm ready for a change."

"So, what will it be? Our specials are on the board."

"Nothing special for me, just something stiff."

"How come before the past week I've never seen you in here?"

Because once I had a full-time job and a family—and no time for a place like this. He looked around at the crowd, a lot of young kids with their lives—and mistakes—ahead of them. He repeated, "Something strong, don't care."

"Coming right up," she said and pranced off.

*   *   *

I'm proud of you," Lyndee said. "Prouder than I've ever been."

Haleya laughed through her tears. "That's crazy, Mom. Everything's so messed up," she sniffed. "I think Thomas is done."

"No, he's not. It doesn't end like this. No, ma'am. You've got something special with that man. He loves you and his family. It's not over. Can't be."

"I'm scared," Haleya confessed. "How can you be so calm?"

"Baby, my parents had the most distorted marriage, and yet, somehow, why I don't know, they stuck by each other. Your dad, he's not always Mister Romantic, but he's the truest a person could ever find. You're part of a long line of people who don't give up."

"I just quit my job."

Haleya told her mother about her conversation with Candice. Haleya had asked Candice to cover the speaking engagement in Maryland. She started explaining everything she needed to get caught up. Candice interrupted and began naming her priorities and commitments. Somewhere in the middle of what sounded more like Candice's review of her resume and her aspirations than anything substantially time consuming, Haleya heard herself say that she'd contacted her prior nursing supervisor. "You know, Candice, I hate to interrupt you, but I've been thinking about the value of the nurses in our hospital. I've been fortunate to get to train them. They're appreciative, and it's really rewarding. I think that I'd like to work alongside them again." She let Candice know that she'd be forwarding her resignation and didn't wait for a response.

"Mom, I quit," she repeated.

"No, you didn't. You just started a new chapter."

*   *   *

Lyndee watched Gina thumb through a wedding magazine though she'd never had a boyfriend.

"I wike this one." Gina held up the magazine for Lyndee to see. "It looks wike your dress." Gina pointed to a framed picture of Lyndee's wedding day.

150

Lyndee's mind drifted while Gina continued talking. Kent was helping hundreds, yet she couldn't help just one. Whitney had slammed the door and left with her hands full of her stuff earlier in the week. Lyndee's heart sank, and Gina had lots of questions.

"Where's she going to go?"

"I don't know."

"Does she not wike it here?"

"She does. But it's hard for her to be happy. She gets happy, and then she gets scared."

"Why?"

"Because in her mind, it never lasts. It's the beginning of the end when it starts to feel good—when it starts to feel like home. She'd rather leave before she gets hurt. If she likes it here, it'll hurt when she has to leave."

"Who's going to make her weave?"

"No one here. She just remembers all the times it happened to her in the past."

"Then why did she weave?"

"She's just been hurt so many times. She doesn't trust that we really care. She thinks we are going to quit on her too."

"I don't understand."

"I don't either. When you're hurt, you're sad, but you forgive in the blink of an eye. Whitney doesn't."

"Who hurt her?"

"Oh, very few people intentionally. But she never knew what it was like to have a mama and daddy."

"I had a mama and a daddy."

"You had a wonderful mama and daddy."

"Daddy got sick."

"Yes."

"Mama had to take care of him."

"Yes."

"Now they're boff in heaven, and nobody is sick," Gina said.

"Yep, and then they shared you with me and that makes me very glad."

"Wet's play that game."

"Which one?" Lyndee asked.

"Where we rhyme."

"Okay."

"I say fun, ooh say—" Gina started off.

"All done! I say snap. You say—" Lyndee followed.

"Map. I say apple. Ooh say—" Gina continued.

"Scrabble. I say nice. You say—"

"Sugar spice!" Gina said, clapped her hands, and went again, "I say Caca-doodle-do!" Gina giggled big.

"I say I love you!" Lyndee pulled Gina in for a hug.

Chapter 32

Haleya tried to hold her hand steady as she applied mascara. After a couple of attempts, she gave up. *Is that what she was doing, giving up?* She'd walked away from the responsibilities instead of sticking through them. One minute her thoughts rationalized her decision, and the next they chastised her. She'd accepted failure, admitted defeat, caved to the pressure; but ultimately, she'd realized this time was different. *The stakes were too high. Something was going to break, if it hadn't already.*

After she'd quit, Candice had called back, but Haleya was on the phone with her mother. Candice texted asking Haleya to reconsider, and then called Janice, who left a voicemail. As terrified as Haleya was to let go of all she'd worked for, she was more frightened to see what holding on might cost her. Thomas hadn't come home last night. She'd hardly slept. He hadn't answered her calls nor any of her texts.

Though headed to an orientation for a job she'd done before, she fought back fear. The last time she'd felt like this was when she'd taken the State Board Nursing Exam. Even with all she'd accomplished, it had crossed her mind to give up, afraid she'd fail. It was her father's words then and now that came to mind, "I'm not upset when you fail. I'm upset when you don't try." He'd first said this when he'd taught her how to stand on her head.

"Daddy, how do you do that?" She begged him to help her. Standing on his head, Kent's face reddened and his shirt draped showing his belly. His feet wobbled and with the most ungraceful thud, he dropped to the floor proud to show off for his daughter. "Daddy! Daddy, show me! Please!"

She'd gotten so frustrated trying. He'd worked with her each night though, until she'd gotten good. She'd spent most of her evenings after school upside down waiting for her father to get home. He'd taught her if she wanted something, she had to work at it; when you don't get it right, try again. When she didn't pass the exam the first time, he'd been there for her. When she passed the second time, he was there. She'd asked him if he could still stand on his head. He'd answered, "Yes."

She'd said, "Me too."

Haleya checked her phone hoping Thomas had texted. Nothing. As she drove past the University of Kentucky's campus, its Wildcat reminded her of another mascot. When she was seven, her father worked at a hospital south of Lexington. She was in first grade when she met Big Red, the mascot for Western Kentucky University—a big red blob that looked to her like Grimace on her plastic McDonald's souvenir cup. He was huge and waddled, his mouth as wide as his body and his arms ridiculously tiny in comparison. Yet he gave each kid, individually, one humungous hug—the kind where you sway and rock from one foot to the other. That evening, between cartwheels, headstands, and uneven breaths, she told her father that someday she was going to school at Big Red's house.

Now, sitting in her car outside the hospital, no longer a little girl, she tried to push the thoughts of failure away. Her memory of Big Red also reminded her of the second time she'd seen Big Red. It was the *second* year she was in first grade.

*   *   *

Thomas sat in his truck outside the tin building, a stark difference from T & T Construction headquarters where he'd interviewed yesterday. He hadn't expected anyone to be there on a Sunday, but he thought he'd check it out. He'd worked temp jobs the last few months, his savings were dwindling, and last night, he'd stumbled into a hotel only a couple of miles from where his family slept. His phone rang. This time he answered.

"You okay?" He heard his wife's voice.

"Yeah."

"Where were you last night? Did you get my texts?"

"I stayed in a hotel." Anticipating her next question, he added, "Alone."

"Why?"

"Why alone?"

"No. Why didn't you come home?"

"It just doesn't feel right there anymore."

"And a hotel room does?"

"No."

"Come home." Her voice was weak.

"I'm going home."

"Good."

"Ridgewood."

"Oh, Okay. How long?"

"Don't know."

"I took my nursing job back."

"You did?"

"Yeah, I would have talked with you about it but—"

"I understand," Thomas interrupted. He imagined her thoughts were the same as his, still lots of hours and less money.

"I love you," Haleya's voice cracked. "Don't be gone long."

He'd be in Ridgewood in a couple of hours, though he didn't know what answers he expected to find there.

*   *   *

Lyndee taped the picture of Sugani to the wall and promised herself this would be her last. She placed her palm against the picture of Karusa. She prayed for Karusa's heart and the surgery to come—if the rebels would just stay away, but updates about Karusa only came twice a year. Karusa could be well and sharing hugs or holding onto her last breath.

Though Whitney wasn't in another country, Lyndee felt as helpless. "You don't have to be alone," Lyndee had called as Whitney walked out the door. *"And we cling to what we know,"* Lyndee thought, *"even pain."*

Moving her hand to Racco's photo to pray for him, Knox and Elizabeth shot through her front door. "Missed you at church this morning," she greeted them.

"I gotta get this. It's Mom." Elizabeth put her iPhone on speaker.

"I work tonight. I need you to take Knox to school in the morning. Can you do that?"

"Sure."

"Your dad went to see his father in Ridgewood and won't be home tonight."

"Is Grandpa okay?"

"He's fine. This walk-though at the hospital won't take long. I'll be home soon."

"Let's look for bugs." Gina pulled Knox out the front door.

"How are your friends?" Lyndee asked Elizabeth.

"Kara and Sam are so crazy."

"Kara seems like fun."

"She's my best friend ever."

"Do you still talk with Emma Lee?"

156

"Not so much. She's," Elizabeth paused, "well, kind of boring."

"It's good that you can text her to keep in touch."

Elizabeth shrugged. "Is Whitney coming back?"

"Don't know."

"Sounds like I'm in charge tonight. Mom's at work and Dad's out of town. I'm glad. He's been really grouchy."

"Not knowing what's next is hard," Lyndee offered in explanation.

"Like me not knowing if I'm going to get to go on spring break with Kara."

"That's months away. Is that really important right now?

"Yes! I'm only a senior once!"

"Who's going?"

"A bunch of kids. They all know they're going. I mean, they went last year when they were juniors. Their parents don't care. But Dad is 'We'll talk about it,' and 'How are you paying for it? Do you have a job?'"

"Good questions."

"But I'm a senior," Elizabeth insisted. "I can't be the only one who doesn't go!"

"They require you to go?"

"No, not like that. I'm saying it'll be my only chance to go. Kara really wants me to go."

Gina pulled open the front door. "We pound a walking stick bug on da tree. You gotta thee it, Wizzy."

Elizabeth shook her head.

"Come thee!" Gina pleaded.

"I'm hungry. I'm staying inside."

"I have left over spaghetti and meatballs," Lyndee offered.

"No."

"Want some celery and peanut butter?"

"Ew, no."

Elizabeth opened the cabinet. "Pringles!" After eating the last chip, she yelled to Knox, "Let's go!"

Gina waved trying to get Elizabeth's attention.

"Let's go, Knox!"

Knox transferred the stick bug from his hand to Gina's.

"Thee Wizzy," Gina showed Elizabeth.

"Is that really a bug?"

Knox nodded. "It looks like a twig from a tree, so it's hidden from predators."

"It's weird looking," Elizabeth said.

"I doeth't bite," Gina said. "Can I keep it?" she asked Lyndee.

Elizabeth grabbed Knox's hand and pulled him. "Thanks for the money!" she called to her grandmother.

"Oh, wait," Lyndee said and went inside the house. She came back with a box of donuts.

"Thanks, Grandma!" Knox grabbed the box and pulled out a donut.

"Bye," Gina yelled.

Elizabeth pulled away before Knox shut his door.

*   *   *

Thomas remembered being as tall as a tree stump when the big trucks rattled through laying asphalt widening the roads in Ridgewood. That was when his interest in construction began. Someday, he had thought, he'd take these roads out of Ridgewood. He'd done just that, only to return to find what he'd left here. He wanted the youthful hope he'd known before the world took hold of him. He wanted to remember why it had felt so right to cash a check given to him by his mother and build a home for someone who was left with nothing but twisted scraps and the clothes they wore. That had come from Ridgewood. That had come from his mother.

Holding the steering wheel tighter than necessary, he revved his truck engine at the stoplight. As his mind raced, he realized that he'd returned with the same frustration that he'd left with as a teen. Thomas slowed as he passed the new elementary school that now stood in place of his father's wood mill. Turning into the church's parking lot, he saw Colton.

"You've got to be lost, brother!" Colton looked up from working on the air-conditioning. "Everything okay?"

"Better than ever."

"Well, you look great. I can't believe you're here."

"Me either, actually. How's Dad?"

"Lonely," Colton answered.

*   *   *

After Knox had taken out the trash that afternoon, he kept walking. There was still enough daylight to see the small beetles in his hand.

"What are you doing?" he heard from behind. "I've seen you at school. Your name is Knox, right?"

Knox turned.

"I'm Alicia. Whatcha got? Lady bugs?"

Knox nodded.

"What are you going to do with them?"

Knox shrugged expecting her to make fun of him. In his head he heard her say, "Bugbee Boy," but her lips didn't move and her smile seemed genuine. He shifted his hand closer so she could see. "Some people believe ladybugs are good luck," Knox said, holding her glance for only a second.

"What do you mean?"

"In some cultures, they believe whatever a ladybug touches will be made better."

"Do you think that's true?"

Knox shrugged.

"My little brother needs lady bugs then. He's really sick," Alicia said in a big breath.

"What kind of sick?"

"Duchenne Syndrome. Have you heard of it?"

"No."

"Muscular Dystrophy?" she asked.

Knox nodded.

"He's 10. His muscles are weak. They say it's genetic and it just gets worse."

"I don't think lady bugs fix that."

"I wish they could. I wish something could. They say that it can't be fixed."

"Do you want to hold one?"

Alicia nodded. He helped the ladybug onto her palm. "The boys give you grief, huh?"

Knox turned and began searching for more ladybugs.

"Jerks." She hesitated. "I like bugs too. Our favorite thing to do before my brother got too sick was to catch fireflies at night. You know, lightning bugs?"

Knox nodded and bent down to let the ladybugs he'd found crawl from his hand onto the sidewalk.

"We'd cup them in our hands and peek inside to see their lights flashing. Once, we put them in a jar. We even put holes in the lid, but they died."

"Don't put holes in the lid. Airholes dry out the air. They need damp air to survive. Then after a couple of days, let them go." They began walking together.

"Seriously?"

Knox nodded and pointed to ants scurrying across the sidewalk in the glow of the streetlights. "What do you know about ants?"

"They're tiny," Alicia laughed. "Okay, so not much."

"Ants have superman strength. They don't have lungs, but they have two stomachs."

"No way!"

"Yes, way. There's more. They don't have ears either."

"How do they hear?"

"By feeling vibrations in the ground through their feet." Knox stopped and bent down to an ant colony. Alicia squatted beside him and asked one question after another.

Chapter 33

MARCELLA—1962—age 14

Roxie stacked the scoops of ice cream so high that she had to hold the cone at her belly button to lick the top one. Roxie counted the flavors: Strawberry, Chocolate, Raspberry, Fudge Swirl, Pineapple, Orange Sorbet, Butter Pecan, and Vanilla Bean topped off with a cherry. A perfect treat for a perfect day.

Marcella struggled to carry the water hose. It trailed down her back like a dinosaur tail. She watched the mud flow from the truck like melting chocolate. The top of the truck was the hardest to reach. Thankfully, no one could tell the difference between the old dents and any new ones her knees made. Getting down from the truck, she lost her balance and tumbled into a pool of mud. "What the—" her grandfather yelled. That night she dreamed of chocolate because she got no supper.

MARCELLA—1972—age 24

Marcella's eyes opened. From the top bunk in the cinderblock room, she knew exactly where she was. She didn't miss Randall, her freedom, or her baby she'd left behind. She missed the drugs. She pressed her head with both hands wanting the pounding to stop, whispering Roxie's name over and over.

MARCELLA—2010—age 62

The doctor read aloud the nurse's notes. "Bluish coloring around the nails and lips. Chest pain. Weak cough. Shortness of breath. Fever. Fast heart rate."

The nurse nodded.

"Increase her oxygen. We need to add a second antibiotic," he directed.

Thankful for the oxygen that helped her breathe and the medication that dulled the pain, she rested. The needle woven through Marcella's scarred veins gave her life. She had a bed and a blanket to keep warm. She thought she might be in heaven. Marcella mumbled. The nurse placed her hand on Marcella's shoulder and said, "Just rest."

Chapter 34

When Ben answered his door, Colton stepped aside, and he saw Thomas. Ben's lonely tears flowed. Thomas handed his father the note that his mother had written.

"I've always been loved. The best blessing ever. Though my heart has broken more times than I can count, I've never felt the pain without someone to give me hope. Be that for someone. This money was put in my care by someone who never let the world know his heart was big. Yours is beautiful and full of love. Your choice: touch someone's life when they would never expect it. He did mine."

Ben handed the note back. "You did good, son."

"This isn't good. I'm not good! When I built the house, nothing ever felt more right, but I'm so confused now." Thomas, sitting across from his father, looked away. "There's no more Kage Construction." He shared how he'd treated Haleya. "She deserves better."

"Don't think that the past is all you've got. You write your future. Your mama raised you better than this." He reached for the spiral-bound notepad. "I've nearly committed this to memory. Take it."

Thomas wasn't sure what his father handed him, but he recognized his mother's handwriting and knew he'd spend the night reading every word.

*   *   *

Gina jumped from the couch and dashed to the door when she saw Whitney. "I prayed this morning por you to come home," she said.

Lyndee stopped mid-slice of an apple. "You've got your stuff with you?"

Whitney nodded.

"Are you still angry?"

Whitney shook her head.

"Do you want a hug?"

Whitney dropped her stuff on the floor and nodded. Together they had a three-way hug that lasted until the apples Lyndee peeled turned brown.

"I'm sorry," Whitney mumbled.

"Why are you sorry?"

"I mess up everything."

"We all do that sometimes," Lyndee said.

"I do it all the time."

"Not *all* the time," Lyndee assured her.

"You know what hurt the most over the years?"

"What?" Lyndee listened.

"The promises that this time it was really home, that I was good enough."

"I'm sorry so much went wrong for you."

Whitney shrugged. "They didn't want me."

"That wasn't it."

"I was a lot of trouble."

"Okay, then that wasn't it *every* time," Lyndee chuckled and handed her a freshly cut apple slice.

"I wasn't always a bad kid."

"I know you weren't a bad kid."

"Why didn't anybody want me?"

Lyndee didn't answer right away. *"I guess you drew the short straw."* Though callous and not the right answer, in some ways, that was exactly it. And it wasn't fair. "I really don't know."

*   *   *

As Haleya was getting ready to leave for work, Elizabeth had bopped down the stairs to say goodnight. What had sparked the argument, Haleya couldn't even remember. Elizabeth blamed her mother for raising her voice. Haleya tried to remember what Elizabeth had said that set her off. Was it just the tone of her voice, a specific sentence, or Elizabeth's entitled attitude? "Wait until your father gets home," Haleya had said.

Elizabeth didn't miss a beat. "He's not coming home." She'd stomped off.

"Haleya, you're back!" a nurse said passing the nurses' station as Haleya's phone rang.

"Dad!"

"You sound great," Kent said.

"It's great to hear from you. Is everything okay?"

"Yep, I just wanted to make sure that you're still standing on your head."

"So, Mom told you."

"Just a little."

"I miss you."

"Come home. You've been gone for almost a year!"

"I'm ready to be home. I'll be there before Christmas," Kent assured her.

"I told Santa to bring you something really good this year."

"I can't wait!"

"Love you, Dad."

"Love you, my girl."

Haleya noticed she was cradling the phone to her ear like she'd hug her teddy bear when she was small. She felt safe hearing her father's voice. "Thank you."

"Thank you for what?"

"The call. Perfect timing." Stepping into room 301, Haleya glanced at the screen and read the profile: *Jane Doe #94.* She carefully pulled off the old bandages and brushed

166

the dry skin from the lady's forehead. She'd taken a beating, her cheek still raw and bruised. The gash on her forehead would be tough to heal. Her labored breathing was concerning. As she cleaned the woman's wound, careful so the stiches wouldn't break through her purpled, thin skin, she wondered what had happen. *Who had done this to her?*

"Haleya–" The voice over the intercom startled her, but Jane Doe didn't move. Hearing her name over the speaker reminded her of another time in collage when Thomas had come to her rescue.

"The schedule's been set," Haleya's sorority sister said as they counted balloons getting ready for Greek Week.

"I know, but I'm just asking to switch with someone so I can study," Haleya explained. "I hate to bring this up, but I put in a ton of hours on the Earth Day float, found our sponsor for the dance, and made cupcakes for the–"

"Study ahead!" Another girl showing no sympathy interjected.

"I am. I mean, I do," Haleya stumbled on her words. "I just thought maybe I could get another shift instead of the afternoon before my biggest exam."

"I'm going to get Mrs. Marsha." Little Miss 'Study Ahead' trotted off.

"Stop, Amber. I'll work it out!"

Mrs. Marsha approached, wearing the same letters on her shirt as the girls but clearly her college days behind her. "Haleya, we've talked about this. The retreats are mandatory."

"I'm not trying to get out of the retreat!" Haleya's voice rose.

"Haleya, if you miss the retreat, you know there's a fine."

"I just asked about trading a Greek Week shift. I'll be at the retreat!"

Haleya heard her name called over the outdoor speaker. "Haleya to center stage. Haleya, center stage." She excused herself.

Jogging toward the stage, she called out, "Hey, did somebody call for me?"

"Yeah, I need you to look at this. It's not getting better," Thomas said.

"Why'd you do that?"

"Seemed like you were being ganged up on."

Haleya turned to see that her sorority sisters had gone back to arranging fishbowls and sorting balloons. "Kinda felt like it."

"And I have an emergency—no Snoopy Band-Aid." Thomas pointed to his arm.

"Are you serious?"

"Are *they* serious? What's the fine for missing a retreat?"

"You were listening?"

"Hey, you were the one screaming, again."

"Oh, dear. I'll have to go apologize. Chances are I'll have to take clean-up duty after the dance to get back in their graces."

"Just skip the dance. Or is there a fine for that too?"

"No, silly. That's the fun stuff, getting all dressed up—"

"No Red Wings allowed? I do have another pair of shoes, if you'd like to see them."

"I thought you said you weren't in a fraternity."

"I'm not."

The guy adjusting the sound equipment yelled to Thomas, "Try it again."

"Test. Test one, two, three," Thomas said into the microphone.

The guy nodded thanks. Thomas gave a quick salute in return. "It's much easier just being friends with them; I don't have to pay the fines and all. Just stopped on the way to my apartment." He pointed in its direction.

"And again, you come to my rescue. That's two in a row."

"But I owed you one."

"How do you see that?"

He pointed to his arm. "Could have died from this gash if you hadn't been there."

Haleya's thoughts of Thomas were interrupted when the nurses' station called again. "Haleya, report your location, please."

"Hurry home, Thomas," Haleya whispered to herself. "My heart needs rescued."

*   *   *

Knox was sitting at his computer when his sister barged in.

"Hey, punk, Mom left for work. I'm supposed to take you to school in the morning."

"I know."

"And Dad's at Grandpa's, so it's just us."

"I already did the paper for you. Why are you in here?"

"What's wrong?"

"Why would you care?"

Elizabeth walked over to Knox and sat on the floor. "Because you're my brother."

"So?"

"So, I don't like it when you look like that. All sad and stuff."

Knox looked at her, analyzing his sister.

"Tell me."

"Tell you what?"

"What's wrong. Maybe I can help."

"Don't act like you care. You don't."

"Knox, that hurts. I do too."

"Whatever. You are always bossing me around or insulting me. I know when you're lying."

"I'm not lying," Elizabeth insisted.

Knox ignored her.

"Okay, I know I haven't been nice to you. I'm supposed to treat my little brother that way."

"Whatever. That's stupid."

"No, you're stupid," Elizabeth shot back.

"See."

"Oh, okay. Hmm," Elizabeth thought. "I could be nicer."

"You bully me. It makes you happy. You're proud of yourself. I get angry and wish—" He stopped mid-sentence.

"You wish what?"

"Never mind."

"No, you were going to say something. What was it?"

"Sometime I wish I were an only child."

"You mean, you wish I wasn't your sister."

Knox didn't answer. He could tell Elizabeth was hurt.

"I don't know what to say," Elizabeth's voice cracked.

"Kip's big sister gives him hi-fives as they pass in the hallway. Roland's sister sneaks him ice cream even though he's lactose intolerant and spends his next class in the bathroom. Chris and his sister share clothes—not the girly ones, but her Green Day T-shirts.

"Wow, you've thought a lot about this."

Knox shrugged.

"I'm sorry."

Knox looked at his sister.

"I am. I didn't know—"

"Yes, you knew."

"I mean, I didn't know that it really bothered you."

"Sometimes you only think of yourself. Other people matter too."

170

Elizabeth's iPhone rang, and she silenced it. "So are you saying that I shouldn't eat that last donut Grandma gave you?" She pointed to the open box.

"How would you feel if I took the money Grandma gave you?"

"Oh, that's already gone. I got new fingernail polish." She wiggled her fingers.

"Maybe if you *ask* for the donut instead of just taking it."

"Oh, okay. I get that." Her iPhone buzzed. "Kara's got guy problems. Well, actually, she doesn't have a guy and that's her problem." She cut her phone off. "I wish you'd tell me what's wrong."

Knox shook his head. He didn't trust her. He wanted to, but he didn't.

She stood up. "Then can I have a hug?"

Knox hesitated. He wasn't sure this was his sister, but it looked like her. "You want a hug?"

"You're my brother. I love you."

"Who are you?"

"Your sister who wants to give you a hug."

"Okay, but if you put me in a headlock, I'm never trusting you again."

Elizabeth reached out her arms and slowly Knox edged toward her and into them.

She rocked with him in a playful hug and asked, "Can I have one of your donuts?"

"My last one?"

"Yeah, that one."

"Okay, but only because I made myself sick eating so many."

"Good. Oh, I don't mean 'good, you made yourself sick,' I mean 'good, I really want that donut!' See, I'm already being nicer."

Chapter 35

MARCELLA—1963—age 15

Roxie Applesauce posed for the camera—tilting her chin, lifting her eyes, and adding a spunky smirk. The flashes nearly blinded her, but she continued without falter. She cupped her chin with her hand, fingertips out; and the camera man responded by getting on his knees to position himself closer. "Click, click, click," the camera sang. She ran her fingers through her hair and pulled it back into a ponytail, exchanging her smirk for a shy gaze. The photographer called to her, "Perfect. I love it!"

Marcella found the make-up in the trash at school.

"What do you have on your face?" her grandmother scolded the next morning. "Hey, Roger. Come look at this."

Her grandfather stepped into the kitchen. "What's she trying to be? It's not Halloween."

"Nothin' but a whore with that stuff on her face. She ain't pretty, anyway. At least it covers up some of that ugly that we've gotta look at."

MARCELLA—1972—age 24

She didn't know which was worse, the jail cell or the court-ordered treatment program. She'd been part of a similar program when she was homeless and pregnant at 20. She'd obeyed the rules required to stay at the halfway house, but after her baby was born, she left the first chance she got. That's when she met Randall. He wanted her as his wife; they'd be a family. Now she didn't know where he was, and she didn't care.

MARCELLA—2010—age 62

"Lucky to be alive," Marcella heard the nurse and felt the doctor's touch. It was nice to be touched so delicately—as if she could break—as if she wasn't already broken. The needle in her arm fed her life and, for a reason unclear to her, she prayed to live.

"Has she said anything?" the doctor asked.

The nurse shook her head.

"Vital signs good?" he asked.

"Improving."

"Set her up for chest x-rays." The doctor peeled back the bandage on her forehead to look.

He asked the nurse, "Pain medication sufficient?"

The nurse nodded.

He started out, but turned. "Glad to have you back," he said. "How are the kids?"

"Growing up. Elizabeth's 17 and counting the days until she's 18, and Knox turns 13 soon."

"They are two lucky kiddos. Tell Thomas I'm ready to beat him at another round of golf."

"I'll let him know."

The nurse rubbed a warm washcloth along Marcella's neck. She'd never been to a spa before. She couldn't wait to tell Roxie about her day.

Chapter 36

Thomas didn't wake his father though he had a hundred questions. He turned to the first page and began reading again. First about his mother and what had happened—how she'd lost her hand and so much the night of the fire. Then about his father, only 19, and how he'd stumbled into Ridgewood with no intention to stay. And from its last pages, the note from his mother finally made sense. But it was the message to his mother from his great-grandfather, his namesake, that inspired him the most. *"You won't be one to miss the view from the top of the mountain. Keep climbing."*

* * *

"Miley Cyrus or Selena Gomez?" Elizabeth asked, on the phone with Sam as she flipped through *Seventeen* magazine.

"Neither. Taylor Swift. She wants me."

"Dream on."

"How come you're up so late?"

"Dad's out of town, and Mom's at work."

"Party at your house!"

"Seriously?"

"Does your dad have any liquor he wouldn't miss? We can make it a party of two."

"You'd come over right now?"

"Yeah! I'm on my way," Sam said and hung up.

Elizabeth opened the front door when she saw Sam's Trailblazer park on the street. *"Smart,"* Elizabeth thought. He jogged through her front door with a hug that almost knocked her down.

"What's got into you?" Elizabeth whispered, "Shhh!"

"Smokin' more than cigarettes."

"What? I just got off my phone with you."

"And I just got done smokin' a joint. Sorry, none for you."

"We've got school tomorrow!"

"Nah, I'm fine." Sam trotted upstairs. "Just fakin' it to weird you out. It worked!"

*   *   *

Knox looked at his alarm clock—2:30 a.m. Opening his bedroom door, he looked out expecting what he'd heard was his mom coming home early, instead, he saw Elizabeth's friend Sam. Crawling back in bed, his stomach hurt thinking of the guys who called him "Bugbee Boy." *What if Bugbee Boy was a superhero,* he thought. *I'd have the power to sting through beams from my five eyes. I bet none of those idiots at school know that bees have five eyes.* He imagined a scene where the mean boys were picking on Alicia. *Faster than a dragon fly, more powerful than a horned dung beetle, able to leap a Redwood tree in a single bound, it's "Bugbee Boy."*

*   *   *

Before her shift ended, Haleya checked on Jane Doe. "Can you hear me?" Haleya asked, placing a clean bandage on her head wound. "What's your name?"

Jane Doe didn't answer, though her respiratory rate was improving and she'd opened her eyes once.

"Haleya, I heard you were back." Sandra leaned in the doorway. "Look!" She draped her left hand showing off her ring.

"Wow! We *do* have to catch up."

"Is she doing better?" Sandra pointed to Jane Joe.

"A bit."

"Wonder what her story is?" Sandra asked.

"She's somebody's daughter, somebody's sister, somebody's mama. We just gotta find out whose."

Chapter 37

MARCELLA—1963—age 15 ½

Roxie Applesauce sniffed the scented lavender envelope and admired the crushed flowers embedded in its fibers. She hesitated before ripping it, not wanting to disturb its perfection. But then again, what was inside would surely be even better. "A party!" she exclaimed. The invitation read:

> *Come dressed for a royal occasion.*
> *Only the most elite received this invitation.*
> *We'll be dancing the night through,*
> *and drinking champagne too.*
> *Bring a friend, a guest if you like.*
> *The party starts at six and ends at midnight.*

Marcella rode her bike as though it could take flight. She'd gotten away. She'd out-smarted and out-run him. A freedom that only Roxie had experienced! Marcella knew better than to turn and look. She focused every ounce of energy on reaching the hidden path ahead. Taking cover, she heard gravel popping beneath the tires of his truck as her grandfather passed.

MARCELLA—1972—age 24

The 12-step program wasn't difficult. Marcella showed up, listened, and spoke when asked. The first, *admitting she was powerless,* was no stretch. She had always felt powerless. The second—*believing that a power greater than herself could restore sanity*—well, she'd always been a dreamer. The third, *turning her life over to a higher power*—God, if she chose. *Sure, why not?* Fourth—*make a searching, fearless moral inventory of herself*—not as bad as she thought it would be with the support from the group.

It got harder when she came to the fifth step—*admit to God, herself, and another the exact nature of her wrongs.* Marcella thought, *"Where to begin?"*

MARCELLA—2010—age 62

The nurse made notes on the computer as the doctor spoke. "High risk pneumonia. The X-rays show multiple fractured ribs. Need to rule out internal bleeding."

The nurse nodded.

"Set her up for a CT Scan. Has she said anything?"

"Nothing coherent."

"No contact from anyone looking for her?" the doctor asked.

"No, not yet."

Chapter 38

"Elizabeth!" Haleya shouted, dashing through the front door and up the stairs. Elizabeth's car was still in the driveway.

Dressed for school, Knox stepped out of his room.

"Why didn't you get your sister up?"

"Tried to. She wouldn't open the door."

Haleya pounded on Elizabeth's door. "Open up! You were supposed to be at school an hour ago. Open this door now!"

"What?" Elizabeth sluggishly opened the door.

"School! Today! You and your brother are supposed to be there!" Haleya pointed to the clock.

"Okay, okay! I'll get in the shower."

"Elizabeth! I trusted you to do what you were supposed to do this morning! This is not okay!"

"Mom, chill! First period's a joke anyway."

"Who are you to determine—" Haleya followed Elizabeth. Elizabeth closed the bathroom door, locked it, and turned on the shower.

Haleya stomped to Knox's room. "Ugh!" She slapped the door facing with her hand and leaned in. "What are you missing first period?"

"Algebra. A test. I tried to call you."

Haleya pulled her phone from her purse. She'd put it on silent. "Get in the car. I'll take you."

*   *   *

Back in Lexington Monday morning, Thomas slowed his vehicle as he passed the house he'd built for the family. The shrubs had grown, and they'd added a stepping-stone sidewalk. When Thomas pulled up outside the construction office trailer that he'd stopped at the day before, the door stood open.

"Come in." The man sitting at a metal desk stood and extended his hand.

"Name's Thomas. Your wife suggested I check about a job."

"Been hopin' you'd drop by. Have a seat. I'm Walt." Sitting down, he asked, "What's your favorite number?"

"Excuse me?"

"Give me a number, two-digit."

"Is this a pass or fail interview question?"

"No," he chuckled. "Powerball." He lifted the card to show his selections.

"52 then."

"52, it is. When I win, we'll split this." He set the card aside. "How much do you want to be paid?"

"You just said we'd split it. That's half, right?"

"No, for working here."

Thomas looked around the trailer and smirked. "Doing what? Errand boy? Running to the gas station to collect your quick-pick of the day."

"I like you. That's why this is going to work. Charisma, guts, skilled in the trade—"

"Bring me up to speed. We just met, right? Either you've got me confused with someone or—"

"Nope, Thomas Kage. I know exactly who you are." Walt opened his desk drawer and pulled out a Kit Kat and the newspaper clipping of Thomas and the family he'd help. He pushed the article across the desk, opened the candy wrapper, snapped off a section, and placed it between his fingers. "Want a smoke?" He pushed the Kit Kat package toward Thomas.

"No, I'm trying to quit."

Walt put the Kit Kat to his lip and pretended to take a draw from it. "Understand. Now let's get down to business. How much are you going to cost me?"

"Nothing at this rate. I have no idea what I'm even doing here." Thomas wondered what that Kit Kat was laced with.

*   *   *

"Where were you this morning?" Kara asked as she fumbled through her purse at the lunch table.

"Overslept."

"Bad day to oversleep. We reviewed for the Art Appreciation test."

"So?"

"So, I guess I forgot how smart you are," Kara quipped.

"And you assumed that I care what grade I make in that stupid class."

"Yeah, it's pretty stupid."

"Forth period bell," Elizabeth said. She pulled her book bag over her arm and picked up her lunch tray. "You didn't eat anything."

"Yeah, I did. I ate the dessert."

"The dessert was tiny."

"Yeah, that's why I ate it." Kara swallowed a pill.

"What's that?"

"A laxative."

"You keep laxatives in your purse?"

"Yeah, it helps." Kara pulled at the waistline of her pants. "These didn't even fit me last month. Look now! A pill a day keeps the pounds away."

Elizabeth's phone rang. "Knox, stop screaming at me!" Elizabeth held her iPhone from her ear. "What happened? He won't let you take the test? What test?"

"I missed my algebra test. I got a zero. You know what a zero is? No points, not even a flipping failing grade. It's completely nothing!"

"Oh," Elizabeth was quiet. She wanted to brush it off, tell him that he's a big enough nerd and that it didn't matter, but his words from the night before ran through her mind. Now he wasn't just sad about something, he was angry, and she'd caused it. "Mom took you to school. She'd didn't tell him why you missed your test?"

"Mom didn't go in with me. I'm not in kindergarten."

"I'll talk to your teacher. I'll fix it."

"Whatever. You caused this. You and the stupid boy you had over. I saw. I didn't tell. I didn't screw you over! Just don't ever talk to me again!"

*　　　*　　　*

"Thomas already gone?" Colton asked when he stopped to see his father.

Ben nodded. "Any word from Caleb? I've left messages at the—" his voice trailed off.

"Nope." Colton sat next to Ben.

"Did Thomas tell you about shutting down his business?" Ben asked.

"Yep." Colton took the framed photo of his mother from his father's hand. As a pastor, Colton listened to heartache regularly, but these he shared.

"Thomas got enough money to take care of his family?"

"Dad, I don't know."

"Before you say anything, I know I missed church yesterday, and I *am* intentionally avoiding the subject."

"Okay."

"Oh, go on and tell me. What'd I miss?"

"Esli came forward to be baptized. That was something special! Took three of us to be safe."

"How far along is she now?"

181

"Nine months, could have the baby any day. Trying to find her a place to stay when Michael comes home on leave."

"Esli's mother still want nothing to do with him?"

"Won't even acknowledge that the baby has a daddy. There's no way she's letting him step foot in their home."

"Michael ain't a bad guy."

"Last time he was in, he said he was going to marry her and wanted me to preside. Doubt Esli's mama ever talks to me again after that."

"And that's a bad thing?" Ben kidded.

"I see your point."

"You know you don't gotta visit me like you do the shut-ins. I'm not completely crippled yet and still know my name."

"*I* know your name. That's why I visit, *Dad.* That's what family's supposed to do. I do need to head out though, I've got a few shut-ins that like it when I visit."

*   *   *

When Thomas got home, he found Haleya in the laundry room.

Haleya pulled clothes from the washer. "The kids are home. They aren't speaking to each other."

"Sorry," Thomas said.

"Sorry about the kids?"

Thomas shook his head. He pointed his finger toward her and stepped closer.

"Like sorry a little or sorry a whole, whole lot?" Haleya asked as she stuffed the last of clothes in the dryer.

He stepped closer. "A whole, whole lot," he said, his eyes searching hers when she turned to him.

"Like bunches and bunches?" she asked taking a step closer.

"A whole bunches," Thomas said, putting his hands on her shoulders and leaning his forehead against hers.

Haleya pulled him into her arms. "I am, too," she whispered.

"It's been hard," Thomas said.

She tightened her grip. "I know."

"I'm hurting," he mumbled.

"I know."

"I loved owning my own business."

"I know."

"I want to be able to take good care of our family."

"I know."

"I think of Caleb every day. I wish he hadn't gotten into trouble. He's smarter than that."

"I know."

"I really miss my mama."

"I know."

Chapter 39

MARCELLA—1964—age 16

Roxie ducked behind the tour bus. Fans were everywhere. She'd taken a year off from performing so she could travel the world. She wasn't surprised so many people had come to greet her upon her return. She was so loved.

No prodigal son welcome awaited Marcella's return home after she ran away. She wondered if they'd even tried to find her. "What's this?" Her grandmother grabbed the satchel from Marcella's shoulder. "Fancy leather or something?" She sniffed it.

"What's in it?" Grandma growled. The high heeled shoes didn't fit her grandmother, so she stuffed them with newspaper and lit them with her cigarette lighter.

MARCELLA—1972—age 24

Steps six and seven—*ask God to remove all defects of character* and *humbly ask God to remove her shortcomings*—weren't as bad as she'd expected, mainly because everyone had to do it. The next two threw her into a tailspin of emotions. The eighth, *make a list of the people we've harmed*, was followed by the nineth, *make direct amends whenever possible*. She didn't know where her baby was, and she knew that was for the best.

MARCELLA—2010—age 62

The doctor reviewed the results of Jane Doe's CT Scan. "Reduction of fluid on the lungs—"

The nurse adjusted Marcella's oxygen and leaned toward her. "The fluid on your lungs has reduced significantly. That's good news."

Marcella nodded.

"Are you feeling a little better?"

Marcella nodded.

"Good. You're looking a little better too."

Marcella nodded.

"Can you tell us your name?"

Marcella shook her head.

"In addition to the pulmonary laceration and rib fractures, the CT scan shows a grade 1 ruptured spleen. Internal bleeding minimal," the doctor shared. Then he squinted for a closer look. "I'm concerned with the lung mass I see here." He pointed. "If she gets strong enough, let's consider scheduling a lung needle biopsy."

Chapter 40

"Okay. Let's make a deal," Thomas said on his second visit with Walt. He reached for the Kit Kat on Walt's desk. "I could use one of these right now."

"Trying to quit smoking too?" Walt asked.

Thomas nodded, ripped the wrapper, and separated the chocolate bars with a clean break. "Whatever this is that you've got in mind, I need to be able to provide for my family." He placed the Kit Kat between his teeth.

"Got it."

"Evenings and weekends, I'm my own boss."

"Okay."

"Why you think I'm the one for *whatever* this is?"

Walt took his Kit Kat from his lips. "Because I was you once. I woke up to tackle the world and anything less from a day left me unsatisfied. Then I got sick, and I couldn't do anything for myself. I had to call for my wife when I had to pee, and well—we won't go into detail as I couldn't much do anything for myself. I'd like to say that I was humbled, but that would be padding the truth. I was angry. Oh, and mean. So, she left me. Didn't divorce me or anything like that, but she wasn't sticking around for a verbally abusive, helpless man. She paid some stranger to come take care of me, and she went to work. Not just any job, but she took over my business. Now *talk* about being truly humbled against your will. I was broken. She was taking care of us financially and coming home every night, but she was done with me thinking and acting like I was king when I couldn't get myself to the potty to poo."

186

Thomas laughed, nibbling on the Kit Kat.

Walt continued, "I had to admit defeat. I had to find a new me." The Kit Kat rested between Walt's fingers like a lit cigarette. "She says I'm a better man. I like to think because I was already incredible it wasn't much of a stretch." He chuckled. "Our marriage is better than it's ever been. I learned to listen and can admit I'm smarter for it."

"Not my strong point either, so my wife says," Thomas interjected.

"You," Walt said leaning forward, "did something big for someone you didn't even know *before* you were crippled and brought to your senses. You have that something special."

Though Walt paused, Thomas said nothing.

Walt rested his Kit Kat on the edge of an ashtray. "I didn't believe my wife when she said that God can bring something great from unfortunate circumstances because she's never known or seen what I've seen." He pointed to photographed soldiers and framed medals. "Vietnam."

"You fought?"

Walt nodded. "She's right though, and they need us. We've got an opportunity to build our vets a village!"

Thomas looked at the men in uniform, glanced at the Kit Kat in his hand, and looked at Walt. "What's in these things?"

"Calories. Actually, 106 calories to be exact."

"All I know right now is that I need a cigarette." Thomas tossed his Kit Kat in the trash and nodded goodbye.

*   *   *

"Mr. Logsdon," Elizabeth hustled alongside him. "Knox said that you aren't letting him take the test he missed. I was supposed to get him to school. I didn't get up in time."

Mr. Logsdon slowed, and Elizabeth was thankful. With a deep breath she continued, "School is so important to him. He's devastated. He's never made a zero on a test before.

187

Shoot, he's probably never made less than a ninety. It's my fault. Please let him take the test."

Mr. Logsdon looked at Elizabeth, shook his head, and picked up his pace.

"Please, please—" she begged.

"It's an unexcused absence."

"I can't believe this!" Elizabeth threw up her hands and scurried away. "What am I going to do? He's going to hate me forever. I hate me!" She scolded herself as she willed back frustrated tears.

*   *   *

"Good afternoon, Ben," Aaron greeted as he walked in the grocery. "Heard Thomas was in town. Hate that I missed seeing him." Aaron took an empty grocery cart and wheeled it to Ben.

"Yep. He didn't stay long."

"Bet it was good to see him."

"It was." Ben pushed the cart down the closest aisle.

"Have you heard from Caleb?"

"Nope."

"Doesn't seem right for him to be in jail. I still see him as a boy running on the church lawn."

"He grew up."

"I know that you and Gracie raised him better than this. How many years until he gets out?"

"Several."

Staring at the selection of apple cider, he could hear the conversation at the end of the grocery aisle.

"He will not stay at our house!" Esli's mother took the groceries out of their cart and put them back on the shelf.

"But, Mom, he has nowhere to stay when he's here."

"Then tell him not to come."

Esli dropped her head, rubbed her belly, and said in a weak voice, "But he's the daddy."

188

"And that's your fault. Tell him he's not welcomed."

"But it's his baby too," Esli pleaded.

"Ain't that a shame!" Esli's mother spouted. "Your baby'd be better off if he never met his daddy. I wish I'd never laid eyes on him. I hope he's deployed to another country and—"

"Mom, he's a good man. He loves me."

"He gets you fixed up like that and runs off."

"Please, Mama."

"That boy ain't no good for you. He can't take care of you because he can't even take care of himself."

"That's not true."

"He's a 19-year-old kid who's got nothing. Don't," she paused and shook her finger in Esli's face, "ever bring him into our home."

Esli tucked her hands under her belly and took off down the aisle, past Ben, and out the sliding doors.

*   *   *

Thomas slowed as he neared the home he'd built with the money from his mother. Her words from the note played through his mind: *Your choice. Touch someone's life when they never expect it.*

Brother and sister were playing outside on the swing set. "Push me faster," she said pushing her legs out and kicking them back.

"Okay!" Brother pushed. When her swing was high, he ducked and fell flat under the swing. She lifted her legs as she passed over him. When the swing slowed, she let her toes drag along his head to his ankles.

He knew his mother would have been pleased. Pleased with what he'd done—and pleased with what he was going to do.

*   *   *

"Mom, can I ride the bus to school from now on?" Knox asked when she got home from work.

189

"Sure." Haleya put out her arms. "Can I have—a—hug?" She took a breath between each word like he'd done when he was a little boy, crying and wanting a hug. She got a laugh and a hug.

"How's Dad been?" Haleya asked.

"Okay," Knox muttered dragging his feet.

"That 'okay' was less than okay."

Knox shrugged his slumped shoulders.

"He told me that you helped him work on the shed."

Knox nodded.

"He told me that he wasn't very patient with you and thought that he probably hurt your feelings."

Knox fiddled with the edge of the tablecloth near where he'd sat down.

"He knows that he needs to do better. We both need to do better."

Knox looked up. "I hate swim, Mom," he blurted out.

"You do?" She moved a pan to the stove to start an omelet. When she pointed to the eggs, he nodded and smiled weakly. They were the only two in the house who liked omelets, and she knew just the way he liked his.

"Can I quit?"

Haleya thought for a second, probably the same thing Knox was thinking. Thomas was the one for Knox to convince.

"Will you say something to Dad?"

Haleya nodded as she sliced the mushrooms. "I will."

"I'll figure out how to hammer a nail. I just need practice. I'm not going to get it perfect the first time."

Haleya dropped her head. There was so much she wanted to fix that she couldn't. "I told your dad he had to be patient. He forgets that he had to learn too."

"He acts like he's always been able to do everything."

"Yes, he does. I explained that teaching you to drive a nail while standing on a ladder wasn't the best starter lesson."

Knox nodded. "I got a zero on my Algebra test."

"What?" Haleya nearly cut her finger with the knife.

"The test I missed when Elizabeth didn't get me to school, Mr. Logsdon gave me a zero."

"Oh no!" Haleya turned toward him. "I know you don't want your Mama calling your teacher, but can I?"

Knox nodded. "I made a new friend."

"A new friend?"

"Her name is Alicia."

"Alicia?"

"Mom, it's nothing."

Haleya listened as Knox shared about his week. *This is what she'd missed.*

Chapter 41

MARCELLA—1965—age 17

Roxie leaned out the treehouse window, and a bright yellow butterfly fluttered toward her extended finger and landed. Though she'd seen incredible things on her tour around the world, nothing was as pretty as this butterfly. She spent the day reclined on the chaise with her butterfly friend resting on her big toe.

Marcella crawled over the broken washer stored in her bedroom, passed the useless air conditioning unit, and wound through the tunnel she'd made to her bed. When she'd asked her grandmother why they'd stored so much stuff in her room, her grandmother replied, "It's where we keep the junk."

MARCELLA—1994—age 46

Marcella preferred the homeless shelter to the jail. Neither had long-term plans for her. She glanced around the room. Just like the times that she's spent in jail, she'd learned who to avoid. She took a seat.

"You want mine?"

Marcella ignored the vagrant offering her his Jello.

"You come here often?"

Marcella picked up her tray and searched for an empty table. She spotted a table with only one person—younger than most in the room and scraping out her Jello cup with her finger.

Marcella sat down and handed her Jello to the teen girl. "Your generation likes Jello, right?"

The young girl nodded.

Marcella stood up, waddled over to the man offering his Jello, and took the cup from his plate. "I'll take your Jello. Don't think that I'm interested in anything else." Marcella shuffled back to the table and handed it to the girl.

She nodded in appreciation.

"Can I ask you a question?" Marcella asked.

The girl shrugged her shoulders.

"How old?

"Nineteen," she answered.

"No, I mean, how old when you first left home."

"Oh, about 2 months ago. But I ain't alone. It's Chris and me."

"Chris?"

"Yeah, we take care of each other. He's my man."

"Where's he now?" Marcella asked.

"Making money."

"What does he do?"

"Don't know." The girl pointed to Marcella's cookie, and she passed it over. It felt good to share the little she had.

MARCELLA—2010—age 62

"We're working to help get those ribs healed. I need you to concentrate on breathing. This is a spirometer." The nurse showed her the breathing device. "It's really important that you try every time we do these breathing treatments." She guided her through a set. "They are coming to get you in a minute for a biopsy. They want a closer look at your lungs. You'll do fine. We need you to tell us your name. Do you remember your name?"

Marcella didn't answer.

"That's okay." The nurse said and turned to the student nurse beside her. "Once in a while, we'll get a Jane Doe like this lady. There should always be an explanation in this

193

section." The nurse pointed to the computer screen. "She came in as a result of what appears to be a physical assault rather than a bad fall. Blunt force trauma to the head and ribs. They told us she was found in an abandoned home, suspected to be homeless. They've estimated her to be in her 70's. She could be younger or older. It's difficult to predict."

"What happens to a Jane Doe?" the nursing student asked.

"Hopefully, once she's cognizant, she can tell us her name and what happened. If she has family, we'll contact them. We've contacted the police to check into missing persons reports with no luck. Right now, we do what we can for her. There are several concerning elements." The nurse lowered her voice, and Marcella made out portions of what she said. "High risk of complications—specifically pulmonary. Frailty is a major driver of adverse outcomes in elderly. Pneumonia is a big concern. Mucous and moisture can build up in the lungs and lead to infection. Overall state of health prior to the incident, of course, plays a significant role in recovery. In this case, there's a history of drug use we've determined by the track marks on her arms."

Marcella felt the nurse's touch as she continued with the instructions. "We are administering pain medication, keeping her hydrated—" She enjoyed the company.

Chapter 42

"I took the test today thanks to *Mom's* call to my teacher. They agreed that I shouldn't be punished for you being irresponsible."

Though Knox was berating her, Elizabeth breathed a sigh of relief into the phone. "That's great."

"Where are you?" he asked. "It's loud there."

"The carnival with Kara. Yeah, I can hardly hear you."

"Okay, bye." Knox hung up.

The carnival had drawn a large Friday night crowd.

"I want it." Kara pointed to the baseball cap on the street cart.

"Buy it."

"I don't have enough money." Kara glanced behind her and then to her right and left. "Distract him for me."

"What?"

"Go talk to him. The guy at the register. He's kinda cute."

"I guess."

"I mean, *go* talk to him. Distract him," Kara said with a subtle point toward the hat.

"Are you serious?"

"Yeah. Do it." Kara gave Elizabeth a nudge in the direction of the guy.

"Okay, okay. But if you get caught, I don't know you."

"Deal."

Elizabeth tried on hat after hat asking the guy to take pictures of her with her iPhone. Elizabeth left the carnival with several cute pictures and the guy's number. Kara left with a new hat tucked under her jacket.

Saturday morning, Ben gathered what he needed and loaded the RV in his driveway. He'd called its previous owner the day before and spoken quickly so that he wouldn't change his mind. It wasn't easy for him to let *My Gracie* go. He'd decided to trade his boat for the RV.

"I'll take your offer," Ben had said as soon as the RV's owner answered the phone.

"No negotiating? I expected you to play hard ball."

"That boat was never about the money to me. I'd keep it forever, but I saw something that changed my mind," Ben said.

"Gonna do some traveling?" the new owner of Ben's boat asked.

"I'm not sure what my plan is yet."

Once he'd made the deal, he didn't look back. Overhearing the conversation between Esli and her mother at the grocery store had lingered in his mind. He'd once been what he imagined Michael felt like—in love and confused about how he could ever be a man worthy of her affection.

Ben worked his way around the kitchen, cleaning and organizing. He'd leave the food in his pantry; it could be used. In his bedroom, he stuffed his remaining clothes in a box to store.

Looking at his to-do list, he had only a couple of things to mark off before he left.

*   *   *

Thomas showed Haleya the business card:

HAVHonor
A Village for our Veterans
Help HOUSE A VETERAN
Walt Cummings

"He's starting a village for vets. We'd be partners."

"And you're smiling. This is good, right?"

"Risky, kind of."

"And you like that?"

"Yes and no. Yes, I like the adrenaline rush. It reminds me of when we opened Kage Construction. No, in that we have to get it off the ground, and it's a not-for-profit, which sounds like a dirty word to me, but I'd have a salary.

"You'll build the houses?"

"Yep, they're very small duplexes with only the basics. There's a fundraising component which I know very little about and will have to learn quickly."

"You really want to do this?"

"No, actually, I want my business back, but that's not going to happen right now. I'd never have done something like this, ever! But I never would've built a home for that family either, if it hadn't been for Mom." Thomas glanced at a picture on the wall of him with his brothers, dad, and mom. "Owning my own business made me happy."

"I know."

"The look on the family's face the day we gave them the keys to their new home, that made me happy—like for weeks."

"Yes, it did."

"Somehow this feels like it's both combined."

"Wow."

"Thomas looked Haleya in the eyes. "I want to do this."

"You're sexy when you're passionate about your work." She pulled him close.

"Do you have anything you need fixed in the bedroom?" Thomas playfully pulled her in that direction. "A loose knob on the dresser or a picture frame that needs to be hung?"

*   *   *

In the kitchen, Whitney balled up dough, pounded it flat on the counter, and then rolled it with the rolling pen. Gina waited eagerly, all smiles, with the cookie cutter. Lyndee waved at the computer screen. Kent waved back. He was cleaning his work area and sterilizing the surgical equipment. Though Skype had no sound, they were all together. Gina showed off the cookie she'd cut. Kent gave a thumbs up.

"Everybody's here," Whitney said.

"Wait," Gina ran upstairs. When she came back down, she sat the picture from her room of Jesus on the kitchen counter.

*   *   *

"Is Knox home?" a girl with a glass jar in her hand asked when Haleya opened the door.

"He is—" Haleya turned to Thomas. Thomas raised his eyebrows and stood from the couch where he and Elizabeth were watching TV.

"Knox?" Thomas called for him.

"Yeah, Dad?"

"You've got company."

"Look!" Alicia held up the jar as he came down the stairs. "I caught these lady bugs. I need to know what they eat and if they can live in this jar and for how long. Can you help me?"

"Can Alicia come to my room so we can use my computer?"

Haleya looked at Thomas, and he nodded. Knox and Alicia ran upstairs.

"Ice cream coming up!" Haleya listened to Thomas and Elizabeth as she scooped ice cream into three bowls.

"Lizzy, how was the carnival?" Thomas asked.

"Good."

"It's El," Haleya corrected.

"Yeah, El," Elizabeth repeated.

"What the El?" Thomas quipped. Throwing his arm around her shoulders, they pumped their fists in the air to the rhythm of the Sunday Night Football theme song. Haleya took a mental snapshot as she sampled the ice cream. The ice cream was good. Being home—that was the best ever.

Chapter 43

MARCELLA—1966—age 18

"*Happy Birthday to you,*" *Roxie belted out. She'd selected a special dress for the occasion. It shimmered with all her favorite colors.* "*Sweet eighteen,*" *Roxie sang twirling about the room.*

Marcella shouldn't have been surprised when no one remembered. She thought that maybe a birthday cake would be a good hint. Rummaging through the cupboard, she'd found most of the ingredients. *Who'd miss vanilla extract anyway?*

"What have you done?" her grandmother knocked open the screen door at first whiff.

"Birthday cake—"

"Ain't my birthday!" Grandma hobbled over, tobacco juice dripping from her lip. "You shudda been getting the laundry done," her grandma scolded as she peeled her clothes off and added them to the pile in the floor. "We're in the tobacco patch workin' and you in here playin' around." Grandma dumped the baked cake in the dog's bowl.

"But—" Marcella started.

"Ain't done a thang today, have ya?" Grandma pulled Marcella's clothes from the pile and stumbled out the back door, dumping the clothes in the trash barrel. "Didn't take out the trash today either, did ya?" She lit the clothes. "Now you got less laundry to do."

That night Marcella, wearing a gown she found, tiptoed barefoot out the back door, past the smoldering trashcan, and into the night with Roxie by her side.

MARCELLA—1994—age 46

Marcella carried her tray to a crowded table, which wasn't her preference. She sat down beside the teen girl she'd met once before and handed her the chocolate chip cookie from her tray. The girl looked up—a bruise on her forehead and a healing cut on her cheek.

"Any advice?" the girl asked.

"Don't trust a man you don't know where his money comes from," Marcella paused. "And, if ever at home you heard the words 'I love you,' then go home."

MARCELLA—2010—age 62

"Haleya, call the nurses' desk. Haleya, call the nurses' desk," the words came through the room's overhead speaker.

Marcella's lips moved to the sound of the nurse's name. Was this another LSD induced trip or had she heard correctly?

She'd never heard the name before the day that she named her baby girl Haleya. She'd stared at the line that said "name" on the form that they'd asked her to complete at the hospital. Down the hallway someone yelled, "Hey, Leah, get back here! You aren't supposed to be back there." A 3-year-old ran past her door with a jog as awkward as the lopsided ponytail on her head. Marcella had watched as the little girl giggled and her father snatched her up, kissing her on the neck. The girl's giggle turned into a broken snicker. Marcella didn't know how to spell it, or if she'd even heard it right, but it sounded pretty. She wrote H A L E Y A on the paper.

The nurse asked Marcella to tighten her fist and then loosen it. "Now the other one, please."

Marcella spoke, "Your—name—again?" Marcella's swollen jaw slurred her slow speech.

201

"Haleya," she answered. "My name is Haleya Kage. Glad to see your eyes open. What's your name?"

Marcella repeated, "Haleya." Her voice unrecognizable to her own ears.

"No, that's *my* name. And you are?"

"Happy." Marcella couldn't remember her own name, but she knew she was happy.

PART TWO

Chapter 44

NOVEMBER 2010

"Can I ask you a question?" Jane Doe asked.

"Sure—" Haleya said as she unwrapped the blood pressure cuff from her patient's arm.

"Are you happy?" Her mouth barely moved.

"Am I happy?" Haleya repeated. Had it come a few days earlier, she would have burst into tears.

"Yes, dear." She worked to clear her throat. "Are you happy?"

"I'm very happy."

"Oh, that's wonderful!" The tired, sunken edges of her lips turned upward.

"The other day when I asked you your name, you said that you were 'happy.' Is that your name?"

"What?"

"Happy?" Haleya repeated.

"Yes, I'm happy."

Haleya smiled. She had no idea if the lady understood what she was asking, but in Jane Doe's profile, she typed "aka Happy."

*   *   *

"This it?" Thomas asked, getting out of his truck.

"Yep, and this is Art." Walt slapped his friend on the shoulder. "Don't be thinking that he's anything special just because he saved my life once."

Art's handshake was strong, its strength telling of the man he was once.

203

"Art's got this land. He could do lots of things with it, but he wants to give it to us." Walt stuck a Kit Kat between his lips and put his arm around Art.

"I gotta do this," Art said.

"You gotta do what?" Thomas asked.

"I gotta make good," Art declared. "I ain't been a good man. I can say that if I want." Art glanced at Walt. "I've done good people wrong. I ain't worth—what is it that I'm supposed to say now instead? Crap? I've been trying not to use bad language."

"Poo-poo," Walt suggested.

"What?" Thomas was amused by them.

"Poo-poo. That's the word you're looking for," Walt said.

Art nodded, satisfied. "Since I started reading the Bible Walt gave me, I've changed. He'd told me to pray. I laughed. I wasn't gonna pray. I wasn't gonna pray for nothing. I didn't deserve nothing, and I didn't want nothing from nobody. One night when I was too drunk to argue with him, he got me on my knees, and we prayed. We prayed for stuff I didn't remember and about stuff I didn't want to remember. Then he said 'Bring something great from this man.' He meant me. He said that I saved his life and that he wanted Jesus to save mine—to give me hope and a purpose. Well, I'll be honest, all I wanted was another shot of whiskey. The next day when I woke up nothing felt the same. I called Walt and said 'I don't know where this is coming from, but I feel different, and I got land.'" Art chuckled. "Walt here said 'So?'"

Walt laughed.

"I said, 'I got land, and that's all I know to say,' and I hung up. The next week a politician—in a suit and tie, no one I'd regularly give the time of day—spoke at the VFW. He was advocating for this and that. He handed me pictures of tracts with assisted living homes for veterans. And here we are!"

"Art's donating the land," Walt said. "All we gotta do is put the other pieces together. Still, not a simple project."

"I prayed, Thomas," Art said, his eyes damp. "I prayed for a person who could help make it happen—who could build this community and care about its mission."

"Wow," Thomas said.

"I'm ready," Walt said. "You in, Thomas?"

"In!" Thomas said.

*   *   *

Knox launched his goggles at the bathroom cinder block wall. It wasn't okay that his coach kept calling him out. It wasn't okay that his father made everything sound easy when it wasn't. It wasn't okay that he felt stuck: stuck with a bully for a big sister, stuck with parents who didn't understand, stuck in class with kids making fun of him, and stuck on a swim team where he stank compared to the others. He didn't want to be at swim practice any longer or ever again. He didn't want his sister to pick him up from there or anywhere ever again. Wet hair and no shirt or shoes, he walked out.

*   *   *

"Mom, another one!" Haleya leaned close to the photo tape to the wall.

"I know, I know, but—"

"Let me guess. He was the last one that needed to be sponsored for them to hit their 100th child goal."

"No, but close," Lyndee admitted.

"Don't even tell me." Haleya pointed to his dimples. "He's a cutie. How's Whitney?"

"Confused. Hurt. Sad."

"How long do you think she'll stay?"

Lyndee shrugged. "No way to know. I just hope long enough to figure out that the lies she's being told out there in this crazy world aren't going to make it any better."

"Drugs?"

205

Lyndee nodded. "And everything that promises but doesn't provide."

"I was lucky."

Lyndee reached out to her daughter. "*I* was lucky."

*   *   *

"Can you help with the dishes?" Haleya asked as Elizabeth started up the stairs.

"I've got homework."

Haleya looked at Thomas.

"That's fine. Get your schoolwork done; I'll help." Thomas stacked the dishes. "How was your day?"

"Great. Yours?"

"Awesome."

"Who *are* we?" Haleya giggled. "I love this!"

"Knox, phone," Thomas yelled answering it.

"Who is it?"

"It's a girl."

"It's a *girl*," Elizabeth cooed stepping out of Knox's room.

"You're supposed to be studying!" Thomas scolded, seeing her goofing off.

Haleya swished him away. "Don't get all worked up. Lizzy can help finish up."

"She's pushing her luck." Thomas tossed the dishtowel on the counter.

"Go, before you say something and a good night goes downhill."

"Elizabeth—" Haleya called.

"What?"

"Come downstairs, please."

Elizabeth walked down the stairs and stood in front of her mother.

Haleya handed her the dishrag. "If you aren't studying, then help." She pointed to the table for Elizabeth to wipe it down. "You haven't said much tonight besides taunting your brother. How are you?"

"Okay."

"Do you have homework?"

"It's done."

"I thought you said you had homework."

"I thought I did, but I don't." Elizabeth finished cleaning the table.

"Trash?" Haleya pointed to the trashcan spilling over its edges.

Elizabeth took it outside and headed back upstairs.

"Elizabeth—" Haleya pointed with her sudsy finger to the empty trashcan.

Elizabeth looked confused.

"New trash bag," Haleya said.

Elizabeth put in a new bag without a word and headed upstairs.

Chapter 45

"Dad," Colton said. "Don't do it."

"Don't do what?" Ben loaded his suitcase in the RV.

"Think that looking up Caleb will fix anything."

"This isn't about Caleb."

"I know it's hard. He's never returned our calls. He doesn't want to see us."

"I said, this isn't about him," Ben insisted.

"Then what are you doing?"

"The right thing."

"What on earth does that mean?"

"Exactly what I said."

"But that tells me nothing."

"Well then nothing is all that you need to know," Ben declared.

"Dad, you're so stubborn!"

"Did you say Suburban? No, son, it's an RV."

"Okay, whatever. I'm not playing this game with you."

"Good, love you, son." Ben got in the RV. "I'll be back."

"When?"

"About 10 minutes." Ben backed out of his driveway.

*   *   *

Marcella's memory was coming back. She was young when she'd chosen a better life for Haleya. She wanted more for her baby. She wanted Haleya to live like Roxie.

"Where's the pretty nurse?"

"I'm not sure how to take that," Sandra chuckled.

"She's coming back, right?"

"Yes, it's her day off. I think she's pretty too."

"Are you friends?"

"She's like a second mom to me. How are your ribs? Better?" Sandra asked.

Nodding, she said, "My name's Marcella."

"You remember!"

"I'm starting to remember lots of things."

"That's good. Really good!" Sandra encouraged as she updated Jane Doe's profile.

"I remember my daughter."

"Do you want us to contact her?"

"No, no—" Marcella insisted. "She doesn't remember me. She was a baby when I last saw her. I don't want—"

"Want what?"

"Want her to see me like this. She doesn't know me."

"We need to contact your family, if you'll help us."

"There's no one to contact. But there is something that you can do for me."

"What?"

"Do you pray?"

Sandra nodded.

"Pray for Raquel."

"Is Raquel your daughter?" Sandra asked.

"No, just someone special. But I don't think her name's really Raquel."

"Oh?"

"God will know who you're praying for though, right?" Marcella asked.

Sandra nodded. "I'll pray you get better too, Marcella."

"You can call me 'Ella,' if you want."

"Do you like to be called 'Ella?'"

"It's the sweetest sound."

*   *   *

Ben placed the baby diapers on the grocery conveyor belt along with the other newborn essentials. He didn't know

209

particularly what he was buying, but if it looked useful, he'd tossed it in the cart.

"You got news to share?" Aaron teased walking up to the register.

"Just making sure she has everything she needs," Ben said purposely vague, mainly to play with Aaron since he had the chance.

"Who's that?"

Pulling a *Parenting* magazine from the rack, Ben said, "The baby. It's a girl, they think." Ben's phone rang. "Hello?"

Aaron, stepping in to help bag Ben's groceries, squinted his eyes as if that might help him hear Ben's conversation better.

"Absolutely. Stop crying. Oh, please, stop crying," Ben said. "Well, have him call me. I'll tell him everything he needs to know." Ben pulled out his debit card to pay. "Yes, well—" Ben nodded as he listened.

Aaron, leaning closer, placed the bags of baby supplies in Ben's cart.

"Not really sure," Ben said and nodded bye to Aaron.

Aaron followed Ben outside. "You got yourself an RV," he yelled to Ben.

Ben might miss Ridgewood. He wouldn't miss Aaron.

* * *

The front door's slam startled Lyndee.

"I hate everything!" Elizabeth threw her book bag on the recliner.

"Everything?" Lyndee saw her granddaughter sprint up the stairs. Gina started to follow her, but Lyndee asked her to stir the soup.

Lydee had learned from many unsuccessful efforts how to delicately approach a teenager when everything's horrible. She rummaged in a drawer and found a Laffy Taffy, Sweet

Tart pack, and a stick of gum. She started up the stairs slowly as timing was important. Showing up too soon only resulted in an argument because the frustrated teen sees that as confrontation. Then, the conversation never gets past the 'You got a problem with me?' encounter. Pausing to listen, Lyndee edged up the stairs. No heavy pacing footsteps, long-restrained whimpering tears, or bull-like grunting.

Lyndee had calculated two minutes was enough to avoid a confrontation, yet wasn't long enough to cause the 'You don't even care!' argument. Analyzing the best approach, she chose the "nonchalant arrival." Lyndee flipped on Gina's TV and turned down the volume—a subtle announcement of her presence. Elizabeth, sitting on Gina's bed, wore headphones blaring the beat of Black Eyed Peas' "Boom Boom Pow." Lyndee sat at Gina's desk thinking, *"Gotta get this kid to smile."*

The next 10 seconds would give her the information she needed. There was no "What do you want?" *Good.* There was no complete breakdown. *Good.* She finished her count *... nine and ten.*

Lyndee took a piece of paper and wrote: *Mocha Almond Fudge or Black Cherry Vanilla?* and passed it to Elizabeth.

Elizabeth pointed.

Lyndee tucked the candy beside Elizabeth and headed down the stairs to scoop a bowl of Black Cherry Vanilla.

*   *   *

"Something's wrong with Elizabeth," Haleya said over her shoulder to Thomas as she turned on the bedroom light.

"And that's different, how?"

"I know. It's just that it's both Elizabeth and Knox. Neither seem very happy."

"Are you happy?" Thomas asked.

"That's funny you ask. One of my patients asked me that. And what was even odder, when I said 'yes,' she seemed to care."

"I care. Are you?"

"Yes, I am."

"And you still love me?" Thomas extended his hand, reaching out for her to come closer.

"I do."

"Because I *really* love you."

"Good." She nestled closer.

Are we good again?" Thomas asked.

"We've always been good." Haleya lifted her face and looked into his eyes.

Chapter 46

"Small-cell carcinoma confirmed. Lungs, extensive," Dr. Walden read the report.

The medical team nodded.

"Not a candidate for surgery. Health and recent injury restrict chemo options," he continued.

Haleya was reminded of what she hadn't missed about hospital nursing. Sometimes they couldn't make people better. Happy Lady had a lot more working against her than cuts and bruises.

"No longer a Jane Doe. We have name."

"Marcella Ciscal," Haleya confirmed, though she still preferred to refer to her as Happy Lady.

"But no legal identification, named family, or record of medical history?"

Haleya shook her head.

The doctor looked to the RN assigned as case manager. "Doris, are you working with the social worker for an accommodating respite facility?"

Doris reported on her efforts and concluded, "When I originally contacted them, we were skeptical that she'd make it a week. I don't think they expected to be working this case. I'll get them back on it."

*   *   *

"Art, are you ready for this?" Walt asked.

At the law office, Thomas sat in the lobby sure that he was the most anxious about entering the partnership.

"I'm past all this and ready for the celebration," Art pointed toward the bar across the street. "A Bible-reading man still gets thirsty."

"Save some celebrating for the groundbreaking," Walt said.

"Do you have your speech written?" Thomas asked.

Art squinted his eyes at Thomas. "I don't understand a word you just said."

"We've got 15 minutes on the agenda for you," Walt teased.

"Fifteen minutes of silence," Art scoffed.

"Seriously," Thomas said. "You have nothing to say?"

"Hallelujah only takes a second," Art declared.

*   *   *

"Elizabeth," Mr. Bratcher called her to the front of the class. "We are ready to hear your opening paragraph."

Looking down at the paper in her hands, she muttered, "I am supposed to write *My Story*. This is what was assigned to me in class. So, I am to pick something that has affected or influenced me in my life. Something that made a difference. For some people this is easy. They had a heart transplant or someone left them a load of money when a family member died. But nothing has really affected or influenced me. I did eat something that was spoiled one time. That made for a really bad night. I was fine the next day, though." Elizabeth started walking back to her seat.

"That's it?" Mr. Bratcher asked.

Elizabeth nodded.

"I know you can do better than that."

Elizabeth didn't answer.

"That's all you've got for us?"

"Yep."

Mr. Bratcher made a few notes, and then he looked up at Elizabeth who'd taken her seat. "I'd like you to do that over again. Spend a little more time with it tonight and show it to me tomorrow morning, please."

"I have to?" Elizabeth challenged.

"Yes," Mr. Bratcher answered.

*　　　*　　　*

"I see they ran more tests today," Haleya said taking a new IV needle from its package.

"I know. It's bad. My lungs."

Haleya took a deep breath and nodded.

"Can I ask you a question?" Marcella asked.

Haleya tried to thread the IV needle, concentrating. She was having a tough time. Haleya expected the question was if she could have another nurse.

"Is your husband good to you?"

"What?"

"Is he good to you?"

"You really want to know? Seriously?"

"Yes."

Haleya, focusing on what she was doing, finally answered, "He's really good to me."

"Oh, tell me about him."

Frustrated with the IV, Haleya sat back. "You know my conversations this morning have been about bed sores, vomit, and constipation."

"Go on," she encouraged.

"Okay, so this morning, I fixed oatmeal for breakfast. I remembered that I'm supposed to be watering the neighbor's flowers. I turn off the burner, letting the oatmeal cool, while I step out. I, maybe, am gone four minutes. I rush back through the door and the oatmeal's gone."

"He ate your oatmeal?"

Haleya laughed, realizing that would be more probable. "No! He'd dumped the oatmeal in the garbage disposal and had the pan soaking."

"Dumped out your oatmeal?"

"Yes, he thought he was helping by cleaning it up. He's not your everyday guy. Sometimes it's great. He's never, not even once, left the toilet seat up. He loves to cook, has never forgotten my birthday or our anniversary, and sends me a dozen roses every Valentine's Day. He says his pretty wife isn't going to have a Valentine's Day without roses."

"Oh, he's a good man. Thank God." She closed her eyes and nodded her head. "He sounds so precious."

"Precious, I suppose. Not every day is great, but his heart is good. Most women I know complain their husbands are lazy and never help around the house, but I have to leave a note by my oatmeal so he won't clean it up before I take a bite."

"Oh dear, that is a sweet story."

"Okay, your turn. Tell me about your husband, was there a Mr. Ciscal?"

"Yes, my father. That would be Earl Ciscal. I never met him, but let's just say he was probably the kind who would have eaten the oatmeal. I never had any luck with marriage. Tried it twice, two times regretted it dearly. Tell me more about your wonderful husband."

Now more relaxed, Haleya had luck with the IV—just as she heard a call over the intercom to come to the front desk immediately.

*   *   *

Thomas's phone, on silent, continued to vibrate. He excused himself from the meeting with the real estate agent, banker, and attorney finalizing the partnership. Stepped into the hallway, he answered, "Hello—"

"Are you Elizabeth Kage's father?"

"Yes."

"This is Officer Prats. Your daughter has been in a car accident."

"Oh, God!"

"The ambulance has taken her to the hospital for observation. Injuries don't appear to be serious. She was wearing her seatbelt and the airbags deployed. I have her cell phone and her purse. The car is banged up pretty good. We've called a wrecker."

Thomas sped out of the parking lot.

*　　　*　　　*

Lyndee couldn't understand a word Haleya was saying. "What? You're talking too fast. I can't understand you."

"She's at the hospital."

"Who?"

"Elizabeth!"

"What happened?"

"Car accident, Mom!"

"Is she okay?"

"Yes, but she's bleeding and all bruised up."

"Isn't she supposed to be at school?" Lyndee glanced at the clock.

"Yes!"

"So, how'd she get into a car accident?"

"I don't know how it happened!" Haleya shrieked.

"Are you okay?"

"Yes, Mom. I wasn't in the car. I was here at work!"

"But you don't sound okay."

"I know, because I'm not okay!" Haleya said.

"You just said you were okay."

"Well, I didn't mean it. I mean I'm okay, like I'm not the one bleeding!"

"Why was she not at school? She should be at school," Lyndee repeated.

"She skipped school!" Haleya screamed into phone.

"Oh." Lyndee finally understood.

"I gotta go!"

"Are you sure you're okay?"

"Mom, my daughter skipped school, totaled her car, and showed up by ambulance at the hospital!"

"I'm coming. I'll be there in a few minutes."

"I need you to get Knox at school."

Lyndee pulled her keys from her purse. "I'm leaving now. Where's Thomas?"

"On his way."

* * *

Colton knew there was no changing his father's mind.

"He'll arrive tomorrow afternoon," Ben handed his house keys to Colton. "Make sure he has everything he needs."

"And you'll be gone?" Colton asked.

"Yep, headed out now."

"This is what you want to do?"

Ben nodded, saluted his son farewell, and turned on his heels. Colton watched as his father drove off in his RV—*My Gracie* painted on its side.

Chapter 47

"Is the car really totaled?" Haleya asked, after Thomas brought Elizabeth home, and they'd helped her into bed.

"Yeah."

"Thank God, Liz is okay."

"And the stray dog too, huh?" Thomas scoffed, referring to Elizabeth's supposed reason for the car accident.

"Yeah, tough lesson."

"Expensive lesson," Thomas added.

"She could have rolled the car and really been hurt bad."

"I know. It just seems like—" Thomas paused.

"Things have gotten so complicated with her."

"Exactly."

"So, what do you think?" Haleya asked.

"I think you're beautiful."

"No, I mean what do you think about Liz?

"Who?"

"Your daughter?"

"Yeah, she's pretty like her mom. I'll take care of getting the bills paid. You take care of the punishment."

"Great, take the easy part."

*   *   *

"Were you scared?" Knox asked his sister.

"Yes. Well, I mean it happened so fast."

"Why'd you skip school?"

"Because I hate it. Kara and Sam are the best, but school's stupid. I know you love it, but everyone there's stupid."

"You say 'stupid' a lot."

219

"Yeah, because everything is stupid. Well, not you. You're smart."

"But still your stupid brother?"

"See, you get it! You're so smart that you actually get it."

"I'm sick of school too. Do you think I should skip tomorrow?"

"Oh, don't you dare! You're kidding, right? I'm in so much trouble."

"I'm gonna be too," Knox said.

"What do you mean?" Elizabeth asked.

"I quit the swim team."

"What?"

"I left in the middle of practice. Broke my goggles and tossed my gear in the trash."

Elizabeth winced as she pushed herself up in bed. "You what?"

"Yep. Remember when I told you I caught a ride home? I walked out."

"Oh, wow! What'd Dad say?"

"I haven't told him."

"Oh, don't. Not right now. Bad timing," Elizabeth paused. "Oh wait, on second thought, that might be a good distraction. Take some of the heat off me. Yeah, tell him, please."

*   *   *

Ben didn't have his path planned out, but he ultimately knew where the road would take him. Memories of the mean orphanage caregiver ran through his mind. Maureen, growled, "You got a tender heart, boy." Though he hadn't known what a 'tender heart' was, he knew by the sound of her voice it was bad. Had it not been for Lattie, the kinder caregiver, he wouldn't have learned that a tender heart wasn't something to be ashamed of.

Had he over emphasized the need for his sons to be tough? He worked them hard at the wood mill. He'd had high expectations and not listened to any excuses. He wanted to help them do well in life, but he questioned if he'd done it right. If they had tender hearts, he gave all the credit to Gracie. Had he had a father, maybe he would have known when to back down and when to just let it go—when it was okay for them to be boys instead of men.

Thomas had left first. He headed out without a glance back. He'd done well in college though, met Haleya, and made a family. For Colton, there wasn't the inner battle. Colton loved people like his mama did. He trusted strangers and put others first. Colton gave in at age 19 to his tender heart and went into ministry.

Then there was Caleb. "God," Ben spoke to the sound of the rain against his windshield, "I can't exactly say that I've given up, but I don't believe he'll turn things around or that he'll ever come home. I don't want to let Gracie down, but I think he's gone." Ben pulled into the KOA, parked, and crawled in the bed of the RV.

Chapter 48

"Can I ask a question?"

Haleya took hold of the lever on the side of the bed. It didn't budge. Her 6 a.m. shift came early. She hadn't slept. Elizabeth was on her mind all night.

"Ugh?" She pushed and pulled as she gritted her teeth.

"What was your childhood like?" Marcella asked.

Haleya tried to wiggle and push the latch. "I miss it!"

Marcella motioned for Haleya to stop working with the bed. "Tell me about when you were little."

Haleya conceded. "What do you want to know?"

"First thing that comes to your mind."

"I loved making dandelion bouquets. I had vases of dandelions in every room of the house. I even had dandelion print pajamas."

"I like dandelions."

"I loved the soft round cotton heads too. I'd blow them into the wind. I still do that sometimes," Haleya confessed. "Okay, your turn."

"Oh, you want to know what my childhood was like?"

"It's only fair. I shared."

"Yes, but your memories are good ones, dear."

"Oh, you have to have a good memory."

"There was one."

"Okay."

"I ate a butterscotch once."

*   *   *

"You know she hates school."

"How'd you find that out?" Haleya asked when Lyndee visited for lunch in the hospital cafeteria.

"Black Cherry Vanilla."

"What?"

"Ice cream. It's my secret weapon. They don't even see me coming."

"Thomas thinks she's lying about the dog. He says she was driving recklessly. I want to think he's wrong, but he's usually right." Haleya hung her head. "Why does she hate school?"

"The teachers."

"Which teacher?"

"All of them."

"What?" Haleya shrilled.

"Yeah, but especially Mr. Bratcher."

"Her English teacher? Why?"

"She said he told her she wasn't trying."

Haleya threw up her hands. "That's because she's probably not!"

"Not according to her. She said the assignments are stupid."

"Oh my goodness! That is all I hear! Everything is stupid!"

"She's not stupid."

"Right! No, she isn't stupid. So why does she keep doing stupid stuff?"

"Is that rhetorical or do you want me to try to answer it?"

"If you have the answer, yes!"

"No, I don't have *the* answer, but I might have a little insight. Not saying it's going to be helpful, but with the girls we've had in our home—"

"Mom, she's not homeless, beaten, or pregnant," Haleya spouted. "Well, not yet! Oh my God, I don't know if I can do this! I called to check on her earlier today. Do you know what she asked me? She asked, 'Am I going to get a new car?'"

Lyndee pushed their food trays away and leaned in to hug her daughter. "It's tough."

"I was a good kid, Mom."

"Well, not perfect."

"I know, but I didn't treat you like the enemy. I didn't lie to you and then ask for a new car." Haleya pulled away from Lyndee. "Do you know she snuck a boy in our house the other night? Knox told me. He didn't mean to tell me, but he let it slip. I haven't even told Thomas yet."

"Oh, that's not good. So see, she doesn't tell me everything. Just that she hates her teachers."

"So you were telling me what you've learned over the years." Haleya reached for the brownie on her tray and took a bite.

"I can, but I told you that I don't know if it'll be helpful."

"Go for it. I'll take anything at this point."

"Well, not by choice, but I do know their music, favorite foods, and what tattoo they want to get."

"So what tattoo does my daughter think she's getting when she turns 18 and can legally do it without our approval?" Haleya stuffed the last piece of brownie in her mouth.

"Figuring out their code takes time. Time has as much to do with it as anything. And because they're teens, the codes change, and you have to stay on top of it. What's cool today isn't tomorrow."

"Exactly!" Haleya agreed, chocolate brownie on her teeth.

"The other day when Whitney was with me, I turned the radio from the Christian station to the pop station she likes. Then she proceeds to tell me that station is lame, and rap is all that she listens to now."

"Perfect example," Haleya said. "Somebody blurts out vulgar language and calls it music, and my daughter sings along!"

"Exactly," Lyndee agreed and continued with her point. "Well, I needed to talk to Whitney about where she'd been the night before and why she skipped the visit with her case worker. So, we listened to Kanye West."

"And?"

"And that's it."

"So you did nothing?"

"I left a note on her door that said Gina and I missed her here with us on game night, and if she skips her visit with her case worker, then that is her choice, but not coming home for the night when she said she was going to was not okay. She was supposed to at least let me know that she was okay."

"So, she willfully disobeyed you. But she's 19 and not your legal responsibility. It's different."

"You're right," Lyndee agreed. "I reminded her in the note that we need to know she's safe because we care. I said to think about it and either come talk to me or just write me a note that she understands that if she lives in our home, we need to know she's safe at night."

"So that worked?"

"Still waiting."

"So, no note and no conversation? Mom, you're no help!" Haleya said exasperated. Reaching for the brownie on her mother's plate, she took a bite of it.

"I warned you that I didn't know if it would help."

"And you're okay with her not doing what you asked? Why?"

"Because she's been home each night since, which was the ultimate goal—to have her safe with us at night. She even offered to help with dinner."

"I'm not sure what to do with that scenario. Your point, please. My head hurts."

"I have to assess where I am with Whitney. My guess is that if I push the point with her about the expected conversation or the returned note, then she'll rebel and probably leave again which we all know isn't best for her, but she'd do it. She'd leave just to prove that she was in control. If it makes her feel empowered by doing this her way, that works for me."

"And what makes you think it's going to work this time?"

"Well, I know now Whitney no longer wants the skull head tattoo that she'd been saving up for. It's now a dragon with fire coming out of its mouth."

"What?" Haleya tossed her hands up.

"She's talking to me. Being updated on what's on her mind is as important as the signed paper or forced conversation."

"So you talk tattoos and listen to Kanye West and that fixes everything?"

"Not exactly, but kind of."

Haleya shook her head. "I love you, Mom. But I think you're losing your mind with age. I won't tell Dad."

"Now worrying about him—that's going to make me lose my mind."

*   *   *

When Ben woke, he was alone, but not lonely. His knee didn't hurt or his heart. He'd let his tender heart have its way the night before on a winding road, through the town where he'd been born, and then Thistle Creek where he'd grown up. Ben's cell phone rang.

"I picked up Michael from the airport," Colton said, referring to Esli's baby's daddy.

"And?" Ben asked.

"I wish you could have been there. You're a good man, Dad."

"So, he had no idea?"

"No idea," Colton repeated, sharing the details with his father.

226

Michael had talked about Esli the entire way to Ridgewood. Colton broke the news to him that Esli's parents weren't going to let him stay at their house. Michael began stressing over the fact he didn't have money for a hotel.

"I pulled up to the front gate at your place and told him to hang on a minute because I had to run inside and get something," Colton said.

"Yeah, yeah, I like it. That was good," Ben interrupted, and then insisted, "Go on! Tell me about it!"

"Well, I wish I could say that I got inside and walked Esli out for the big surprise, but she bolted out the door."

"And?"

"And Michael stumbled out of the truck like a kid who forgot how to use his legs. He nearly fell out, and she was in his arms before he got his feet steady."

"Perfect," Ben said.

"It was," Colton assured him.

"You told him to read the note, right?" Ben made sure Colton had remembered. "It should have everything he needs to know about the place, but he's welcomed to call me."

"Yep, he knows."

"You showed Esli all the stuff for the baby?"

"Yep. She cried."

"Perfect," Ben said again. "Make sure they know that they can stay as long as they need. I'm fine. I've got *My Gracie*."

Chapter 49

"Can I ask you a question?"

"Absolutely." Haleya had become accustomed to the routine.

"When your feelings got hurt as a little girl was someone there to make it better?"

"My parents. They'd hug or kiss the hurts away," Haleya said as she straightened the blanket around Marcella's feet. "Tell me about you."

"You mean a time when my feelings were hurt?"

"Yeah, and what made it better?"

"Roxie Applesauce."

"Was that a friend?"

Marcella nodded. "She is."

"Has she been by to see you?" Haleya asked curious, hoping maybe the lady had someone.

"Yes."

"Well, I'd like to meet her."

"She'd love to meet you. I've told her all about you."

"Really? That's nice," Haleya said as she read the recent notes in the computer. "Did Dr. Walden talk to you about your test results?"

"Yes. He said I'm sick."

"We hope to do everything we can. You keep healing, especially those ribs. You've got to get strong."

Marcella nodded.

"Do you have someone who can take care of you? When you get better and leave the hospital."

Marcella nodded again.

"Who's that?" Haleya asked.

"Roxie."

*　　*　　*

"Shhh, just a minute," Lyndee quieted Gina so she could hear the CNN World News reporting from Haiti.

> Though it has been 10 months since the seven-magnitude earthquake, resulting in billions of dollars of damage, took the lives of more than 100,000 people, Refugee International characterized the aid agencies as dysfunctional and inexperienced saying, "The people of Haiti are still living in a state of emergency. Humanitarian response is essentially paralyzed." Gang leaders and landowners are intimidating the displaced, and sexual, domestic, and gang violence in and around camps is rising. Additionally, at least 50 people per day are dying from the cholera epidemic that has broken out. It is estimated that numbers will reach well over 3,000 by year-end. This has the potential to be the most-deadly modern cholera outbreak. *Byron Webb, reporting to you from Haiti.*

"What doth that mean?" Gina asked.

"It means that I want Kent to come home. I wish he'd come home," Lyndee pulled Gina into her arms.

*　　*　　*

Elizabeth made her way through the aisle of the bus. She found an open seat toward the back, slid in, and tossed her bag beside her, hoping to send the message that the seat was taken. She knew that Knox would sit in the front, like a nerd. Of course, he saved his seat for Alicia.

"Hey, Elizabeth," someone called from the back seat.

Elizabeth turned. "Who are you?"

"We're in English IV together," he said. "I've never seen you on the bus before."

"Because I don't ride the bus." Elizabeth turned back around in her seat.

"I thought your English intro was the best," he said.

"It sucked," Elizabeth said.

"Nah. It's like you said, 'This assignment is the dumbest ever' without actually saying those words. That's poetic, if you ask me."

"I didn't ask you." Elizabeth made a face and sank back down in her seat.

"Ah, come on. I know your type."

"What's my type?" Elizabeth bolted up and challenged.

"The get-out-of-my-pretty-little-face type, just like you're doing now."

"How do you know what I'm doing now?" Elizabeth shot back.

"Because you think you're too good for guys like me."

"What does that mean?"

"I *don't* ride the bus," he said in a high-pitched snobby tone.

"Shut up!" Elizabeth regretted wrecking her car more than ever.

*   *   *

Ben made his way along the interstate thinking of when his grandson was little.

"You can't find me!" Knox had rolled under the bed. His toes and nose tickled by dust bunnies. He let out a sneeze, and his cover was blown.

Ben placed his hand on his knee to steady himself as he crouched down and lifted the ruffled bed skirt. "Found you!"

"Pen-Pa, you can't see me. *I'm inbisible.*"

"Oh, I wish I had my fancy vision-ray glasses so I could find Knox. All I can see with these old glasses is that big black spider hanging from his web right where I imagine your big toe might be."

Knox swatted his arms and knocked his head against the wood plank that supported the mattress. "AHHH," he squealed, his tiny frame rolling from under the bed onto Ben's toes and right into his grasp.

"I got you now," Ben growled.

"Noooo!" Knox fought his way out of his grandfather's hold and sped out of the room. "Zooomm," he started his motor, feet taking to the hardwood like the Road Runner on his pajama shirt.

*　　*　　*

"Chemotherapy or anything an option?" Dr. Walden reviewed the patient's file with Dr. Harper.

"She's got to heal from the broken ribs and make sure that ruptured spleen is good," Harper said.

"They've got to find short-term care," Walden concluded.

"They? The family?" Harper asked.

"Social services," Walden clarified. "There's no family. Homeless by what we can determine. I told Haleya I'd check with you. She's been caring for her."

"Injuries like these," Harper paused. "Complications are always an ongoing threat. I'd be surprised if—"

"That's what I was thinking," Walden broken in. "She may never make it out of where she goes next. And then what's next, if she actually does?"

"I've seen this uphill battle before," Harper glanced at the x-rays and CT Scan one last time. "Then," he pointed, "add in the advanced lung cancer; she's in her final days, either way. Tell Haleya she's done a great job taking care of this one. Odds were against her surviving at all."

*　　*　　*

231

"Elizabeth's looking better," Thomas said to Haleya. "Knox's avoiding me though. Do you know what that's about?"

"Could be he quit swim."

"What?"

"It wasn't working for him."

"So what if it wasn't working for him. He has a month left before the season's over—"

"I know. Just talk to him." Haleya thought of her mother's words. "No, don't talk. Maybe listen to him instead."

Chapter 50

"Good morning, Happy Lady. You may be moving out of here soon," Haleya said. "That's good news, right?"

"Can I ask you a question?"

"Of course, you can. I'd expect nothing different."

"What is your favorite book?"

"That's an easy one. I needed an easy one today. It's been a long week. *The Notebook* by Nicholas Sparks. Have you read it?"

"Oh no."

"Have you seen the movie?" Haleya asked.

"No, no. I've never seen the movie."

"We were at the beach when I read the book. I read it in two days. I remember sitting on the balcony listening to the ocean and wiping my nose with my t-shirt. I cried so hard my husband thought something was wrong. That's a book worth reading if you ever get a chance."

"Oh, I'd like that."

"The movie isn't just like the book, but it's really good too. I made my husband go with me to see it. It's not his kind of movie, but he went."

"Because he loves you."

Haleya nodded. "And what's your favorite book?"

"The Bible. I tried to read it, but there were lots of big words. I started reading Proverbs but never got to finish. My Bible and high heeled shoes were burned in a fire.

* * *

Before Ben could say hello, Colton blurted out, "Esli had the baby. She's a beautiful little girl."

"Just like her mama," Ben said. "How's Michael?"

"Working while he's here, all that he can. Odd jobs for extra money. And taking care of Esli and now the baby."

"Perfect."

"Have you found what you're looking for out there?" Colton asked his father.

"Not yet, but getting closer."

"You are coming back, right? Someday?"

"Probably. But I've been homeless before. This is really all I need."

"Dad, seriously. Are you just driving around, all by yourself?"

"Yep."

"Why?" Colton persisted.

"Do you know whose birthday it is this week?" Ben asked.

"No."

"Well, I've got a present to deliver."

"And then you'll be home?" Colton asked.

"Nope."

"Dad!"

*   *   *

Thomas waved from his truck as Knox exited the school doors. Knox sped up.

"Hey, Dad, why are you picking me up?" Knox got in.

"Well, Lizzy doesn't have a car to take you to swim. Thought you might need a ride."

"Oh, ahh, Dad—" Knox started.

"I know. Your mother told me."

"Sorry, Dad," Knox stammered. "I just—"

"Hate it?" Thomas asked.

Knox looked up at his dad. "Yeah, I hate everything about it."

"But you used to like to swim. I remember when you loved it."

"That was before, well, before I learned that I wasn't any good at it."

"Why do you say that?"

"Everybody is better than me. I always come in last. Even when I improve my time, the others keep improving theirs. So, I'm still the loser."

"Okay."

"Okay, what?"

"Okay, fine," Thomas said.

"I can quit?"

"Didn't you already."

"Yeah," Knox said.

"Okay then."

"Where are we going?" Knox asked.

"You'll see."

*   *   *

"Liz!" Haleya was waiting for Elizabeth when she got off the bus. She shoved the credit card bill into Elizabeth's hands and pointed to the circled line.

"Yeah, Mom, it was the dress I wanted."

"That's not the price we talked about. Return it."

"No tags," Elizabeth shrugged.

"What?"

"We tore the tags off them," Elizabeth said.

"We? Them!" Haleya questioned, feeling her heart rate rise.

"Yeah, Kara said she'd pay us back."

"Us?"

"Her dress didn't cost as much. Half the price of mine."

"So I trust you with the credit card and you put 3 times what we agreed on it!"

"Your mistake for giving me the credit card, I guess!" Elizabeth shuffled around her mother and up the stairs.

*   *   *

Thomas pulled up near the construction trailer on the site of the property Art had donated.

"Why are we stopping here?" Knox asked.

"I want you to meet somebody." Thomas motioned for Knox to get out.

"Who?"

"The guy that I'm partnering with on this project." Thomas opened the door to the construction trailer. "Hey, Walt!"

"Is this the young man?" Walt asked, looking up from the desk.

"Yep, this is Knox."

"So, you think he can do the job?" Walt stood and offered Knox his hand.

Knox looked up at his dad and then extended his hand to shake Walt's.

"The man just asked if you want a job," Thomas said.

"I don't know," Knox answered, confused.

Walt offered Knox a Kit Kat.

Knox took it, opened the wrapper, and crunched on a bite.

"I'm looking for someone to work in the afternoons from 3 - 5:30 p.m. It's more than just keeping the trailer cleaned up and toilet paper in the porta potty, but that's part of it. You'll have a list to do each day. Are you interested?"

"I'd get paid?" Knox asked.

"Yep. Willing to pay a little better than minimum wage for someone I can count on."

Knox looked at his dad. "Can I?"

"I think we can make it work. Walt, do you have something for him to get started on?"

"Well, now that you mention it. I got these receipts that need to be logged—" Walt named several more office tasks and pointed around the trailer with his Kit Kat between his fingers.

"He can do it. He's smart." Thomas winked at Knox. "Made a 99 on his last algebra test."

Knox added, "And I skipped 1st and 3rd grade." Looking to his dad, he asked, "Am I going to have to hammer anything?"

Walt jumped in, "You know how to use a hammer? That'd be mighty helpful."

"No, not really. I mean, not yet. But I want to learn. I'll get better."

"So, he's smart *and* willing to learn new things?" Walt scratched his head as if he were thinking. "He's hired!"

Chapter 51

"What?" Elizabeth asked as her mother entered the bedroom. "I have to catch the bus," she grumbled.

"This is what you'll do to pay off the credit card bill." Haleya handed her a note.

Read Proverbs to Happy Lady
Room 301
Every afternoon after school

"Read *Proverbs to Happy Lady,* what kind of book is that?"

"The Bible."

"I don't get it." Elizabeth shook her head.

"Read—the book of Proverbs—in the Bible—to Happy Lady at the hospital," Haleya spoke in fragments.

"Still don't get it!" Elizabeth opened her eyes wide.

"There's a lady at the hospital. She couldn't remember her name at first, but she said she was happy, so I call her Happy Lady."

"I'm glad somebody is."

Haleya ignored Elizabeth's comment. "Each day you'll read several chapters to her."

"Every day!"

"Yes, until you've read her all of Proverbs."

"How will I get there?"

"City transit."

"Mom, seriously?"

"Sure, walk to the pick-up point near the park and jump on the bus."

"You're kidding, right?"

"Not at all. People who don't have cars use public transportation."

*   *   *

Kent, we want you to come home! Lyndee texted Kent a picture of Whitney, Gina and herself posed Sunday after church.

You all look great! I am. Got to finish here. But I want to be home too. He responded.

Are you safe? Lyndee asked.

Yes. Kent answered.

But it's not a safe place to be, right now.

I know, but I'm okay.

You're needed here too.

I know.

Come home soon, please.

Before Christmas. Love you!

*   *   *

"Your mother told me about the credit card charges," Thomas said to Elizabeth that evening.

"And did she tell you my punishment?"

"Yes, it sounds like a really nice thing to do. There are worse punishments than reading to an elderly lady who's bedridden."

"Dad, but I can't get there. I don't have a car."

"You don't have a car. You do have transit bus access."

"D-a-a-a-d? It's not safe on there."

"I'll tell you what's not safe. It's not safe driving over the speed limit on curvy roads—"

"Dad, there was a dog."

239

"Elizabeth, let me explain something clearly. Your mother and I have tried to stay calm through this, but you need to understand that we are very disappointed."

"Dad!"

"No. I'm talking. You're listening. I don't believe a dog ran in front of you. I honestly believe you're lying. I can't prove it, so you can hold on to your dog story if you want. What I do know is that you were skipping school, so you were already being dishonest about being where you were supposed to be. Skipping school for a first time isn't the end of the world. I've done it once before too, but blowing off school isn't okay."

"Dad, it was the first and only time."

"Good. Then it's also your very last time. So, why'd you skip?"

"The teachers are—"

"The teachers are what?"

"Stupid. They give us dumb stuff to do. It's like they just want to keep us busy with projects and deadlines."

Thomas could tell he was getting frustrated. He'd promised Haleya that he wouldn't make it worse by getting angry with Elizabeth again.

"I'll tell you what. Let's just come clean. I know you've had your brother do you schoolwork, and I know you've had a boy in our home in the middle of the night without our permission."

"Knox!"

"So that you know, he didn't want to tell us. And there's really only one person to blame."

"That's yourself," Haleya said as she walked into the room.

"Mom! Knox is a traitor!"

"And you're what?" Haleya shot back.

"Haleya," Thomas said turning to his wife. "I can tell this isn't going anywhere good. Lizzy is upset when she should be the one apologizing and," Thomas paused, "and that makes me upset. Because I see a kid who keeps bullying and blaming others, and I know that she used to not be like this."

"Until she got a car and the freedom that came with it," Haleya interjected.

Thomas nodded. "Well, she no longer has a car. We trusted you, Elizabeth. The car being wrecked is one tough blow for us both, by the way. Cars cost money. But a boy in our house and not getting yourself and Knox to school the next morning on time—"

"Dad, I'm sorry! I messed up!"

Thomas put his hand on Haleya's, indicating for her to stay calm. They were both angry, hurt, and disappointed.

Thomas said sternly, not breaking eye contact with Elizabeth, "Then understand that because of all this, things have changed. The freedom we entrusted you with will have to be earned back." Thomas took Haleya's hand and started out of the room. Then he turned and added, "And the worst thing you can do right now if you want to try to get back on track with us is give your brother any kind of grief for what he told us. Understand?"

Elizabeth coldly nodded.

*   *   *

Knox was surprised when he asked his sister to borrow her cell phone and she let him without any stipulations.

"Can you talk right now?" Knox asked Alicia.

"Sure."

"I saw a praying mantis today," Knox told her.

"What's that?"

"A big, green bug. Well, it's not that big, but it's interesting."

"How big?"

241

"Oh, some are six inches long. This one is probably almost four inches," Knox estimated. "It's unusual to see one at the beginning of November."

"Why?"

"It didn't get cold yet this year. They've predicted that this November may be one of the top 10 warmest recorded in over 100 years."

"How do you know this stuff?"

"Don't you listen to the news?" Knox asked.

"Sure, but I'm not actually paying attention."

"Well, I caught the praying mantis in a jar, but I gotta get it a bigger space to live."

"You're keeping it? Like a pet?"

"Kind of. It's different from a cat or dog, of course. But it's interesting to watch it. I'll be home around 5:30 tomorrow. Do you want to come see it?"

"That sounds fun!"

"Okay, read up on them because we'll have to take care of it to keep it alive."

*   *   *

"Life just seems so strange these days," Haleya said.

Thomas, sitting in his recliner, picked up the remote to turn down the TV volume. "Why do you say that?"

"Well, for example, there's this lady at the hospital. I call her 'Happy Lady' because when I asked her what her name was, she told me she was happy. Remember me mentioning her?"

"Is this the lady you asked Elizabeth to read Proverbs to?"

"That's her."

"It'll be interesting to see if Lizzy follows through. Really, I don't know what to expect."

"I know." Haleya sat down next to him in his recliner, edged half on the chair arm. "So, this lady has a question for me every day. It started with her wanting to know if I was happy, remember?"

"Uh-huh."

"But it doesn't stop there. She wants to know if *you* love me, what my favorite book is, if I enjoyed my childhood. It's a different question every day."

"That's not so strange."

"You don't think that's strange? Her questions aren't ones like if she's going to be okay, what's the weather like outside, or when she's going to get to leave."

With a quirky grin, Thomas picked up the open Kit Kat on the table beside him, broke off a bar, and tucked it between his fingers. "I don't think that's strange at all." He placed it to his lips and gave it a mock puff.

"Are you smoking a Kit Kat?" Haleya shook her head in disbelief.

"Actually, I'm trying to quit."

Chapter 52

"Can I ask you a question?" Marcella asked.

"Always."

When she began to speak, she broke into a round of coughs.

"Does that hurt?" Haleya asked and typed.

Marcella nodded. "What was the best day of your life?"

"That's a tough one. My best day ever? I really don't know. Can we go back to basic questions like favorite foods?"

Marcella laughed. "Answer it like this then, which one? Too few special days to remember one or is it too many special days to choose one?

"Okay, I can do that. B. Too many good ones."

"Good."

"Okay, your turn. Your best day ever?" Haleya asked.

"That's easy. What day does that computer say was my first day here?"

"You're kidding?" Haleya asked.

"Definitely the best day of my life."

"The day you nearly died?"

She'd been barely conscious and yet that was her best day in all her years. "Yes."

*   *   *

Ben felt older than he actually was, moving slower than he used to and thankful to wake up with only a few aches. As he pulled onto the highway, a conversation he'd had with Knox when Gracie was sick came to mind.

"Pen-Pa, are you sad?"

"Just thinking."

"Thinking about what?"

"Your grandmother."

"Why?"

"She always made apple cider when any of us were sick."

"To make you better?" Knox asked.

"She thought so."

"Does it? I'll give some to Waffle when he throws up so he'll feel better."

"Waffle's an old cat. I bet if you'd brush him every day, he'd get sick less."

"And fix him some apple cider?" Knox asked.

"Nope."

"Why?"

"Apple cider smells good, tastes good, warms your throat and belly, but it's not gonna fix old."

"What fixes old?"

"Sometimes old can't be fixed," Ben remembered saying.

*　　　*　　　*

"Beautiful flowers!" Haleya got out of her car.

"Got the last ones they had." Lyndee arranged the mums on her front porch. "Can I ask you a question?"

"Oh, my, you sound like a patient of mine."

"Which color? Yellow or Orange?" Lyndee asked.

Haleya pointed to the yellow one. "Every day she asks me a question."

"Sounds fun," Lyndee listened as she repotted the yellow mum.

"First she wanted to know if I was happy. Then she wanted to know if my husband was good to me. Then she wanted to know if I enjoyed my childhood—"

"Did you?" Lyndee interrupted.

"Did I what?"

"Enjoy your childhood."

"You know what came to mind when she asked me that? Dandelions."

"You wore out those dandelion pajamas." Lyndee pinched off a yellow bloom and handed it to Haleya. "Looks like a dandelion, huh?"

"Yep." Haleya twirled it between her fingers. "When you were little, what was one of your favorite things?"

"My baby doll," Lyndee said. "I always wanted to be a mama."

*   *   *

"So, they really will starve rather than eat a dead fly or cricket?" Alicia asked. She was waiting at Knox's house when he got there.

"Yep, it has to be a live one."

"I don't want to watch you feed it."

"Why?"

"I thought we'd feed it sunflower seeds or something like that."

"Nope, we'll have to hunt and capture crickets and other soft bodied insects."

"Maybe I'd rather have the cricket as a pet."

"Finding a bug and feeding it to another bug, that's cool. Guys can handle that kind of thing," Knox bragged.

"Do you know if it's a boy or a girl?" Alicia asked.

"It's a girl."

"How can you tell?"

"It's got a big abdomen. See the bumps on it, underneath its belly. Girls have six segments and that last one is the biggest one. That means it's a girl." Knox pointed so she would see. "Boys have eight."

"I read up on them last night like you said to."

"Good." Knox situated his old oblong fish tank he'd found to be the praying mantis's new home.

"Do you know about what can happen?" Alicia asked.

Knox stopped and looked at Alicia. "What?"

"They—die—sometimes." She stretched out the sentence.

"Yeah, they live about a year usually. I don't know how old this one is. But, yeah, it won't live forever."

"I mean, sometimes the boys are killed, you know—" Alicia lifted her chin in hopes he'd get her hint.

Knox thought for a second. "Oh, you mean, like when—"

"Yeah, by the girl." Alicia covered her face, peeking out between her fingers.

"Oh, yeah. That."

"It seems so wrong."

"Yeah, but they're bugs."

"I'd rather have a caterpillar or something."

"Come on!" Knox handed Alicia a stick to place in the tank along with the praying mantis. "Well, look at it this way. With her in here, male praying mantises are safer tonight."

"What if she's already, you know?"

"Killed her suiter as they say on the nature shows." Knox lifted his eyebrows.

"Well, that, but I meant, pregnant. They have tons of babies, right?"

"I hadn't thought of that. Now that would be way cool!"

*　　*　　*

"Where are you going?" Thomas asked Elizabeth after dinner when she bopped down the stairs with her bookbag.

"Kara's to study."

"Did you go after school to read at the hospital?" Haleya asked.

"No." Elizabeth opened the refrigerator for a water bottle.

"Did you ask if you could go out tonight?" Thomas countered.

"It's studying," Elizabeth scoffed. "Kara's picking me up."

"Why didn't you go to read to—" Haleya asked, but Elizabeth interrupted.

247

"The bus schedule is all messed up."

"You mean, it's not convenient. You have to be there when it runs. It doesn't cater to your schedule."

"Elizabeth!" Thomas pointed upstairs. "You didn't ask permission to go to Kara's tonight. See if you can catch her on the phone before she gets here."

"Really, Dad?" Elizabeth shifted her eyes to her mother. "Mom?"

Haleya shook her head. Thomas pointed to her room again.

Elizabeth mumbled on the way upstairs, "I liked it better when you two weren't here as much."

Chapter 53

Tucking her nose in the bend of her elbow, Elizabeth vowed never to be a nurse. The room smelled like a concoction of bleach cleaner, joint pain ointment, and bad breath. "Happy Lady" didn't look happy to Elizabeth. The frail woman nearly vanished into the white sheets.

Elizabeth, sitting in the chair, used her weight to scoot it away from the bed.

"Hey," Elizabeth whispered. "Can you hear me?"

Nothing.

"Whatever." She pulled up the Bible app on her iPhone.

The title in large font on her screen read: *Wisdom for young people. The first few chapters are Solomon's fatherly advice to young people.*

Elizabeth rolled her eyes. "And I guess *you* need to hear this?"

No movement.

"Like you can even hear me," Elizabeth mumbled and began reading, equally muffled.

No movement.

"*... but whoever listens to me will live in safety and be at ease, without fear of harm,*" Elizabeth ended the first chapter. "That's it. I'm done." She left.

*   *   *

When Thomas answered the phone, Ben hesitated and then spoke. "Hi there, son."

"Hey, Dad. You okay?"

"I need to ask you something."

"Sure," Thomas said.

249

"Do you remember when you said that I should visit sometime?"

"Yeah."

"Remember that boat I used to have?"

"You don't still have it?"

"Nope, traded it."

"For what?" Thomas asked.

"An RV."

"Whatcha gonna do with that?"

"Come see you."

"Alright. When are you thinking?"

"Your boxwoods need a trim, you know."

"Dad! Are you here?"

*   *   *

"My daughter read to you this afternoon." Haleya stepped into Room 301.

"Oh, that was your daughter? Thank you."

"If it goes well, then she'll be doing that every day until she finishes reading Proverbs to you. Do you remember telling me about what happened to your Bible?"

"Yes. Can I ask you a question?"

"Of course, as always," Haleya chuckled.

"Do you enjoy being a mother?"

"Honest answer—yes and no."

"Why do you say that?"

Haleya flipped the identification badge over on the lanyard around her neck. Tucked behind the clear plastic was a family photo. "Well, I thought it would be easier than it is to tell you the truth. This is Knox. He's 13 today. Elizabeth is 17 and counting the days until she turns 18. Of course, you met her."

"May I hold it?"

Haleya unclipped it.

"He's precious. Has your beautiful smile."

"Thanks, he looks a lot like his daddy too," Haleya said and leaned in to look at Knox's picture along with Marcella—their heads side by side.

*   *   *

The 15-minute walk from the city bus transit pick up/drop off point to Elizabeth's house was exactly the length of Lady Gaga's "Poker Face," Beyonce's "Single Lady," Katy Perry's "Firework," and her new favorite, "Forever" with Drake, Lil Wayne, Eminem and Kayne West—the explicit version.

As Elizabeth's house came into view, she slowed. An RV was parked in her driveway. She took off running when she saw her grandfather step out.

"Oh, this is so cool!" Elizabeth took a tour. "You live in this?"

"For now."

"Oh, wow! I wish I had a place like this. Look, you have a bed, a kitchen sink, and a bathroom. It's got everything a person needs."

"Yep."

"Do you want to trade rooms? I'm serious. You take my bedroom. I'll move in here."

"You got a TV?" Ben played along.

"Yep, one even bigger than that one." Elizabeth pointed to his.

"What about a fridge?"

Elizabeth opened the fridge. "A refrigerator doesn't mean much if it's empty."

"Good point. That reminds me, I'm hungry. Let's go for a ride." Ben pointed to the passenger's seat and got behind the steering wheel.

*   *   *

"Happy Birthday!" Walt leaned through the office trailer doorway. "You're doing great."

"Thank you." Knox checked off his to-do list.

"You ready to go?" Thomas asked.

"Yep." Knox neatened up the papers by the computer.

"You know how you tell me sometimes that you miss seeing Grandpa Ben."

"Yep, can we go there sometime? He goes snake hunting with me."

"And why would someone hunt for snakes?"

"It's fun to watch them. Most snakes aren't dangerous, Dad."

"Well, I guess you can go snake hunting if you want to."

"What? Are we going there?"

"He's here," Thomas said.

"Really?"

"Yes, at our house. Just promise me if you two find a snake that you don't bring it home."

"But I want to show it to Elizabeth." Knox, pretending he held a snake, jumped toward his father.

"Ohhh, now she might deserve that, but please don't."

"Dad, please—"

"No, son."

"Well, actually snakes aren't often found this time of year. They are in brumation. How about a rat?"

"What? Brumation? No rats either, Knox."

"What if Pen-Pa tells me that I can?"

"Then both you and Pen-Pa are in trouble."

"Just—how much—trouble?" Knox quizzed.

*   *   *

Haleya answered her phone as she got in her car to head home.

"Hey, mom! "What do you want for dinner?" Elizabeth asked.

"Is this my daughter? It sounds like her but that doesn't sound like something she'd ask me."

"Me and Grandpa Ben are going to pick up dinner."

"I'm confused. Where are you?"

"With Grandpa Ben. There's Fazoli's or Wendy's or—"

"Wait. So, Grandpa Ben is here?"

"Yep."

Looking at her phone, Haleya saw a notification of a voicemail from Thomas.

*　　*　　*

"I'll light the candles," Haleya said.

"No, no," Knox said. "I want to open my present first."

Haleya had a piece of chocolate cake on her mind and had forgotten what it was like to be 13.

Knox tore the wrapping paper. "YES!" he shouted.

"MOM!" Elizabeth squalled. "It's an iPhone 4!"

Haleya nodded.

"That's nicer than mine!"

"When we got you yours, we bought you the newest one," Haleya said, already prepared for Elizabeth's reaction.

Knox thanked his mom and dad, then smirked at his sister.

"Now can we eat cake?" Haleya asked.

Ben leaned over in his chair and picked up a box near his feet. "I got something for him too," he said.

Knox's eyes lit up. "This is the best birthday ever!"

"It's not as great as one of those gadgets," Ben said. "Just something that I made."

Knox took no less time ripping the paper. He pulled out the hand-carved letter K. "I like it!" Leaning over to hug his grandfather, he said, "Mom, hurry up. Light the candles. I want to set up my new iPhone and put in Pen-Pa's number and Alicia's."

"And ours," Thomas added.

"Yeah, yeah. Even Lizzy's, I guess," Knox grumbled.

"It's El," Elizabeth reminded.

*　　*　　*

253

"I read to that old lady today, Dad."

"Good."

"She was asleep. I don't think she even heard."

"What was it about?" Thomas asked.

"I can't remember."

"Well then, I guess you'll have to start over the next time you're there."

"What?"

"I'm kidding."

"Good. I mean, I really can't make her listen," Elizabeth insisted.

"Right, as long as you do your part," Thomas stated.

"Right," Elizabeth agreed. "So after I finish reading to her, then we'll talk about a car?"

"Your mother asked you to read to the lady at the hospital as a consequence for the credit card bill. That's what I understood. When you get done reading Proverbs, however long that takes you, then the fact that we trusted you with the credit card to an agreed amount and you did otherwise is in the past. The idea is that you learn a lesson from this."

"So what do I have to do to get another car?"

"Let's see," Thomas thought for second. "You could get a job, which probably would pay minimum wage, say about 20 hours a week, use city bus transit to get to and from work after school and weekends for about," Thomas calculated in his head, "the next 3 years, and then you'd have enough saved up to buy a car like the one you had."

"Dad!"

"But also, there is gas and car insurance. You're a senior this year, right?"

"Yes!"

"So actually, you can work full-time at a fast-food joint after you graduate and," Thomas scratched his head, "in two years, you'll have the money saved up to buy a car and pay insurance and gas."

"What about college?"

"I don't make the money I used to and your mother is working too many hours already. Do you have a scholarship?"

"Dad, seriously?"

"Oh, I'm being serious."

Chapter 54

Thomas peeked into room 301, hoping he'd caught up with Haleya.

"Hey, handsome—"

The voice wasn't Haleya's.

"Are you looking for Haleya?"

"Yes, have you seen her?" Thomas stepped into the room.

"Thank God, yes, I've seen her!" The fragile woman reached out toward him.

"Are you Haleya's Happy Lady?"

"Yes, but you can call me Roxie."

"Okay, Roxie. Have you seen Haleya?"

"Oh, I have, and she's beautiful. Sit down, please."

"She's my beautiful wife."

"I know, dear one. Let me look at you. Oh yes, Knox does look like you. I can see it."

"You've met Knox?" Thomas sat on the edge of a nearby seat.

"No, but Haleya lets me look at his picture while she tugs on these tubes."

Thomas noticed her struggling to get her other hand free from under the covers. "Here." Thomas scooted closer and helped.

"Strong hands." She took hold of his hand.

"Thanks." Her grasp was weak, and he was careful.

"You love her?"

"Yes. Do you have a list of questions for me too?" Thomas asked.

"Only one, if you don't mind?"

"Okay."

"Does Haleya ever mention her birth mother?"

"Her birth mother? Not really. Why?"

"She has good parents?"

"Some of the best," Thomas said.

"Thank God. She's been so good to me. Tell them thank you."

*   *   *

"You just missed him."

"Who?" Haleya asked.

Marcella smiled. "Your husband."

"Oh, he found me," Haleya assured her.

"Tell me about it."

"About what?"

"How he found you."

"You mean by the nurses' station?" Haleya pointed outside the door.

"No. I mean how you met."

"Well, that's a long story and a big misunderstanding. I thought he was someone else and started yelling at him, or so he tells the story."

"I bet that's a good story. Did he take you on a date?"

"On our first official date we went to a restaurant downtown. We go there each year for our anniversary. I love their yeast rolls. Oh, and their pecan pie—yum!"

"You talk about food with the same passion you do your husband."

"That just goes to show you how much I love my husband." Haleya pinched her belly.

"I would have given anything to have been your size when I was your age."

"It's just that I used to not have this," Haleya patted her stomach.

"Sweetie, at your age, I barely broke a hundred. You, my dear, are beautiful. Your skin, your hair, and your stomach."

"Were you bulimic?"

"What?"

"Or did you just not eat?"

"I fed my body all the wrong things."

"Did you have a favorite food? Something heathy?"

"Applesauce."

*   *   *

Knox read a text from Alicia as he worked his way through the crowd and out the school doors. *Told my bro about the praying mantis. He thinks it's cool. Not the head bite thing. Can you bring it over?*

Knox texted *Sure!* and looked up. "Pen-Pa!" Knox took off running when he saw his grandfather's RV lined up behind the buses. Knox jumped in the front seat.

"I didn't know if you'd be embarrassed of this big contraption."

"Are you kidding! Riding with Liz is embarrassing. This is cool!" Knox waved at his friends. "Where's Dad? Did he ask you to pick me up?"

"Yep. He's busy with lions, tigers and bears, oh, my."

"What?"

"Bankers, lawyers, and real estate agents," Ben clarified.

"I can show you my office, I mean, the construction trailer where I work."

"Great."

"Oh, uh—" he hesitated. "When I get home, I have plans."

"Plans?"

"It's just Alicia."

*   *   *

Sandra flipped through the bridal magazine showing Haleya wedding dresses.

258

"You'd look great in that," Haleya said. "So elegant."

"Or what about this one?" Sandra flipped the page.

"That's gorgeous!"

"See! I have no idea how I'm going to decide, and I can't afford these so why am I even looking?" Sandra shut the magazine.

"There's the perfect dress for you. You're going to find it, and you're going to look beautiful!" Haleya gathered her things from the nurses' station.

Doris, Marcella's case worker, approached. "Haleya, sorry we didn't get to finish our conversation earlier. It's been that kind of day."

Sandra chimed in, "It's been that kind of week."

"Tomorrow, I need to meet with you about the patient in room 301," Doris said. "I think social services has finally had some luck with a respite facility." She turned, pulled into another conversation.

Sandra frowned, "I knew that was coming."

"Me, too," Haleya said. "Sometimes luck needs a hand. I made a few calls."

*   *   *

"Yah, yah, hey listen, I gotta go," Elizabeth said. "I'm here to read to this near-death lady so my parents will trust me again." Sitting in the chair, she used the tips of her toes to push the chair away from the bed. "The things I do to make them happy," she mumbled, selecting her Bible app. "I'm here. You're still here. Let's do this! So, where were we?" She looked up. "Like you'd know!"

Clicking on Proverbs 12, she read, *"... The LORD detests lying lips, but he delights in people who are trustworthy.* Oh, dude, that reminds me of a great song." Elizabeth started humming. "Hold on and I'll play it for you." With a tap the song played, *"Just gonna stand there and watch me burn, but that's alright, because I like the way it hurts."* Elizabeth sang

259

along, *"Just gonna stand there and hear me cry, but that's alright, because I love the way you lie; I love the way you lie."*

She pushed pause. "See, I told you it was awesome! Eminem goes into a rap next. I'd sing that part, but I'd have to bleep out the bad words. They make clean version for old people like you. Oh, no offense, of course." Elizabeth flipped back to the Bible app.

* * *

Knox opened the RV door before his grandfather came to a complete stop. Alicia waited in a golf cart. "I'll be right back," he called to her and ran inside. Less than a minute later he carried out the fish tank.

"Need some help?" Ben called.

"Nope," Knox yelled over his shoulder and scooted next to Alicia. "If your brother wants, after we feed it, he can keep it overnight. I can pick it up tomorrow or whenever."

"Great!" Alicia backed out of the driveway.

"Do I just talk to your brother normal-like?"

"English is fine," she teased.

"Sorry, I just don't want to do, you know, anything wrong."

"Just be you."

"I do know some French."

"Along with what insect is most prevalent in France."

"Woo, 'prevalent.' Big word," Knox teased. "Well, I didn't bring crickets to feed Carolina, so lucky you. These bugs aren't so lucky." Knox pointed to the plastic container where several flies scurried around trying to get out.

"You named it?"

"Yeah. Well, Carolina is the species type."

"Carolina Kage? That has a nice ring to it."

"I wouldn't go that far."

"Bugs don't get last names?"

"There's a long process to officially adopt a praying mantis."

"Whatever. Shut up." She pushed him on the shoulder and then quickly took hold of Carolina's tank, even though Knox had a firm hold on it.

*   *   *

"When I was at the hospital, I met your Happy Lady."

"You met her?"

"She asked me to call her Roxie."

"Really?" Haleya chuckled. "Did she ask you a bunch of questions?"

"A couple." He pulled last night's leftovers from the fridge.

"It's odd what she wants to know. I'm not even sure *you* care what my favorite food is or about my most memorable birthday."

"She asked if you talk about your birth mother."

"What?" Haleya turned to Thomas.

"Yeah."

"Thomas, I never mentioned I was adopted. She asked me about my parents, but I don't remember sharing that with her."

"Maybe Lizzy told her?"

"That makes sense, but at the same time, it would be strange for Liz to talk about anything but herself."

Thomas chucked, "Good point."

*   *   *

"We have a proposition," Thomas said to Elizabeth after dinner.

"Okay?"

"First, grades and school have to be a priority."

"What does that mean?"

261

"It means you show up to class. You do the work *yourself*. I also need a list of scholarships you applied for and other financial aid options from your school counselor."

"Then what?"

"You want—or I should say, you *think* you need—a car, right?"

"Yes."

"One more thing," Thomas said, pulling out the dog-eared, spiral-bound notepad. "Type this, and we'll go looking at cars. Don't misunderstand me, just another one to get you around, not something super nice."

"So an old clunker. What's this?" She took the notepad Thomas offered.

"This is what your grandmother Gracie wrote. It's her story. I want to get it printed and give it to your grandfather."

"Type all of this?"

"Yes."

"Every word?"

"Yes, and spell check it and even proofread it, now that you asked so many questions."

Elizabeth flipped through the pages. "Or?"

"Or what?"

"What are my other options? I mean, this is a lot to type."

Thomas, perturbed, responded sternly, "You do realize school and your future is something you should be concerned about with no incentive."

"Okay."

"We aren't helping you with another car without seeing more responsibility," he continued.

"I know."

"So, yes or no?" Thomas asked.

"What do you mean?"

"Yes, to schoolwork, grades, getting your college finance plan in order, and typing this before Christmas."

Elizabeth flipped through the wire bound notepad. "Okay."

"*Okay, thank you—that's a good deal.* Or *okay—if I have to?*"

Elizabeth looked up. "It's a good deal," she said, though not enthusiastically.

Chapter 55

"Can I ask you a question?"

"What today?"

"Have you ever walked on a beach?"

"I have. Remember, I read my favorite book there, and I got married on the beach."

"You did! Tell me about your dress."

"I wore a simple, tea-length white dress with lace capped sleeves."

"Can I look at your ring?"

Haleya extended her left hand. "He did good."

"He surely did."

"What about you? Have you ever walked on the beach and seen the ocean?" Haleya asked.

"No, but Roxie has."

*   *   *

Scooting away the chair from the hospital bed, Elizabeth ranted. "I don't have time for your chit-chat today. You see, my brother isn't doing my homework for me anymore, and it's putting me in a bind because tonight is Senior Sneak Out. I have places to be like the top of the water tower instead of behind a stupid computer. He's such a lamea—, oh excuse me, lame butt. Life stinks sometimes! Nothing's ever fair! Okay, short and sweet. Wherever my finger falls. Here we go. *Who plots evil with deceit in his heart, he always stirs up dissension? Therefore, disaster will overtake him in an instant; he will suddenly be destroyed, without remedy.*"

"Do you believe that?" Marcella asked.

"You're alive?" Elizabeth jerked, startled by her voice.

264

The lady snickered and coughed.

"You okay? Can you breathe?"

"Yes, I'm breathing. Do you believe that?"

"Believe what?

"Evil people get what they deserve."

"Seems fair," Elizabeth said.

"I've seen evil win before."

"Depends on what you think evil is. Evil to one person might not be considered evil to another person," Elizabeth declared.

"Sounds like you know a lot. Keep reading; I need to know."

"Wait, you've been hearing me read?"

Marcella nodded.

"Every time?" Elizabeth asked.

"You have a pretty singing voice too. Do you know something from Guess Who?"

"You want me to guess?"

"Before your time, I bet. "American Woman" or "These Eyes?" Heard those before?"

"I'm just supposed to read." Elizabeth continued where she'd left off. "*There are six things that the Lord hates—*" She stopped mid-sentence. "You know I have a lot to do, can we finish this next time?"

"Your homework that your brother didn't do and sneaking out?"

"Exactly!"

"Will you read the six really quick?"

"*Haughty eyes*, whatever that means." She continued, "*A lying tongue. Hands that shed innocent blood. A heart that devises wicked schemes. Feet that are quick to rush into evil. A false witness who pours out lies. And a person who stirs up conflict in the community.* Okay, done!" Elizabeth stood and dashed from the room without a goodbye.

265

"Knox likes his job," Ben said as he worked with Thomas on the shed.

"You know, I don't always understand that kid. I'm trying to do better."

"I see that."

"I mean, he's a good kid, but he's not athletic, and he doesn't pick up on things quickly."

"Your kind of things, you mean."

"There's so much more he needs to know in life besides being all brainy and bug loving."

"He's super smart."

"You know who he reminds me of?" Thomas glanced at his dad.

Ben nodded. "And he was a good kid too."

"What happened, Dad?" Thomas stopped staining the door. "Why'd Caleb choose that life when he had so much potential?"

"That's what I'd like to ask him."

They worked, quiet for a minute.

"Elizabeth thanked me for sharing Gracie's story with her," Ben broke the silence.

"Oh really? When *I* gave it to her, she didn't act very thankful."

"I enjoy talking with her," Ben said, spraying the window with glass cleaner.

"She's got a lot to learn about life."

"We all still do," Ben said, seeing his faint reflection in the window.

* * *

Knox and Alicia searched in the grass for bugs to feed Carolina while Austin looked up bug facts on his iPad.

"Yuck! I hate them." Alicia had an accidental encounter with a stink bug. "Why are there stink bugs anyway? What good are they?"

"I can tell you," Austin said pecking on his iPad. "I have it right here. *The stink bug quite frankly doesn't have a lot of redeeming qualities. It is a pest that causes a lot of problems to fruit and vegetable crops.*" He ran his pointer finger along each sentence. "*The stink bug's smell,*" he tried to sound out the next word. "Knox, read this."

Knox walked on his knees checking the grass along the sidewalk for bugs. Taking the iPad, he scanned for where Austin left off. "*The stink bug's smell, emitted when it feels threatened, comes through its abdomen. Unfortunately, any touch or any handling will cause it to release the odor.*"

"No joke!" Alicia rolled her eyes.

"*You shouldn't squash stink bugs when you kill them because doing so releases their pheromones which smell bad and, more importantly, attract other stink bugs,*" Knox giggled.

Austin smirked and covered his mouth, "This is great!"

"*The smell from the stink bug has been characterized as a pungent odor, and some have described the stink as a scent that smells like cilantro.*"

"Hey, I like cilantro!" Alicia crossed her arms. "Not the same!"

"*Or skunk,*" Knox continued.

"Yeah, a skunk!" Alicia agreed.

Knox pointed to Austin and then the iPad. "You gotta see this!" He passed the iPad to Austin.

"What?" Alicia asked.

"It says—" Austin, laughing too hard to read, handed it back to Knox.

"It says that hundreds of stink bugs may hibernate in your home through the winter."

"Let me see that!" Alicia grabbed the iPad. "*The bugs are not able to tolerate the cold weather of winter. In October, hordes of stink bugs make their way inside homes through windows, doors, chimneys, and cracks.*" Alicia covered her mouth. "*They send out a scent which is undetectable to homeowners as an invitation for other stink bugs to join them.* What!" Alicia squealed. "I'm going inside." She tossed the iPad on Austin's lap.

"Did you hear that, Alicia? Hundreds of stink bugs," Austin repeated. "Knox, can I keep one as a pet?"

"Sure. Some are even carnivorous, but don't let Alicia know that." Knox raised his voice as Alicia stomped inside.

"Fabulous, more bug-eating bugs!" Alicia let the door slam behind her.

"Great night!" Austin raised his hand for a high-five.

*   *   *

"Pen-Pa? Are you out here?" Knox called out the back door.

"You found me." His grandfather sat by the firepit.

"Are you out here by yourself?" Knox asked.

"Your dad was here a bit ago."

"I'll sit with you. Whatcha doing?"

"Whittling something."

"What?" Knox asked.

"Can't tell ya."

"Okay, then I got something I can't tell you."

"That's fair."

"So, we'll just sit here and say nothing," Knox declared.

"Sounds pleasant enough. That's what I was doing before you came along."

"Pen-Pa, but I have a question."

"I don't have that many answers. Maybe you should ask your dad."

"Dad doesn't really listen."

"Parents aren't always the best listeners."

"Alicia's a good listener."

"She is?"

"Yeah, and we like a lot of the same things."

"Well, that's good."

"So, my question—"

"I'm listening."

"Why do kids get sick? The really bad kind of sick that can't be fixed. I mean, I know Grandma Gracie got sick, but she was a grandma. Even if everybody kept saying she was too young, still she was a grandma."

"Thankfully, she was a grandma." Ben paused. "You know why? Because you and Elizabeth made her a grandma."

"Not everybody gets to be a grandma or a grown up, huh?"

"No."

"I guess I've always known that but never really thought a lot about it."

"What's got you thinking?"

"Alicia's brother, Austin, is sick."

"What kind of sick?"

"It's called Duchenne. It's where his muscles gradually stop working. He uses a wheelchair now. Alicia said that he got by without using it last year, but this year he got worse. He's just a kid. I don't understand."

"I don't understand either."

"He's a lot like me. I met him. He's fun!"

"I bet."

"But he can't crawl in the grass and bug hunt with us."

"Was he sad?"

"Actually, he had the best time ever. Alicia found a stink bug. She was so mad, and he thought it was hilarious."

"Good times?"

"Yep. I always thought I wanted to be a vet." He shuffled a small pebble with his toe.

"Why not a bug scientist?"

"You mean an entomologist? Yeah, that, too. But then I started working with Dad, and I thought maybe I'd be an architect."

"I can see that."

"But I don't think so."

"Why not?"

"Have you ever heard of the Shriners Hospital here in Lexington?"

"I have."

"Our church youth group visited once. I think I'd like to work there."

*　　*　　*

Elizabeth, putting on her favorite jeans, sweatshirt, and ball cap, tiptoed down the stairs. When she reached for the door, a device hung from it—a motion sensor. Elizabeth clinched her fists and headed to the back door. Along with an identical device was a note. *The windows have alarms too. Go back to bed.*

Pacing, Elizabeth sent Sam a text. Too impatient to wait for his reply, she dialed. When he answered she whispered, "I'm locked in!"

"How's that?"

She could hear giggling in the background. She was missing all the fun. "My dad put motion sensors on the doors. Someone must have tipped him off."

"Oh, that's a bummer," Sam said.

He didn't hear what she said next. "Sam!"

"Hey, listen. I gotta go." He hung up.

Elizabeth climbed the stairs with less effort to be quiet, shut her door, and locked it.

Chapter 56

"They found you a cozy new place to stay," Haleya told Marcella. "They're getting the details worked out."

"Can I ask you a question?"

"Always."

"Have you been to Disney World?"

"I went when I was a kid, and we took our kids." Haleya smiled at the memory. "I remember that everything was so real to me. The Cinderella's castle was my very favorite." Haleya glanced at the monitors and typed notes in the computer. "Did you hear me say that they are finding you a room in the rehab facility nearby? That's good news."

"So Elizabeth got to go to Disney World too?"

"Yes," Haleya gave into her conversation. "She dressed like Cinderella, and we had breakfast in the castle."

"Oh," Marcella gasped, "she really got to do that?"

"Yeah, I guess we spoiled her." Haleya shook her head. "Have you ever been to Disney World?"

"No, but Roxie has."

*   *   *

"... *An unplowed field produces food for the poor, but injustice sweeps it away,* okay, whatever. I think Happy Lady is a stupid name. What's your real name?" Elizabeth asked.

No answer.

"Were you even listening? I mean, I read all that and—"

"I was listening."

"Good, okay. Back to your name. So my friends think it's funny when I call you Happy Lady. I tell them about my visits with you, and they laugh the whole time. We came up with a better name. Nothing like Martha or Frances, which is something like what it probably really is. How about Gee Gee? Kara came up with it, and it's Sam's favorite. Can I call you Gee Gee?"

"Oh yes, Roxie would love that."

"Okay, great! And you can call me El."

"El?"

"Yeah, El. That's what my friends call me. Instead of Elizabeth, Sam yells down the hallway at school 'Hey, El,' and then says something like 'Camino.' Then the next day it's 'Hey El Paso.' He's so funny!"

"El Shaddai," Marcella mumbled. "The angels sing it."

"Actually, Amy Grant sings it, but he wouldn't know that song. So you're Gee Gee, and I'm El, right?"

"Yes. You aren't done reading, are you? I like it when you read to me."

Elizabeth rolled her eyes, touched her iPhone screen, and continued, "*Those who spare the rod hate their children, but those who love them are careful to discipline them.* Gee Gee, I'm so ready to leave home! One day they're going to wake up, and I'm not going to be there anymore."

"I ran away when I was 15. Well, me and Roxie did."

"Lucky you."

"It's a great story. Wanna hear it?"

Elizabeth clicked on her iPhone. She had 10 minutes. "If I don't have to read anymore, then okay."

Marcella began, "Roxie knew the cool places to go. She'd once lived in the big city. She'd done it all. Those are great stories for another time. But it was me who took Roxie to church for the first time. I'd never been before either, but I hadn't done lots of things. We didn't go in. We hid behind the bushes and watched the families go in and come out. We tried to guess which person it was. Could it be the lady whose hat nearly blew from her head each Sunday as she left church, even though she held it tight? Roxie said it was the big ring on her finger that kept it weighted down."

"What do you mean by 'which person it was?'" Elizabeth broke in.

Marcella shook her head. "I'll get to that."

"Okay." Elizabeth rolled her eyes.

"Then I thought maybe it was the floral-dressed grandmother, with the knowing look, who had the face for such a deed. Roxie told me that too many people had to stand close, keeping her balanced down the stairs, for it to be her. Roxie then pointed to the handsome young man. I probably wouldn't have even considered him, but Roxie was confident he was the one who had been leaving the food outside the church's outhouse door for us. Roxie was wrong though. But every Sunday we'd watch for him to enter the church doors and help the floral-dressed grandma down the stairs. He was something to see."

"Was he hot?" Elizabeth asked.

"I never got to touch him."

Elizabeth laughed. "No, not hot like that. What'd he look like?"

"Striking in every way. Dressed sharp and—"

"Like Liam Hemsworth?" Elizabeth broke in.

"Who's he?"

"A hot actor. Miley's boyfriend."

"Who's that?"

"Oh, how about Justin Bieber? He's hot!" She sang, *"Baby, Baby, Baby, oh ..."*

"Who?"

"Okay," Elizabeth thought hard. "Like Tom Cruise."

"I think he probably looked like all of them put together and a touch of Elvis's charm."

"Oh, yeah. He was hot then."

"Yes, then, 'hot' I suppose." Marcella smiled and continued, "Roxie once said to me, being silly, 'If he likes apple pie, I'll bake him one.' We laughed for days about that."

"Oh, that so sounds like me and Kara. She says things like, 'If his shirt needs ironed, I'm available.' We crack up! Roxie sounds so cool!"

"Roxie is cool?" Marcella questioned.

"And church dude is hot! You get it." Elizabeth giggled and for a second she felt like she was with Kara, but instead it was Geriatric Gee Gee as Sam called her. "I've got to share this with Kara and Sam—that we didn't talk Bible today, but instead, we talked about hot guys. They won't believe it." Elizabeth starting texting.

"They're good friends?" Marcella asked.

"Oh, yeah. The best."

"Can you ask them then what it means when someone is warm?"

"That's great!" Elizabeth exclaimed and texted. Sam's answer came back first.

"Oh," Elizabeth leaned forward in the chair, laughing. "Sam says that if a person is warm, it means he needs to take off his hot-as-crap sweater. But he didn't type 'crap.' And, here's Kara's. She says to check him for a temperature, because if you get closer, he might actually be h-o-t!"

"Funny friends," Marcella nodded.

"Oh, the best!" Elizabeth kicked back in her chair like a cushy couch.

Marcella felt *warm* all over.

Elizabeth looked at the time. "I've gotta go! Next time, can you tell me who was bringing you the food?" She dashed out the door, texting as if her life depended on the device in her hands.

*   *   *

Marcella couldn't wait to tell Roxie about her *new friend* Elizabeth and that she'd picked a fun name like "Gee Gee" to call her. But she'd have to wait. Dr. Walden stopped by, and he wasn't alone. After he'd poked around on her and asked questions, he left, but the two ladies stayed and asked more questions.

Marcella did her best to answer.

"No, I don't remember my last address."

"Yes, I'm over 60. No, I'm not 65 yet."

"I don't have a phone number."

"No, there's no family you can call."

"I don't have any money."

"I can't remember the last time I've seen a doctor."

After they left, she was too tired to tell Roxie about her visit with El.

*   *   *

Haleya dropped by her mother's. "Elizabeth called me all upbeat today."

"Well, that's good news."

"It's strange how she can go from miserable to carefree within hours."

"That's true." Lyndee sliced a piece of sourdough bread and buttered it for Haleya.

"You know that I stop by to see you because I love you and not just because I know exactly what time you pull the freshly baked bread from the oven." Haleya took a bite. She sank back in her chair savoring it.

"I know why you stop by," Lyndee said. "Because you want to make sure that I haven't boarded a plane to Haiti."

"That, too, actually. I just wish Dad was still in the Northwest part where it's safer." Haleya took another bite.

"He's in Leogane this week." She rubbed her head with her palm. "Traveling is so much more dangerous. I just don't know what I'd do without him, I mean, *really* without him."

275

Putting down the knife, Lyndee ripped off a big piece of the soft, warm bread. She pushed the loaf to her daughter.

Haleya pinched off a large piece. Mouth full, she mumbled, "But this helps."

Lyndee nodded.

"Mom, do you remember when I failed first grade?"

"You did not fail first grade. The teacher said you'd have a better chance if you repeated first grade."

"Yeah, yeah," Haleya said. "My point exactly. You told me that Mrs. Harris asked if she could keep me for another year to be her big helper."

"You were a big helper," Lyndee said.

"She let me take attendance in the mornings, lead the class line, and collect the library books. I felt so important."

"Why are you thinking about that?"

"Because I worked extra hard because I didn't want to disappoint Mrs. Harris. She'd chosen me," Haleya said.

"You were reading so much better by the end of that year."

"It wasn't until the year was almost over that Billy Watson told me that I'd failed first grade and that's why I had to do it again."

"I never liked Billy Watson," Lyndee said squinting her eyes.

"I just wanted you to know that you did good."

*   *   *

"What's wrong? Is Austin okay?" Knox answered his iPhone seeing a text come through from Alicia's at the same time.

"He's fine. It's the bug. You know when I was joking about what if she had, you know, with a boy."

"Yeah."

"Well, when I got home Austin pointed to the fish tank and there was something inside. I thought he'd dropped something in the tank, but he didn't. I just sent you a picture."

The image Alicia texted popped up on Knox's screen.

"It's an ootheca," he yelled into the phone. "Oh, we are having baby mantises! This is so awesome!"

"Are those eggs?"

"I think so!" Pulling on his pants, Knox nearly fell over sideways but caught himself. "I'm coming over."

* * *

"Do you need money?" Ben asked.

"I'm good, Dad." Thomas said.

"I mean, I know—"

"Dad, I don't have a lien on the house or anything."

"You know when I sold the wood mill, I got some money for it."

"Of course, you did, Dad. I'm good. Not as good as I *was,* but business just dried up."

"Your credit is good?"

"Yep."

"You don't owe more than you can pay?"

"Nope.

"Proud of you."

"Thanks, Dad. You taught me how to work. I'm just no longer building big houses and making big money," Thomas sighed. "That was then. This is now."

"I love you, son."

"I know," Thomas looked away.

"I was never good at saying that."

"I get it." Thomas looked back at his dad.

"I didn't grow up hearing those words," he said.

Thomas nodded. "When I read the book that Mom wrote, I got it. I got lots of things that I didn't get before."

* * *

"Knox, you're here!" Austin worked his wheelchair over to his computer and pulled up the information on its screen. *"Expect the egg case to hatch in 3-10 weeks. Once the praying mantises hatch, offer food within 24 hours or they may start eating each other!"*

"What?" Alicia squalled.

"Okay, okay, we have some time to figure this out." Knox assured her. "We have to do this right. Lives are in our hands."

"As soon as the," Austin paused and pointed to the screen.

Knox read the word where his finger pointed, *"nymphs hatch*—that's the baby stage." Knox continued to read, *"You should transfer them to an appropriate container in which you can raise them. Keep the mantis in a well-ventilated enclosure and spray with water. The mantis will drink from the water droplets when it is thirsty."*

Knox pulled a chair up beside Austin and finished the article. "What do we do with them for the 3-10 weeks. Why 3-10 weeks? That's such a big difference. I have no idea what I'm doing!" Knox skimmed until he found what he was looking for and then read aloud, *"Low temperature will arrest the development of the ootheca. Higher temperatures will trigger the development. You can keep air humidity high by putting paper, cloth, white sand or tiny pebbles on the bottom of the container."* Knox looked from Austin to Alicia. "So we can control the length of their development by their habitat. I'm going to take her back to my house." Knox picked up the fish tank. "I'll call you tomorrow!"

Chapter 57

"I know I'm not 'the pretty nurse,' but I did shower and put makeup on." Sandra said to Marcella. "I prayed for Raquel."

"Oh, thank you! I pray for her too."

"You believe in prayer?" Sandra asked.

"I didn't." Marcella said. "But I do now!"

"Do you pray a lot?"

"No. I just started."

"Really?"

"I once knew a lady who taught me to pray. I knew her only a short time. She said she'd always pray for me, but I didn't believe it would make any difference."

"And now?" Sandra asked.

"I have no doubt," Marcella said, "but sometimes evil wins."

"Not in the end," Sandra said with a smile.

"That's beautiful. I want to believe that," Marcella said. "You know, sometimes God uses evil for good though."

"What makes you believe that?"

"Because Tad is evil."

"Who's Tad?"

"Nothing but evil. He took Raquel."

"Is this your family?"

"Oh, no. I only knew Raquel for a few days and met Tad for only a few seconds."

"But Raquel isn't her real name, right?"

"No, I don't think so. But pray for her, please."

"How do you know that Tad is evil?"

"He did this to me."

"He hurt you?"

Marcella nodded.

Sandra gasped. "You need to tell the police."

"That Tad's evil?"

"Yes."

"And that God used him for good?"

"What makes you think that God used him for good?"

"Because I'm here."

*   *   *

"Whatcha doing, Knox?" Ben asked seeing his grandson stooped in the grass.

"Waiting for the school bus."

"Most kids stand at the end of the driveway and just look bored."

"Like Elizabeth." Knox pointed to his sister. "I'm looking for a woolly caterpillar."

"I thought you already had one of those woolly worms."

"Yeah, I've got one."

"Do you need two?"

"I want to give one to Austin. I think he'd take good care of it."

"I'm sure he would."

"He really likes the praying mantis, but I brought the fish tank home because there's an egg sac in it. I've got to keep everything the right temperature. And you know what comes next, don't you?"

"Lots of praying mantises."

"Well, yeah, but I was referring to the fact that she dies soon after laying the egg sac. I didn't want Austin and Alicia to see that. The woolly worm turns into a moth. That's something exciting for Austin to see."

*   *   *

"You got a question for me today?" Haleya asked when she stepped into room 301.

"What's your favorite thing? First thing that comes to mind."

Haleya, surprised by what she thought of, laughed. "Honestly the first thing that came to my mind? Icicles. Not just icicles, but icicles dipped in sugar."

"Tasty."

"Wow, it's been a long time since I thought of that. It couldn't have been very healthy, but my mom would let me pick icicles hanging from the house—big crystal-clear ones. I'd dip it in the sugar bowl and lick the sugar off. I wanted them to never melt."

"But they did?"

"The sun would come out and sometimes within just a couple of hours, they'd be gone."

"Gone, but not forgotten."

"Right." Haleya was going to miss these conversations. "Okay, your turn."

She thought for a minute. "Carousels, I think."

*   *   *

"Can I help you?"

Art opened his eyes. He'd staggered toward home from the lodge and had almost made it. He looked up to see a lady's face. "I'm fine."

"You're sleeping on my front porch step, you know."

"Thought my bed was a little hard." Art arched his back and rubbed beneath his shoulder blade sitting up on the concrete step of his neighbor's home.

"Have you had breakfast?"

"Well, Lana," Art said as he worked himself into a standing position. "If you count the tomato juice in a Bloody Mary."

"I don't." Lana extended her hand.

281

"You wanna dance?"

"No, not with a drunk man at nine in the morning."

"How about Saturday night?"

"You know we already tried that, Art."

"Yeah, and you said that you had a good time."

"And you said you'd call."

"I didn't call?"

"No, you didn't." Lana opened the front door and led him in.

"I'm a dumb, old coot," Art mumbled. "Would you have gone out with me again?"

"Had you called, then you'd know."

"This doesn't count as me calling?" Art asked staggering.

"No." Lana led him to her kitchen table.

*   *   *

Elizabeth finished reading quicker than usual, "... *wisdom's instruction is to fear the Lord, and humility comes before honor.* Okay Gee Gee, tell me about you and Roxie."

Marcella started where she'd left off. "We'd sleep in the outhouse only when it rained, until the food started showing up. Then we were afraid to not sleep there because whoever it was might think that we'd left."

"So, if it wasn't the hot guy, then who was it?"

"That's what I'm getting to," Marcella said.

"Okay," Elizabeth said with an eye roll.

"We'd learned though to get up with the sun on Sunday. Roxie would make small notches on the rotting wood wall of the outhouse to keep up with what day it was. Sunday was when the outhouse got visited."

"Oh, is this like a porta potty of the old days?"

"Yes, built like a little bitty shed. My head touched one end and my feet the other. It had a long plank-like bench with two holes cut in a circle, so two people could go at the same time."

282

"That's super disgusting."

"Yes, Sunday nights were the worst. The potty had been freshly used by people who couldn't hold it until they got home."

"Oh, yuck!"

"The story gets better." Marcella continued, "So we'd watch from a distance, hiding in the bushes nearby. The kids frequented the bathroom the most, and sometimes when two or more were in there, they'd laugh and giggle so loud the wind would carry their words to us. One guy, once, we thought had died because he stayed so long. We thought about knocking on the door and running off. About the time we got up the nerve, he opened the door, peeked out, and went back inside. We fell asleep before he came out a second time."

"I *so* want to meet Roxie."

"You have lots of friends."

"I do. They'd love her too! Where did Roxie live? I mean, when you didn't both live in the poop house."

"She lived in a tree house."

"Your friend lived in a treehouse, for real?"

"Yep, a big, fancy one."

Elizabeth looked at the time. "Roxie rocks! I gotta go." Elizabeth scrambled to pick up her bookbag. "You still haven't told me who's leaving the food." Elizabeth's iPhone rang. She put it to her ear with no goodbye as she became instantly absorbed in the conversation.

* * *

Thomas, picking up Knox at school, answered Art's call.

"Yep, yep," Thomas listened. "I can," Thomas said. "No, I don't mind. Okay, see you in a bit."

"What's up?" Knox asked.

"I'm gonna need to take you to your mom at the hospital so she can get you home. Art needs my help."

"So that's it today? No work?"

"Nope, sorry, Bud."

"No problem!" Knox started texting.

*   *   *

"Whatcha doing?" Alicia asked as she approached.

Ben, sitting in a lawn chair outside his RV, pointed to the chair beside him. "Whittling the letter N. Finishing Knox's name."

"How do you do that?"

"Gotta have the right wood and a little time. You here to see Knox?"

"Yeah, I thought I'd wait if that's okay. My mom works at home so she can take care of my brother and needs the house to be quiet."

"How old is your little brother?"

"Ten, almost eleven."

Ben tossed her a piece of wood and handed her a knife. "Have at it."

"What should I make?"

"It's best to get the hang of it first." Ben showed as he whittled.

"Like this?" Alicia whittled nicks in the wood. "Maybe I'll make something for my dad, but I never see him." Alicia focused on the wood.

"What do you think he'd like?"

"I'm not sure. He probably wouldn't care no matter what I made. He has a new wife and another kid now. He moved away." Alicia blew at her piece of wood and a few flecks settled on her knee. "My mom said she's given up hope that he'll ever be part of our lives again," Alicia said. "She says I shouldn't keep *hoping* for something that's not going to happen."

"I understand," Ben said. "I have a son that I haven't seen in a long time. I think about him every day though. It used to be that when the phone rang, I'd—"

"Think it might be him!"

"Every time."

"But it wasn't," Alicia sighed. "Sometimes I pretend that I see my dad walking through our front door again. If my dad came home, I'd forgive him for leaving."

"That's big that you know you could forgive him. Not everybody forgives so easily."

"Do you think you'll ever see your son again?"

Ben looked into the distance. He'd never been asked that, but he'd thought about it every day. "I don't know that I ever will."

"Knox is lucky. He has a dad at home and now you. He talks about you *all* the time. Well, when he isn't telling me about bugs."

"I'm gonna have to teach that boy how to really converse with a woman."

"I like it. He's my best friend."

*   *   *

"Happy Lady, I want you to meet Knox."

"Oh, my." She tried to push herself up in the bed, and Haleya helped.

"Hi," Knox said.

"Come closer. I want to see you." Marcella reached for him. "Your mother is very proud of you."

Knox tilted his head at his mother.

Haleya shrugged. "I can't help it."

"Are you sick?" Knox, standing by her bed, allowed her to take his hand.

She nodded.

"But you'll get better."

"No, dear. It's bad cancer."

285

Knox looked over at Haleya. She nodded.

"Sorry," Knox mumbled. "You know, I read about this man who was given just a few months to live with chemotherapy, but he refused because it made him feel terrible. Instead, he started eating 40 live Chinese weevils—they look like worms—and he's been cancer free for six years now."

"Knox!" Haleya squealed.

"It's a true story, Mom."

"You told me he was smart."

Haleya winked at Knox and glanced at the time. "I've gotta get back to work. Knox, say, 'Goodbye.'"

"Can he stay?"

"I have more healing insect stories," Knox said.

Haleya waved and left them together.

*   *   *

Thomas knocked on Art's door, then waited while Art fumbled with the lock.

"I woke up to an angel this morning," Art said as he swung the door open.

"The one from Christmas Past, Scrooge?" Thomas stepped inside.

"Have you ever prayed for a woman? I don't mean, prayed for someone to get better. I mean really *prayed* for a woman."

"Like, 'Dear God, where is that special woman for me?'"

"Yes! What happened?" Art asked.

"I married her."

Art rocked on his feet, toe to heel a couple of times, and tucked his hands deep in his jeans pockets. "He answers those kinds of prayers?"

Thomas nodded, noticing Art's smile was the biggest ever. "I thought this was about your truck, not an angel."

"Oh yeah, my truck."

"We'll let's go get it. You said you needed a ride."

"That's the thing," Art stammered. "I'm not sure where it is."

"Did you lose it in a bet or something?"

"No, I'm sure it's still where I left it."

"So you don't know where you left it?" Thomas shook his head.

"That's right," Art smirked. "Did I tell you that I woke up to an angel this morning?"

"You did." Thomas led Art outside.

"She lives over there," Art whispered. "In that house, two down from mine."

Chapter 58

Haleya steadied Marcella as the transporter helped her into the wheelchair for dismissal to the nursing rehab facility. "I got this for you." She held a pillow with "Happy" written in script.

"I like it," Marcella said.

Haleya placed it on her lap. "I saw it and thought of you."

"It's pretty." She started to hand the pillow back.

"It's yours," Haleya explained. "It's a gift from me to you."

"Mine? To keep?" Marcella tucked it against her chest.

Haleya, touched by the child-like expression, bent down to eye level with her. "They'll be good to you where you're going. I know the nurses."

"I like this." Marcella patted the pillow.

"Good." Haleya touched her hand. "And I told the nurses that Roxie would be coming by to see you."

"Will you?"

"I will," Haleya promised as the transport pushed Marcella into the elevator and the doors closed.

*   *   *

Elizabeth found her mom at the nurses' station "Hey, where's Gee Gee?"

Sandra dashed by. "Hey, Pretty Nurse!" Then she turned to ask, "Did she get to talk with the police officer about Raquel and Tad?"

Haleya nodded.

"Mom!" Elizabeth repeated.

Haleya turned back to Elizabeth. "They moved her to Sapphire Rehab two streets over."

"You gotta tell me this stuff!" Elizabeth huffed. "I gotta go there now!" She tossed her hands in the air and walked away.

* * *

Checking on Lyndee, Haleya stopped by on her way home. "Are you coming to the groundbreaking tomorrow?"

"We are. Gina's excited."

"Dad's birthday is today," Haleya said.

"Sure is," Lyndee whispered.

"Did you get to talk to him?"

"Not long. He had a surgery."

"Speaking of surgeries, Happy Lady has cancer. It's advanced. They moved her to Sapphire Rehab." Haleya pointed to the wall of photos of the young faces. "You know, I think I get it now."

"What?"

"When your heart gets wrapped up in something, it's hard to stop." Haleya counted the photos taped to the wall. "One, two, three, four, five, six, seven—"

"Okay, okay. I get your point."

"I made over a dozen calls and wouldn't have stopped at that, trying to find help for her. Mom, she has nothing—no one. I gave her a pillow that had 'Happy' stitched on it. She didn't even understand that I was giving it to her."

"Sounds like you've given her a lot more."

"She asked me if Santa came to my house when I was a kid. Santa never came to her house, Mom."

"She's better because of you."

"She might be better than she was, but she's nowhere without good care. I called Healthcare for the Homeless, a federally funded program and probably talked to seven different people. I called the Fayette County Office for Homeless Prevention and Intervention, and, when we kept

289

playing phone tag, I stopped by and wouldn't leave until I got to talk to someone. They're trying to establish help for short stints in rehab, but it's barely started. I talked with the Hope Center and, oh my goodness, what a good organization, but they can't do for Happy Lady what she needs."

"Wow, you *are* my daughter!" Lyndee said.

"Walking out of the Hope Center I prayed 'God, Happy Lady needs a place to go. Help me, please.' I am not kidding, Carol Ann from church, who works at Sapphire Rehab, came to mind. When I called, she told me that they were recently awarded a grant for a pilot program that would provide someone like Happy Lady 30 days of care."

"That's wonderful!" Lyndee hugged Haleya.

*   *   *

"*...The horse is made ready for the day of battle, but victory rests with the Lord,*" Elizabeth concluded. "Good thing you were the only lady they moved in today, because that's the only way they knew who I was asking to see, since they had no clue your name is Gee Gee."

"I'm glad you found me."

"Okay, so, what did you and Roxie do next?"

"Where did we leave off last time?"

"The stinky poop house," Elizabeth said, holding her nose which made her words sound funny, "and who was weaving da food."

"Oh, yes—Sundays. I heard the preacher yelling from inside when we snuck by the church. The front doors were open, welcoming, but scary to us. Once we set our mind to doing it, I dashed toward the fancy hat lady's house next to the church so fast Roxie couldn't keep up. Roxie had owned hundreds of fancy dresses and shoes. I wanted one pair. I'd spotted the shoes the week before, and this morning she wasn't wearing them.

"Once inside the house—I later learned it was called a parsonage and the preacher lived there—I spotted the bedroom and almost lost focus when I opened the closet. Roxie had told me that there were probably as many shoes in the world as ants, but I hadn't believed her. There were so many pretty shoes. I quickly grabbed the suede pumps. Not that I knew at the time that was what they were called or that I had anywhere to wear them. I dashed out the back door, and as I passed the church, the preacher's words rang out, 'Thou shall not steal.' I told Roxie not to listen."

"You stole the preacher's wife's shoes?"

"I did. I shouldn't have."

"Oh, I can't wait to tell Kara and Sam this!" Elizabeth tapped on her iPhone screen. "Yikes, I need to leave now to catch the bus." Elizabeth stood. "Okay, tomorrow, I'll be on time since I know where to come, and I'll read fast so you can tell me more."

"Not all of my stories are exciting. Some are sad. Some are really bad."

"I want to hear those too."

"Are you sure? I don't like thinking about them, but they're part of my story. You'll need to know them."

"Okay, sure. I watch R-rated movies. I've seen and heard stuff."

"I'm sure you have, dear. But when a person lives it, it sticks in her head and stays there, not in a good way."

"I've seen all the Halloween movies!" Elizabeth said over her shoulder as she headed out.

*   *   *

"Pen-Pa, can you help me do something?"

"Snake hunting?" Ben asked, self-consciously massaging his knee.

"No, I mean, yes, in the spring. But actually, I meant something else."

291

"What?" Ben asked.

"We need to get Austin out of the house to the movies or something. He never gets to go."

"We can do that."

"I asked him if he's seen Ironman 2 because it's at the movie theater. He said he hasn't seen the first one yet."

"What do you have in mind?" Ben asked. "Since it sounds like I'm going to be a part of your plan."

Chapter 59

The mayor welcomed everyone to the ground-breaking, introduced Thomas, and stepped aside.

"I don't like microphones," Thomas said, "but today, what needs to be said needs to be heard."

"First, I'd like to introduce my silent partners, Art Mansfield and Walt Cummings. They aren't silent in the sense that they are secret, but silent in that they declared that I'd do all the talking."

A chuckle arose from the crowd.

"These two men right here are the reason we're here today—in more ways than one. It's their passion for this project and their service to our country!" Thomas started clapping, and the crowd followed. Walt beamed, while Art dropped his head.

Thomas spoke over the applause, "When these gentlemen came to me with this proposition, I was at a crossroads, unsure of what was next for me. That's when I realized that maybe God had prepped me for this moment in my life. When Walt introduced me to Art, I'd recently returned from a visit to my hometown." Thomas looked over at his father. "It was my first time back since my mother passed away a few years ago. In that moment, standing with Art offering his land and Walt sharing the need for this, I realized that it had been too long since I'd listened to my mama."

A chuckle rumbled from the crowd. Thomas paused and nodded toward his father who blinked back tears.

"I feel fortunate to be a part of this. We have a lot of work ahead of us, but today we celebrate the beginning of something great! Let's break ground!" Thomas yelled and pointed to Art.

Art raised his hands in the air. "Hallelujah!"

The mayor handed Walt and Art shovels. Thomas grabbed two more and handed one to the mayor. On the count of three, the mayor yelled, "Break ground!" Thomas wasn't watching where he tossed the dirt or looking at the cameras. His eyes were on Walt and Art standing next to him. He didn't want to miss the look on either face.

*　　*　　*

"*... The generous will themselves be blessed, for they share their food with the poor,*" Elizabeth read.

Marcella interrupted, "Oh!"

"'Oh', what?"

"That just reminds me of Mrs. Milam's Bible and the story of Ruth.

"Who's Mrs. Milam?"

"The preacher's wife."

"The lady who you stole her shoes!"

"Yes, dear. And she was the one leaving the food for us at night. She let me and Roxie stay in their spare room. She called me 'Little Miss Marcie.'"

"Oh, that's awesome!"

"It wasn't Ruth who fascinated me but Boaz. Mrs. Milam had written in the Bible's margin: *Boaz was a good man. He took care of his people. He understood the responsibility of family.* I wanted a Boaz."

*　　*　　*

Knox jumped from the RV, bolted up the steps, and took hold of the door so Alicia could wheel her brother down the ramp.

294

"We've got a DVD we can watch on the TV, and we'll go through a drive-through for dinner. It's your day, Austin," Knox said.

Knox motioned for his grandfather to hold the RV door open so he could help Alicia get Austin out of his wheelchair and into the RV.

"This is awesome!" Austin said, as he pointed to the TV where the first Ironman was cued up on screen.

"Pen-Pa's going to drive us around while we watch the movie."

"You choose where we eat," Alicia told Austin.

"Anything I want? Like a bucket of Baskin Robbins ice cream?"

"Sure! But you have to share," Knox said.

*   *   *

"You look good," Haleya said visiting Marcella.

Marcella reached out her hand, fluttering her fingers for Haleya to hold.

"You've got a roommate, I see."

Marcella nodded, then coughed, wheezed, and cleared her throat. "My pillow." She pointed to it in a chair.

"It looks great in here. I brought you a book. Santa gave it to me when I saw him at the airport. I want you to have it."

Marcella reached for it.

"It's about a girl who has big expectations for Christmas and then nothing goes right. In the end though, everything that happens actually makes it her best Christmas ever."

"I like that."

Haleya read the title, "A Girl's Christmas Gone Perfectly Wrong."

"El can read it to me. I like it when she reads to me."

"She asked you to call her El?"

She nodded. "She calls me Gee Gee."

"I know. She's a mess. I'm glad she's still reading to you. Guess what I brought?" Haleya pulled an individual-sized applesauce container from her purse along with a plastic spoon.

Marcella placed the book beside her and reached for the applesauce. Haleya pulled off the foil lid.

Marcella's hands shook as she took a bite. "I like applesauce."

"I know. Has Roxie been here to see you?"

Marcella nodded.

Chapter 60

"Whoever walks in integrity walks securely, but whoever takes crooked paths will be found out."

"That's fitting," Marcella interrupted.

"Another story? Tell me."

"Okay, I'll try," Marcella cleared her throat. "I was dusting the hymnals in the first two pews of the church. No one ever sat there so dust collected. I figured that people were scared to get too close because of the fear of God that Mr. Milam spoke about. That day, I heard *him* enter the doors of the church."

"Who?"

"It was Mrs. Milam's *lost* brother."

"Was he hot?"

"No," Marcella answered without hesitation. "He'd been staying with us for a week. One night I heard Mrs. Milam crying. Her fancy ring was missing. I was in my room, but I heard the man say he was sorry and that he had to have the money or they'd kill him. I learned the next day that 'lost,' in church language, referred to someone's heart and not their whereabouts. In that church, Mr. Lost took something more valuable than any ring. Roxie sang so loud from the hymnal that she thought for sure Mrs. Milam would hear and save me."

Elizabeth sat still. "You mean?"

Marcella lowered her eyes.

"Oh, that's bad."

Marcella nodded. "I finished filling the communion cups with juice preparing them for Sunday morning, careful that my shaking hands didn't drip any on Mrs. Milam's open-toed, high-heeled shoes I wore. I'd been living in the house by the church for almost four months. That Saturday evening, I told Roxie it was time for us to go."

*　　*　　*

Before Ben had the chance to say hello into his phone, Colton blurted out, "I married Esli today!"

"What?"

"I mean, I married Esli to Michael today. They're married!"

"Wonderful! Was Esli's mama there?"

"Nope, just Esli's sisters and the two of them."

"That's perfect."

"It was something special! And she and the baby are going with Michael when he returns to the military base."

"Great news," Ben said.

*　　*　　*

"Movie night!" Knox jumped out of the RV as his grandfather pulled into Alicia's driveway. Alicia, waiting outside, coasted Austin down the ramp.

Pumping his fist, Austin chanted, "Ironman 2! Ironman 2!"

Knox joined in the chant as they lifted Austin from his chair and into the RV.

Alicia whispered, "Thank you."

Doing something special tonight for Austin was exciting. Looking forward to seeing Alicia—that was a new feeling. He'd rather hang out with her than any bug.

*　　*　　*

Art looked out his kitchen window toward Lana's house as he talked on his phone to Thomas.

"Art, I was thinking HAVHonor could build you a house in Vet Village along with the others."

"This house is fine."

298

"You've done so much to make it happen—"

"Only a small part," Art interrupted. "Just my part."

"I'm glad to know a man like you."

"I'm glad to know you. Otherwise, how would I've found my truck," Art quipped as he said goodbye. Staring at the rotary phone, he knew it was outdated, but at the same time, it still felt right—like his house. He picked up the receiver and dialed.

"I thought I'd make that call we talked about," Art said when Lana picked up.

"What call?"

"Last time I saw you, you said to give you a call sometime."

"Well, you are a man of your word, aren't you?" Lana said in the same kind, caring voice he remembered from the other morning.

*   *   *

"I've been typing the book," Elizabeth said as she relaxed with her grandfather by the firepit. "I didn't know."

"You didn't know what?"

"I didn't know that you grew up like that."

"Like what?"

"With nothing."

"Yep," Ben said. "Nothing good."

"Everybody called you Kage?"

"Yep."

"I think Kage is cool," Elizabeth said. "He wasn't scared of a fight. I mean, you weren't."

"No, I wasn't. I had nothing much to lose back then."

"That guy, Barney, reminds me of a guy who's on the school bus." Elizabeth growled.

"You want me to beat him up?" Ben made a fist.

"That would be great! You should have knocked Barney's lights out."

"I won the prize in the end."

"Still, you should have. I could add that to the book, a scene where you clock him really good!"

"How do you know that I didn't. Maybe your grandmother just didn't know," Ben smirked.

"Oh, I love it!" Elizabeth exclaimed.

"That's between you and me now. Don't add it to the book. That's her book. You write your own."

"I just might do that," Elizabeth said.

Chapter 61

Elizabeth pulled her sleeves over her hands to warm them. She'd lost track of time with Gee Gee and missed her transit pick-up. Jogging in place, waiting for the next transit, her phone rang.

When she answered, Kara said, "Don't talk to him anymore."

"Wait, I don't get it."

"Don't talk to Sam anymore. I don't like you talking to him," Kara repeated.

"What? He's my friend too."

"Yeah, but last weekend at the party his neighbor had, things happened—" Kara explained.

"What things happened?"

"Stuff *between us.*"

"Oh, weird."

"Why's that weird?" Kara shrieked.

"Because we're all friends!"

"Yeah, I've been meaning to talk to you about that," Kara said.

"About what?"

"I don't think we can be friends anymore. It's not going to work."

"*We?*" Elizabeth repeated. "*We* like me and you or *we* like me, you and Sam? I'm so confused. So, you and Sam are like, something now?"

"Something like that."

"That changes things, but what does that have to do with me?"

301

"Well, I'm not okay with *you* being friends with him anymore."

"What? Why?" Elizabeth paced in circles.

"Because you're a girl."

"Kara! This is crazy. Sam's my friend."

"*Was*," Kara corrected.

"Why are you doing this?"

"Sorry, El." Kara hung up.

*   *   *

Art tossed several sweaters onto the bed to bag up for Goodwill. Everything he owned made him look like an old man. He called Walt. "Walt, I need to talk to your wife."

"Why?"

"Because she's a classy lady," Art said.

"Well, of course she is, but that's actually a reason for me to not let you talk to her."

"I don't have any clothes."

"And my wife needs to know that because—"

"Dang it, Walt!" Art blurted out. "Hey, I said 'dang it!' I'm getting good not using all that bad language."

"Now you just need to keep up with your truck," Walt chuckled. "Wait 'til I tell Thomas you called and don't have any clothes. Are you naked, Art?"

"I ain't lost my clothes. They're all something a grandpa would wear."

"You aren't a spring chicken anymore?"

"I'm not anybody's grandpa though!"

"Why the sudden big concern about your wardrobe?"

"I got a date."

"Well, in that case, you're going to need all the help you can get." Walt handed the phone to his wife.

*   *   *

"Where's Elizabeth?" Thomas asked.

302

"She left a voicemail saying she's going to stay and read more to Gee Gee."

"Who?"

"That's what she calls Happy Lady."

Thomas looked at the time. "On a Friday evening? You think she's really there?"

"The phone tracker says she is. She must want to get it done."

"Think it's a guy instead?" Thomas suggested.

"What? You think she's lying?"

"She's smart enough to leave her iPhone there and sneak out with someone."

*　　*　　*

"I'm glad you came back. Twice in one day. Lucky me," Marcella had said when Elizabeth showed up at her door.

"I don't feel like talking." Elizabeth began reading, *"Proverbs 18: An unfriendly man pursues selfish ends; he defiles all sound judgement ... One who has unreliable friends soon comes to ruin, but there is a friend who sticks closer than a brother."* Elizabeth huffed. "Friends! I hate them!"

"What's wrong?"

"Kara and Sam, they got together, and now *they* broke up with me."

"Your friends?"

"Yes, but not anymore." Elizabeth scooted her chair up to the bedside and sat her chin on the raised bed rail. Marcella lifted her hand to touch Elizabeth's face.

"Can I ask you a question?"

Elizabeth nodded. Marcella's hand moved with her cheek.

"So does this mean that Sam is hot?"

Elizabeth lightly laughed yet her whole body shook. "Okay, that was good."

"And she'd like to iron his shirt?" Marcella added.

303

Elizabeth took Marcella's hand from her cheek and held it between both of hers. Squinting her eyes, she leaned closer to Marcella and whispered, "I think she's already ironed his shirt."

"Oh, my," Marcella pulled her hand away and covered her mouth.

*   *   *

"How was your day?" Thomas asked Knox.

"Awesome!"

Ben smirked, "In my day, we gave a girl flowers."

"I gave Austin my woolly worm today, and I'm going to catch a swallowtail caterpillar this spring for Alicia. She can watch it turn into a really pretty butterfly."

"That's so sweet." Haleya looked at Thomas. "You should take lessons from your son."

"You mean I could have just dug in my back yard and given you a caterpillar? I can picture it now, me in my Red Wing boots walking up to Miss Sorority girl. 'Hi, I'm Thomas. I think you're pretty. Here's a caterpillar.'"

Ben shook his head. "Flowers, son. Stick with flowers."

"It's in the presentation. Tell him Knox," Haleya encouraged.

Knox looked at his dad. "You say, 'I want you to have this caterpillar. You can watch it turn into a butterfly. It's super neat!'"

Haleya laughed. "Okay, not exactly what I had in mind, but so much better than your dad's!"

Chapter 62

"Charm is deceptive, and beauty is fleeting; but a woman who fears the LORD is to be praised. Give her the reward she has earned, and let her works bring her praise at the city gates. That's it. The end."

"All of Proverbs?"

"Well, I skipped around a lot. Roxie time! Last time you told me how she sang for President Eisenhower," Elizabeth said, scooting her chair closer.

"Did I tell you about when Roxie toured France?"

"No, tell me!"

"Well, Lawrence, of course—"

"Lawrence?"

"Oh, I haven't mentioned Lawrence to you. He played the cello when Roxie danced and sang. He always waited for her in the back of the room after each performance, sometimes with a rose or holding an umbrella if it was raining. After a performance, they'd get dessert. He drove a long, black limousine with lots of windows for Roxie to see the big city lights at night."

"Was he in love with Roxie?"

"Oh, *everybody* loved Roxie."

*　　　*　　　*

"Did Knox tell you that he's decided he wants to be a doctor?" Haleya mentioned to Thomas Saturday morning as she got ready for work.

"Dad told me Knox asked for a ride in the RV to Louisville to visit Kosair Children's Hospital. Dad might need a wheelchair before the day's over."

"So, a doctor?" Haleya glanced over at Thomas and winked.

"We need to get *him* applying for scholarships," Thomas said.

"He's become good friends with Alicia's brother. Pretty sweet. Like you."

"Don't go ruining my tough image."

"Oh, don't fool yourself. Everyone saw through it at the groundbreaking."

"Changing the subject," Thomas said. "Speaking of tough images, where's Elizabeth?"

"She went to see Gee Gee."

"On a Saturday?"

"Yep."

"So, she's lying." Thomas said.

"I called, and they said Elizabeth is in the room with her."

"And there's no boy?"

"No, I don't think so."

"Hmm? Well, we're in the dark on something. I guarantee you that."

*   *   *

Marcella woke up to the tap, tap, tap sound of fingers clicking on a computer keyboard. "You're here?" Marcella watched Elizabeth's eyes shift easily from the notepad to the laptop, resting on her legs.

Elizabeth looked over her computer screen. "I gotta get this typed."

"How do you do that?" Marcella asked.

"Do what?"

"Type so fast. How do you know what letters to push?"

"You don't know how to type?"

Marcella shook her head.

"Doesn't everybody know how to type?"

"I didn't finish school. I guess they would have taught me. Is that yours?"

El looked around. "What's mine?"

"That computer."

"Yes, I use it for schoolwork mostly, but other stuff too."

"What are you typing?"

"A book."

"You write books?"

"No," she chuckled. "It's something my dad's making me do."

"You don't want to type it?"

"Not really. It's a book that my grandmother wrote about her life. I have to type it for him before he'll take me to look for another car."

"Can you do that for me?" Marcella asked.

"Do what?"

"Type my story."

"Do you have it written down?"

"I'd have to tell it to you."

"Are there more Roxie stories?" Elizabeth asked.

"Oh, yes. Lots of them."

"Good."

"Not everything is good though," Marcella said.

"Like the story about that 'lost brother' that I hate."

"Oh, dear. Don't hate. I mean," she paused, "I made a lot of mistakes. I'll need to tell you about those."

"Okay, I can try, if you want."

"My real name's Marcella," she said. "You'll need to know that for the book."

"Roxie and Little Miss Marcie," Elizabeth said. "That's a good title."

"Oh, I like that!"

"This could be fun," Elizabeth said.

"One more thing. When you finish it, give the first copy to your mother, please."

"Why, because she'll be proud of me for finishing something?" Elizabeth stood. "I need a snack; I'll be back." She blew Marcella a kiss before heading out the door.

*   *   *

"Well, don't you look nice?" Lana said when she opened her front door.

Art stood with one hand in the pocket of the Levi's that Walt's wife had paired with a new brown sport coat, which he wore over a freshly pressed, collared, white shirt. She'd insisted he button only the first of the two buttons on the jacket. Apparently, buttoning none is an option, but buttoning both is a big no-no.

"You are—" Art stammered, "beautiful."

Lana blushed and looked away. "Thank you. I'm ready."

"I'm lucky." Art reached out his hand and led her down the front stairs of her porch.

*   *   *

Elizabeth shot through the front door with her computer bag on her shoulder. She'd just finished typing a chapter of her grandmother's book about Kage and his brothers.

"Where's Grandpa?" She tossed her computer on the couch.

"And *hello* to you, and how was your day?" Thomas asked.

"Great day!"

Haleya and Thomas look at each other.

"Really?" Haleya asked.

"Yep!"

"What'd you do?" Thomas asked.

"I've been with Gee Gee," Elizabeth said as she opened the refrigerator door and searched inside.

"Still reading Proverbs?" Haleya asked.

308

"Done."

"Did you move on to Ecclesiastes or something?" Haleya asked.

"Nope," Elizabeth answered and settled on an orange Gatorade.

"You know the agreement was to read Proverbs. You're off the hook now," Thomas said.

"Yeah," Elizabeth headed for the back door. "Is Grandpa outside?" She pointed. "Hey, Grandpa."

"Come have a seat," Ben welcomed her.

"Okay, so your brothers? That's what I'm typing now. They make me really mad!"

"Me too!"

"I gotta know. Did you ever see them again?"

"Nope."

"Good! Because you would have knocked their lights out for sure."

"That's right."

"As I type, sometimes I forget it's you and then I remember, 'That's my Grandpa? No way!'"

"I was young once," Ben said.

"What if you'd never met Grandma? I mean, she's like the love of your life."

"Yes, she is."

"I've already figured out that there's no treasure."

"Why do you say that?"

"Because, if there had been treasure, I'd have heard about it. Everyone would know."

"Oh, but you aren't to the end of the book yet."

"Really? There's treasure?"

"Without the treasure, me and your Grandma may have never gotten married."

"Shut up!"

"What?"

"Oh, no, I don't mean 'shut up' disrespectfully. I mean it like, 'Tell the truth' or 'It can't be.' I had to explain that to Gee Gee too."

"Who's Gee Gee?"

"The lady who I've been reading to. Well, now, I'm writing her story. You know, like Grandma Gracie did. Her story has more sad than happy. I'm not sure how it can have a happy ending, but she's lived an interesting life."

"Anybody with the name Gee Gee has to have a good story."

"Oh, that's not really her name. That's just what I call her."

Chapter 63

Sunday morning Art got out of bed talking to himself. "I don't know how this happened," Art mumbled. In the kitchen, distracted by thoughts of how pretty Lana had looked and how much he'd enjoyed dinner with her, he forgot what he was doing. Coffee, he remembered. Looking at himself in the bathroom mirror, he patted shaving cream on his face. "I was doing good. Just me. Just fine. Doing my own thing."

Digging through his drawer for dress socks that matched, he held two to the light. "Black, navy, maybe navy—" Then, looking at himself in the full-length mirror, knee socks, underwear, and the whitest t-shirt he could find, he muttered, "Who am I?" He giggled and shook his head. "I could've said '*no.*' I know how to say '*No, thank you, appreciate the invite, but I'll pass.*'" Art talked to his reflection. "But I didn't!"

He got into his truck and drove two doors down, trying to convince himself that he hadn't lost his mind. As he knocked on Lana's front door, he admitted, "I think I have."

"Well, you did show up," Lana teased.

Art stood dressed in a sweater he'd maybe worn once before and a pair of slacks. This time he wasn't concerned with what to wear. He was more concerned about the fact that, without hesitation, he'd accepted her invitation to church.

* * *

"Elizabeth asked me to do a favor for her," Ben told Thomas while they waited for the church service to start.

311

"What's that?"

"Read part of the book that she's written. She started a book about that lady she calls Gee Gee."

"Really?"

"Thomas, it's good. She's a good writer," Ben insisted.

"Like Mom."

Ben nodded.

"Dad, thank you."

"Thanks for what?"

"Coming to see us." Thomas reached to hug his father.

"I'm glad I did too. Can I come back?"

"Are you leaving?"

"After Thanksgiving, I guess I'll head home."

"We'll come see you for Christmas," Thomas said. "Elizabeth is almost done typing Mom's book. I'll have it bound and bring it."

"That would be great," Ben said. He pointed to the man Thomas had introduced him to at the groundbreaking who walked through the church doors.

Thomas's gaze followed. "Art!"

*   *   *

Elizabeth felt like Roxie as she snuck into the church kitchen. She could have asked for the disposable communion set, but she'd thought of it at the last minute. Elizabeth tucked the tiny, prefilled juice cup into her purse. She asked her parents to drop her off to see Gee Gee.

Marcella clapped when she saw Elizabeth in the doorway.

Her big smile made Elizabeth smile, too. "I've been writing your story. Just the easy parts right now."

"Thank you."

"Have you ever taken communion?" Elizabeth asked.

"What?"

"The bread and wine, well, it's really juice and a cracker."

"Oh, yes. I did that."

"When you were with Roxie?" Elizabeth asked.

She nodded.

"Look what I got for you." Elizabeth pulled out the cup. "At church when we took communion, I thought of you. I remembered you telling me about wearing Mrs. Milam's high heels while you filled the communion cups. I got you one."

Marcella's eyes lit up. Elizabeth pulled off the clear plastic seal that kept the perfectly round, unsalted wafer fresh. When she handed it over, Marcella stuck out her tongue.

"Ready for the juice?"

She nodded.

Elizabeth removed the plastic seal. She put her hand behind Marcella's head and helped her take a sip.

"Do you know what that means?" Elizabeth asked.

Marcella answered, "Jesus loves me."

*   *   *

While Elizabeth typed the last chapter of *Treasure atop the Mountain*, she literally couldn't sit still. At her desk, she stood as she typed. There her father was, a part of the book. She'd never really imaged him as a little boy in his daddy's arms or what he meant to his mama. She sat down slowly and hit the save button several times. She didn't want to lose what her grandmother had shared. She wanted to know more.

Elizabeth came down the stairs. "Have you seen Grandpa?"

Thomas pointed out back.

"Oh, Mom, I need to spend more time with Gee Gee. She's asked me to write her story," Elizabeth said over her shoulder as she headed to find her grandfather.

"I finished." Elizabeth walked straight to him.

"You did?"

"All the pieces," Elizabeth paused, eyes wide, "they came together—so perfect. How does something like that happen?"

Ben pointed up. "That's how."

"God?" Elizabeth asked.

Her grandfather nodded. "He has us, child. He's had us from day one."

"I feel so strange." Elizabeth sat next to him.

"Why do you say that?"

"I think I miss Grandma now more than I ever have. Maybe I actually miss her for the first time ever."

"She was my life. She gave me a life. I think of her every day, a dozen times a day."

"Sometimes, I don't know—" Elizabeth paused in thought.

"You don't know what?"

"It's like I can pretend other people aren't real. If it doesn't really make me happy or sad, then it's like everything else is out there happening and who cares."

"That's very honest. Probably true for more people than would admit it."

"Tell me about her. Something I don't know. Something that wasn't in the book."

"Oh, how much time do you have?"

Elizabeth thought of how her week had gone. "I've got nothing more important at the moment." Elizabeth surprised herself and reached for her grandfather's hand.

"She couldn't talk when she got really sick. She was too weak. She'd take her left hand, place it on her heart, and pat two times. I'd do the same."

"What'd that mean?"

"'Love You.' She went through life with only one hand and left this world with no voice, but she did more and left more to be said about life than most people will or can."

Elizabeth lifted her left hand and patted her heart twice. "Like this?"

Ben patted his heart twice. "Just like that."

Chapter 64

"Whitney's beautiful," Gina said to Lyndee.

Whitney, her long amber hair pulled into a low ponytail, wore makeup and a delicate necklace. Her blue sweater matched her eyes.

"When will he be here?" Gina asked.

"Six-thirty," Whitney said, opening a bag of Hershey Kisses.

"Can we show Kent?" Gina asked, pointing to the computer. "He needs to see Whitney."

"The Skype isn't working. I can't get through," Lyndee told her.

"Why?" Gina held out her hand for a candy.

"I wish I knew why," Lyndee said.

"Is it broken?" Gina pressed.

"It's not connecting," Whitney said, passing the bag of Kisses to Lyndee.

"What if we don't get to see him again?" Gina didn't let up.

Lyndee dropped the bag, and Hershey Kisses rolled everywhere.

Whitney, on hands and knees picking up candy, said to Gina, "He's okay. He'll be home safe with us before Christmas."

"You promise," Gina bent down to help.

"He promised," Whitney said. The doorbell rang, and she stood. "I'm nervous."

"And you're beautiful," Lyndee said.

When Lyndee opened the door, Gina said, "Look how pretty she is!"

Whitney blushed.

*   *   *

Marcella listened with her eyes closed. When Elizabeth finished, Marcella asked her to read it again.

> Marcella heard it clearly though the baby she held hadn't spoken, but she was sure she heard "I love you." She wondered where the voice had come from. In fact, she wasn't sure she'd ever heard those words before. *How could a baby say something that no adult she ever met could murmur?* She rocked her baby in her arms. The yellowed ceiling, plastered with spackled, white patches, reminded her of clouds. The sun light beaming through the hollowed, bay window warmed her back like a gentle hug. She looked into her baby's eyes, back up at the clouds, and turned toward the window to feel the sun on her face. *Was that you, God?*
>
> The cat she held purred. There was no baby in her arms. She'd given up her baby so she'd know nothing of a life like hers. Marcella had wanted better for her baby girl.

"Oh, dear," Marcella said. "That's it. You're a writer. God's given you a gift."

"It's your story."

"Oh, oh. I couldn't put it into those words. It's so perfect."

"You really think so?"

"Come closer," Marcella asked. She lifted her hand, though unsteady, and Elizabeth took hold of it.

"What?" Elizabeth leaned closer.

"I love you," she whispered.

Elizabeth hadn't expected those words but realized she needed them. "I love you too, Gee Gee."

*   *   *

"Your grandfather told me about what you did for Alicia's brother," Thomas said to Knox as they headed to the jobsite.

"Gave him my woolly worm? It's okay. I'll find another one."

"Not just that. All the other stuff. I'm proud of you. Sometime dads forget how important that is to say. I want you to know that I'm proud of you."

"Thanks, Dad. I'm proud of you too."

"You are?"

"Sure. And thanks for getting the job for me. I like it a lot better than swimming."

"You're good at it."

"And we get to see each other every day, *and* I get a paycheck," Knox added.

"What've you done with the money you've made?"

"Saved it."

"You got something special in mind?"

"A Christmas present," Knox hesitated before he added, "for Alicia."

Thomas winked at Knox as he pulled to the jobsite. Art stood outside the work trailer.

"Art, do you want to come to our house for Thanksgiving?" Thomas asked, unloading the snacks he and Knox had picked up to stock the office.

"Nope," Art said.

"There's no reason to be alone on Thanksgiving. We'll have a house full and lots of food."

"Nope," Art said again.

"Wait." Thomas looked at Art as he passed him, grocery bags in hand. "That look—"

317

"What look?"

"Your 'I've seen an angel' look. Art? You *have* Thanksgiving plans, don't you?" Thomas squinted at him.

Art's smug expression gave him away.

*   *   *

Elizabeth, in her room, jiggled the computer mouse that brought the screen to life. She began typing her English paper. "My story—I expected it to be all about me. Shouldn't everything be?"

A knock interrupted her thoughts.

Thomas cracked open the door. "Just wanted to say goodnight."

"Night. Tell Mom goodnight for me."

The door pushed open wider as Haleya leaned her head in too, tilting to see around Thomas. She'd been standing behind Thomas with her arms clasped around his waist. They giggled when Haleya leaned in farther and almost lost their balance. Elizabeth rolled her eyes—yet didn't conceal the smile that crossed her face. Elizabeth shooed them out of the room, motioning her hand. Haleya lifted her hand high and waved to her daughter as they scooted out.

Picking up the stack of printed pages beside her computer, she ran her fingers over the words *Treasure atop the Mountain* on the cover page. Then she flipped to the back couple of pages that mentioned her father as a little boy and re-read them.

She pushed the stack of papers aside, jiggled the computer mouse, and began to type again.

Sometimes a person is asked to do something that she doesn't want to do. Afterward, though, she realizes that maybe someone else does know more. And even through the tension and pressure of the situation, she accepts that had she not been a part of it, she would have missed out—which can make saying "thank you" really awkward.

That was me. Well, that is me.

My father asked me to type something for him. It was no small project. I know now that it wasn't just because he didn't have time to do it himself or because it was a creative way of punishing me, but instead, because he's a smart man—maybe, in some ways, I'm realizing that he is actually smarter than me.

But this is not where the story starts. The story starts with who loved my father before he ever knew or loved me. To me, people aren't something special unless the world cheers and everyone listens to what they say. You know, like Eminem and President Obama. This week though, I expanded my list to add someone who you've never heard of before. Her name is Gracie Howard. She's my grandmother.

Maybe some of the most important people with something brilliant to say are those who tell their story not for the purpose of it being about them. A life story means so much more when it's written to bless others.

Chapter 65

Elizabeth opened the computer and pulled up the document she'd titled *Roxie Applesauce* and read what she'd most recently written. Marcella listened.

Homeless again and alone, Marcella scaled her finger nails up her arm and then to her young beaten, beautiful face, as she'd done as a little girl—when she'd hated herself and everything about her life. In the water-damaged broken mirror forgotten against the wall, she saw herself. She looked older than thirty-two and felt three times that. When she was small, Roxie had saved her. Roxie had been the answer to everything. She'd traded Roxie for Rich. Promises abandoned, like this disheveled storage building she'd crawled into through its broken window as glass grazed her belly. The blood trickling to her toes only slightly concerned her. She didn't know where she or her clothes were. Marcella's bare legs—pinched by the discarded recliner's cracked, vinyl upholstery—itched. She scratched her leg, and dry blood caked under her fingernails. She wrapped what she believed was a curtain from the window around her shoulders. She didn't know what day it was or the last time she'd eaten. What she did know was that not even Roxie could save her now.

Elizabeth looked up from the computer screen. Tears pooled in Marcella's eyes. "It's like you were there," she whispered.

*   *   *

Lyndee answered the phone as she bundled up the clothes from the dryer, several pants legs dragging the floor as she walked.

"Kent!" Lyndee yelled. She dropped the load of warm clothes on the floor right where she was and sank into them. "I was scared. I hadn't heard from you!"

"I'm okay. I've been traveling."

"Where are you? I tried the emergency number you gave me. They couldn't tell me where you were. They wouldn't tell me where you were!" Lyndee cried into the phone.

"They probably didn't know."

"Why? Kent—"

"Because I left."

"You left!"

"Open the front door."

Lyndee scrambled to her feet. She swung the front door open to see Kent standing in front of her. Lyndee grabbed him with a glee beyond anything she'd ever known.

*   *   *

Haleya looked over her shoulder when she heard her name.

"Haleya!" Sandra repeated.

"What's wrong?"

"They just brought Happy Lady in! Low body temp, confusion, difficulty breathing ..."

321

Chapter 66

"Roxie—" Marcella mumbled as Haleya tucked in the bedsheets.

Haleya leaned closer. "Do you see Roxie?"

She nodded.

Sandra stepped in the room, and Haleya placed her finger over the lips for her to stay quiet. Sandra mouthed, "Pneumonia?"

Haleya nodded. Sandra shook her head and blew a kiss.

* * *

Elizabeth tiptoed into Marcella's hospital room and whispered, "I brought your 'Happy' pillow."

Marcella mumbled, "Thank you."

"How are you feeling?" Elizabeth scooted the chair as close to the bed as she could.

"Too weak. Can't talk."

"But I don't know how to end the story."

"I don't know, but you will."

"What does that mean? I need to know how you want me to end it."

"Roxie's there," she paused. "All I know—Roxie will be there."

* * *

Ben crawled into bed in his RV. Tomorrow was Thanksgiving, and he'd leave the day after to go home. Esli and Michael had left to begin their lives together. His house was empty now, but his heart wasn't. His emotional "tank" had been filled, and he had Gracie to thank. *Though gone from this earth, Gracie had set all this in motion with a note to her sons and her love story.*

The day Knox came running toward the RV calling out "Pen-Pa!" a small piece inside him healed instantly. Though he couldn't protect Knox from the mean boys at school or those he'd encounter in the future, he'd witnessed the boy's source of strength. He knew it would carry Knox through it all. He'd seen his grandson love like Gracie.

Gracie's story lived on through her granddaughter. Inspired by it, she'd started writing, shared it with him, and already blessed another.

He'd told his son Thomas that he loved him. Words he hadn't said often enough came out easy for the first time. Thomas may have walked away from Ridgewood and the wood mill, but he, like Kage, had found a meaningful life and the love of a women that fixes a man's heart.

Chapter 67

Ben, pleased to be part of the Thanksgiving preparations, designated himself as the taste tester. Haleya, Elizabeth by her side, had outdone herself. She wiped the turkey grease off her hands and ran to her father when he arrived. "I missed you!"

Thomas extended his hand, but Kent grabbed him in a big hug. Lyndee put one arm around Kent, the other round Haleya, and then motioned to Knox, Whitney and Gina. Thomas's phone buzzed, and he stepped around the corner.

Gina pulled Whitney by the hand. "Group hug!"

Ben picked up Lyndee's phone to take a picture, as Thomas stepped back into the room.

Lyndee motioned for Thomas to join the group hug. Instead, he extended the phone to his father. "Dad, it's Caleb," Thomas paused. "He called to wish us a Happy Thanksgiving." His voice cracked, "He says that he wishes he were here. He wants to talk to you."

Ben pointed up and whispered, "Thank you, God!" Nodding his head as tears welled in his eyes, he took the phone and stepped into the other room.

"Son," Ben said into the phone.

"I miss your mama, too," Ben agreed.

"I know you didn't get to say goodbye," Ben sighed.

"Yes, she asked about you. Often."

"She left a note for me to give you, if, I mean, when I saw you again."

"Sure, I'll hold onto it for you. Yes, I understand you'll be there a while longer."

"I know you were scared. You didn't have to run."

"I'm doing fine."

Ben heard Caleb's voice quiver and dropped his head. "I know that you're sorry."

"Yes, you can come home."

*   *   *

Haleya placed the breadbasket in the middle of the table. "Mom, your applesauce cake is wonderful! I had to taste test it." Haleya winked at Ben.

"Oh, that reminds me of something Gee Gee said," Elizabeth shared a Roxie Applesauce story.

"Okay, so that explains why she asked me to call her Roxie," Thomas said.

"Oh, you met Gee Gee?" Elizabeth asked.

"No, I met Roxie," Thomas snickered.

"You mean Happy Lady?" Haleya chimed in, placing the salt and paper in the center of the table and taking her seat.

Kent's head turned in each direction. "Who? What?"

Lyndee turned to Knox. "What do you call her?"

Knox reached for the large turkey drumstick. "She asked me to call her Grandma," he said.

Laughter erupted.

"That's what she asked me to call her," Knox insisted.

"That lady is too much! I love her!" Haleya took a sip of her wine.

Kent shook his head, lost. "So, who is this?"

"Actually," Elizabeth said, "it's all the same lady. She's the lady mom took care of at the hospital. I call her Gee Gee. I'm typing her life story for her, if it's even true. The other day she tells me that she loves me and asked me to call her Marcella—you know, in the book I'm writing. She's still Gee Gee to me!"

"Marcella?" Lyndee asked.

"Yeah, the story is about her, you know. Marcella is apparently her real name. She has this *really* tough life. She creates Roxie in her mind so she can escape. Her childhood is just cruel, really. The men in her life were no good. She gives up her baby because she can't take care of her."

Lyndee brought her hand to her lips.

Elizabeth, seeing her expression, said, "I know, Grandma. It's just sad."

"Haleya," Lyndee gasped. "She's the one who asks you all the personal questions."

Haleya picked up her wine glass for another sip. "Yeah, and now she's spilling *her* life story out to Lizzy."

Lyndee looked over at her husband. "Kent, this patient of Haleya's asked questions every day about her childhood and her life now. So—many—questions."

"Does Marcella have a last name?" Kent asked.

"Ciscal, I think."

Lyndee dropped her fork.

Kent looked at his daughter and said, "Haleya, she's your birth mother."

"Really?"

"Mom!" Elizabeth gasped, looking at her mother. "Is that possible?"

Haleya shook her head in disbelief.

Thomas sat shocked. "So, that's why she asked—" He stopped mid-sentence and reached for Haleya's hand.

"So she is my grandmother," Knox declared.

"Shhh!" Ben nudged Knox to be quiet.

"Dad, you really think so?" Haleya asked again and looked to her mother.

They nodded.

Elizabeth jumped up and grabbed Haleya's keys from the counter. "Mom, I'll drive!" She pointed to the wine glass still half full in front of her mother.

Haleya slowly stood, looking at Thomas and then her parents. "What am I supposed to do?" she muttered.

"Go," Lyndee answered.

"Come with me."

Lyndee shook her head. "You two go," she said, her hand now trembling against her lips.

In less than a minute they were on the road.

"Go faster!" Haleya encouraged.

"Mom, this is crazy."

"Me telling you to drive faster?"

"Yes, that, too. It's *all* crazy. She's your mother. I mean I know Grandma Lyndee is your mother, but this is—"

"I know. I know. It seems impossible. It doesn't feel real. I'm just so overwhelmed right now." Haleya pointed and said, "Slow down in front of the hospital. Let me out." She popped the lock and jumped out.

*　　*　　*

"No uniform," Marcella muttered when Haleya entered the room. "Only ever seen you in it."

Haleya didn't say anything. She couldn't find the words. She stepped closer.

"Your hands shake," Marcella observed.

Haleya pulled her hands to her chest and clasped them under her chin.

"You know? You know who I am?"

Haleya nodded.

"I've wondered my whole life why God let me live." Marcella's voice was low, dry, nearly drained of life.

"What?" Haleya stepped to her side to hear her better.

"I've made so many wrong decisions in my life," she paused for several breaths. "Even tried to end it. Yet, I lay here an old woman, worn by this world."

"Oh—"

"He kept me alive for this mo—" Her vital signs were weak and mirrored her failing voice. "To know peace—that I made one right decision." Her words interrupted by a cough, she jerked as if her body and mind battled for her remaining strength. Her eyes shut, and for a minute she seemed to fade into the sheets. Haleya waited—her eyes shifting from the monitors to her birth mother's face.

"You, beautiful." Marcella's words formed independently as if every letter were an entire word.

Haleya didn't care how long it took. She wanted to hear every word. Marcella opened her eyes and tried to raise her hand toward Haleya. She took hold of it and lifted it for her. Marcella, inching it toward Haleya's face, rested her palm on Haleya's cheek, and Haleya cupped both her hands around her mother's hand, pressing it to her face.

"Your face has youth," she stopped for a breath, "that mine never did." Marcella reached over and took Haleya's soft, shoulder-length hair between her fingers. "Your heart ... the kindest I ever met. You help people." Marcella's eyes filled with tears and one trickled down her cheek. "You called me Ella. You remember?"

"No, I don't remember anything." Haleya tried to imagine the face of a young woman.

"I do, tiny hands, carousel," she said.

"Tell me about it," Haleya said and added, "Ella."

The lady mustered a crippled smile and closed her eyes to enter her own world. Her hand began to hang heavy on Haleya's.

"There you are. You again, waving at me."

Haleya bent down to Marcella's ear and whispered, "I'm waving at you, and I see your face. You look so happy."

Marcella was still, not a movement for several seconds—she'd drifted away. Though the monitor reflected her heart's

328

weakness, larger peaks showed almost in conjunction with her forming grin.

"Ella, I have had the very best ride. I wish I could have made yours easier." Tears welled up in Haleya's eyes.

"You have," Marcella's lips moved.

Elizabeth rushed through the door. Haleya scooted over in her chair, making room for Elizabeth on its edge. She placed her hand on her mother's as Haleya held her own mother's hand.

"She's coming, and we are going to dance," Marcella said to Elizabeth.

"Roxie?"

"Yes."

"Is she bringing Lawrence?" Elizabeth asked, wiping a tear.

"No," Marcella paused. "Jesus."

Elizabeth stood and leaned in carefully to hug her grandmother. Haleya leaned down, lightly wrapping them in her arms.

Marcella whispered, "Today," she sat on the word, "is—the best—day—of my life."

That night Marcella fell asleep holding her daughter's hand—then woke up to meet her destiny, finally in the arms of the One who loved her since He'd created her.

Roxie Applesauce twirled under the lucent bubbles admiring the sun's radiance shimmering through. She stilled and dropped in a peaceful ballet plie. She extended the tip of her nose upward and a fragile bubble bounced and came to rest. The swaying bubble, sparkling with elegant hues, caused a joy that tingled even to her toes. Then, when the delicate bubble couldn't last another minute, it popped and the sprinkles wetted her cheeks and twinkled on her lashes. There were millions of bubbles—enough to keep her happy for eternity.

Thought from the Author

Love, we think we know it; we pretend to understand it. We believe in it. But when love is difficult, can we see beyond ourselves and embrace its path? Do we hold as tightly to the dark unknown, believing light will come? And if we waiver, could we know only a piece of what was planned for us?

Are we so quick to claim that we have seen every hue created? Or that we could actually assist in the infinite possibilities of the colors merging? Because ultimately, those blends and bends aren't in our control. Yet—every so often—we get a glimpse *of the masterpiece He's creating.*

GET WILL

By Tonya L. Matthews

The crowd stood and applauded. El Kage Mercer stepped to the podium and closed her eyes, taking in the sounds of hundreds of hands welcoming her. In that moment, she knew Roxie Applesauce as intimately as her grandmother had. The difference was that the crowd was not imaginary, and the man waiting for her near the door with a rose was not only incredibly handsome but also very real. She had been blessed with everything Marcella had dreamed of as a girl.

Those in the room sat down. El bowed her head for a mere second and looked out into the audience. "Thank you, Dad, for the introduction. I love you too. Before I forget, there are envelopes on the tables. Please consider a donation to HAVHonor, which is the true purpose for this evening. It is such an important mission and run by a worthy man." El winked at her father who'd taken his seat at the head table.

"I am privileged to say a few words this evening. I hope you enjoyed reading about Roxie as much as I enjoyed getting to know her. Nearly a decade ago when I discovered Roxie, thanks to my grandmother, I was younger and knew much less about life. I was angry for no real reason. I was selfish—a teenager with an attitude. I actually thought the world was cruel because I was supposed to do what my parents asked and what my teachers told me to do. It's crazy now to think that I felt cheated in life because I wasn't given everything I wanted, when I wanted it. When I met Marcella Ciscal, that changed.

"Actually, two women changed me forever," she paused, reached behind the podium, and held up a crumpled spiral-bound notepad. "When I was 17, I was given a book, handwritten by my other grandmother, Gracie. She wanted to share her story with her sons and grandchildren. Because of what it meant to me, I wanted to share it with the world. As a girl, I remembered her as Grandma with tight hugs, a big smile, kind words—and without a right hand. I never really *knew* her until I read her story. She wrote about her fears, disappointment, anger, and pain. I had no idea she'd overcome so much. As I typed her story, I couldn't figure out why I, with two useful hands, had so much frustration bottled up inside. As I typed, tears blurred my eyes and all I wanted was to be little again, when a skinned knee could be fixed with a Band-aid, a kiss from Grandpa, and a glass of Grandma's apple cider.

"If you haven't read Gracie's story, do. It blessed me. I didn't write it; if anything, it wrote me. I am fortunate to get to be the one who shares it." El searched in the crowd for her grandfather. "At the same time that Grandma Gracie's story became a part of me—" she paused, looking at her grandfather, she patted her heart twice with her left hand. Her grandfather did the same. "I met Marcella. You know that story now or you wouldn't be here today. I didn't walk hand-in-hand with Marcella through her difficult life. I only experienced Roxie through her wrinkled eyes as she shared her dream world of admiration and joy—to know what love and happiness felt like and to escape life's pain. *And I thought I was cheated in life!*

"That day I rushed into the hospital room and held my mother's and Marcella's hands as Roxie began to dance,

Marcella—with dry, crusted lips—whispered, 'This is the best day of my life.' That's when I knew how her story would end.

"When I'd begun typing Marcella's story in her own words, I was unaware that the baby she'd given up was my mother or that she was my grandmother. I thought I was writing Marcella's story full of her imagination, and then suddenly I was a part of it—and it was real.

"My mother—" El smiled through dampened eyes.

Haleya, sitting with Lyndee, Kent, Gina, and Knox, lifted her hand in a small wave to her daughter on stage. El blew a kiss in their direction.

She started again, "When my mother laid her head against Marcella's, holding her hand, and Roxie danced into the night, along with Marcella, to be with Jesus—I was never the same again. I asked my Grandpa Ben, those of you who've read *Treasure atop the Mountain* know him as Kage, 'What are the chances of something like this happening? How is it even possible that my mother would care for her birth mother in her last days and that Marcella would have that moment?'"

El saw Grandpa Ben point his finger upward.

"I asked, 'What are the chances?' He said, 'It had nothing to do with chance.' And with those words, I thought of what my Grandma Gracie wrote in a prayer in the final pages of *Treasure atop the Mountain* and how perfectly they applied to my life at that moment." El flipped to the last of the spiral-bound papers and read:

Dear God, I have no words for you. I am so overwhelmed. The way You watch out for me. Why me? And the way You have always cared for me. You've placed so many people in my life. Those I never had the chance to thank. Those I never even knew to thank.

El closed the spiral-bound notepad. She took a donation envelope from her purse, placed it on top of Gracie's notepad, and handed it to her father. The crowd applauded.

El made her way back to the podium. "As you leave today, you'll be given a signed copy of *Roxie Applesauce*. Thank you for all your letters and emails about what *Roxie Applesauce* has meant to you. The experiences you've shared mean so much, as I know how much the story means to me. I'd tell you about the book that I'm writing now," El paused, "but I'm still living it. I don't want to disappoint anyone, but I can't stay tonight to meet each of you as I usually like to do." El raised her finger toward the far corner of the room. "You see that man in the back of the room. The one holding the rose. He's here for me. He has a car waiting outside. We are going to have an ice cream sundae with chocolate fudge, nuts, and whipped cream. Because everyone in this room knows Roxie, I believe you'll understand—I must go."

WHAT DID YOU THINK OF *ROXIE APPLESAUCE?*

If you enjoyed this book, please provide a review on Amazon and Goodreads so that others will be encouraged to read it too. Your review helps gain exposure for the book and may connect it to someone who needs to be reminded that God never lets go.

Please share *Roxie Applesauce* with friends and family by posting on your social media platforms. Its sequel, *Get Will*, is scheduled to be released in 2023. Get updates at haleyapublishing.com, where *Treasure atop the Mountain* can also be ordered.

Acknowledgements

If there is any talent within me, it surely comes from God. Through writing, I escape and work my emotions into a life-story where I can find healing and hope. It is an incredible joy when these books mean something to others. Though our paths in life may be different, what tugs our souls is surprisingly similar. The strength we find that pulls us through shows just how great He is! I hope somehow that your reading this book might be yet another part of His great plan, and that, in some way, this encourages you.

I started this book after we adopted our girls and completed it when we experienced an earlier-than-expected empty nest. Again, like *Treasure atop the Mountain*, this book was—for me—a much needed escape from my relentless mind. We try to manage our lives and the lives of others, and then we realize so much is out of our control. Sometimes the thing to do, though hard, is just hold on for the ride.

First, I thank my Haley. In many ways, we were two broken people God put together. Her road hasn't been smooth; it's taken a village. Haley has been loved by all who've been a part of her life. I've told her many times that God has had her since day one.

Since Haley's adoption and certainly through her teen years, we could write a based-on-a-true-story book. We've held on to love when it didn't feel like love at all. Even when she tried to push us away, we kept loving (along with the hurt). And when we didn't get it right as parents, there was still love—deep inside her, along with the pain. We've learned life is a continuous story. We still hang on through all that's unknown.

I am thankful for those who help edit! Cari Small, for one, who read the roughest draft of this book. She suffered through the mess. I love her for that! Also, Virginia Ransdell for every encouraging side notation and her scattered instances of "Wow." I soar for a moment and hold those tight through the difficult but valuable critiquing process. I also appreciate Lynn Wilton and Sarah Caldwell for the professional final edits. You can find them on Thumbtack. Additionally, I'm thankful for those who were willing to review the first-print draft! Finally, I thank my husband, Todd, who gives me a life where I can do what I love.

Made in USA - Crawfordsville, IN
54014_9780578243696
10.05.2021 1732